VIRUS HUNTERS

A MEDICAL THRILLER | PART ONE

BOBBY AKART

PRAISE FOR BOBBY AKART

PRAISE FOR AUTHOR BOBBY AKART and *THE VIRUS HUNTERS*

"Only Akart can weave a story that begins so calm, so normal and before you know it, you are at the end of the book with your pulse pounding in your chest and your mind screaming for more! ~ Amazon Hall of Fame, Top 2 Reviewer

"Under MY version of Wikipedia, under 'Insomnia – Causation', is a picture of Bobby Akart. I have learned not to pick up one of his books near bedtime as I will be unable to set it aside for hours!"

"Akart is a master of suspense, keeping us on the edge of our seats. But, he does it with fact-based fiction that would scare even the most hardened readers."

"Mixing science and suspense is something Bobby Akart is a master of—writing character driven stories that will have you on the edge of your seat."

"I have highly enjoyed Mr. Akart's literary works because his research is comprehensive and he has an eerie prescience of writing fiction and it becoming reality."

"Mr. Akart has become one of my favorite authors joining the ranks of fellas named King, Grisham & Clancy."

"Bobby Akart is one of those very rare authors who makes things so visceral, so real, that you experience what he writes ... His research, depth of knowledge, and genuine understanding of people make his works more real than any movie."

"No one, and I mean NO ONE, does it better!

ABOUT THE AUTHOR, BOBBY AKART

Author Bobby Akart has been ranked by Amazon as #25 on the Amazon Charts list of most popular, bestselling authors. He has achieved recognition as the #1 bestselling Horror Author, #1 bestselling Science Fiction Author, #5 bestselling Action & Adventure Author, #7 bestselling Historical Author and #10 bestselling Thriller Author.

He has sold over one million books in all formats, which includes over forty international bestsellers, in nearly fifty fiction and nonfiction genres.

His novel *Yellowstone: Hellfire* reached the Top 25 on the Amazon bestsellers list and earned him multiple Kindle All-Star awards for most pages read in a month and most pages read as an author. The Yellowstone series vaulted him to the #25 bestselling author on Amazon Charts, and the #1 bestselling science fiction author.

Bobby has provided his readers a diverse range of topics that are both informative and entertaining. His attention to detail and impeccable research has allowed him to capture the imagination of his readers through his fictional works and bring them valuable knowledge through his nonfiction books.

SIGN UP for Bobby Akart's mailing list to receive a copy of his monthly newsletter, *The Epigraph*, learn of special offers, view bonus content, and be the first to receive news about new releases in the Virus Hunters series. Visit www.BobbyAkart.com for details.

Other Works by Amazon Top 25 Author Bobby Akart

OTHER WORKS BY AMAZON TOP 25 AUTHOR BOBBY AKART

The Virus Hunters

Virus Hunters I

Virus Hunters II

Virus Hunters III

The Geostorm Series

The Shift

The Pulse

The Collapse

The Flood

The Tempest

The Cataclysm

The Pioneers

The Asteroid Series

Discovery

Diversion

Destruction

The Doomsday Series

Apocalypse

Haven

Anarchy

Minutemen

Civil War

The Yellowstone Series

False Flag

The Mechanics

Choose Freedom

Patriot's Farewell

Seeds of Liberty (Companion Guide)

The Prepping for Tomorrow Series

Cyber Warfare

EMP: Electromagnetic Pulse

Economic Collapse

ACKNOWLEDGMENTS

Creating a novel that is both informative and entertaining requires a tremendous team effort. Writing is the easy part.

For their efforts in making the Virus Hunters a reality, I would like to thank Hristo Argirov Kovatliev for his incredible artistic talents in creating my cover art. He and Dani collaborate (and conspire) to create the most incredible cover art in the business. Pauline Nolet, the *Professor*, for her editorial prowess and patience in correcting the same writer's tics after forty-plus novels. We have a new member of the team, Drew Avera, who has brought his talented formatting skills from a writer's perspective to creating the multiple formats for reading my novels. Stacey Glemboski, another new member of our team of professionals, for her memorable performance in narrating my novel. I may have written the dialogue, but Stacey has created the voice of Dr. Harper Randolph. Lastly, there's the Team—Denise, Joe, Jim, Shirley, and Aunt Sissy, whose advice, friendship and attention to detail is priceless.

Characters come and go, but lifelong friendships do not. Everybody needs that set of friends. You know, the ones that you can call on in a time of emergency, that without a doubt, will be there for you. We have Mark and Kathie Becker. The story of how we met can only be attributed to fate. In early 2017, I posted a photo of my vintage Land Rover, affectionately known as Red Rover, in The Epigraph. I received an email shortly thereafter from a reader that recognized Red Rover as belonging to his new neighbors. We may no longer be neighbors, but we will forever be friends with Mark and Kathie Becker. As you come to love the character of Dr. Elizabeth Becker, eighty-eight percent of what you read in the novels, is the real Kathie. Another eleven percent is Lizzie, a mix between Kathie and her three-year-old niece. And one percent is Boom-Boom Becker. I hope you love the character as much as we love the genuine article.

Now, for the serious stuff. The Virus Hunters series required countless hours of never-ending research. Without the background material and direction from those individuals who provided me a portal into their observations and data, I would've been drowning in long Latin words.

Once again, as I immersed myself in the science, source material and research flooded my inbox from scientists, epidemiologists, and geneticists from around the globe. I am so very thankful to everyone who not only took the time to discuss this material with me, but also gave me suggestions for future novels. Without their efforts, this story could not be told. Please allow me to acknowledge a few of those individuals whom, without their tireless efforts, the Virus Hunters series could not have been written.

Many thanks to Laura Edison, a Doctor of Veterinary Medicine and a Lieutenant Commander in the United States Public Health Service, a Career Epidemiology Field Officer, or CEFO, at the CDC in Atlanta. She has stressed the importance of tracking the vast number of travelers during an outbreak. Her creation of an electronic surveillance system called the Ebola Active Monitoring System helped the Georgia Department of Health keep tabs on travelers arriving at Atlanta's Hartsfield Jackson International Airport during that outbreak.

Colonel Mark G. Kortepeter, MD, has held multiple leadership roles in the Operational Medicine Division at the U.S. Army

Medical Research Institute of Infectious Diseases, USAMRIID, the nation's largest containment laboratory dedicated to biological weapons. His expertise in all related fields of infectious disease study from the battlefield to the BSL-4 and to the coroner's office was invaluable.

Eric Pevzner, PhD, MPH, a Captain in the USPHS, who is the Branch Chief of the Epidemiology Workforce Branch and Chief of the EIS program at the CDC Atlanta. Years ago, when I was first introduced to Captain Pevzner, he reiterated that the next pandemic was only a plane ride away. Of course, as we know, he was right. In his capacity as the head of the Epidemiology Workforce Branch, he oversees the Epidemic Intelligence Service, Laboratory Leadership Service, Epidemiology Elective Program, and Science Ambassador Fellowship. He works tireless hours to ensure those within our charge have the tools and knowledge necessary to protect us from infectious disease outbreaks.

Finally, as always, a special thank you to the disease detectives, the shoe-leather epidemiologists of the CDC's Epidemic Intelligence Service, who work tirelessly to keep these deadly infectious diseases from killing us all. They are selfless, brave warriors, risking their lives and the loss of their families in order to fight an unseen enemy more powerful than any bomb.

This is why I wrote the Virus Hunters.

Because you never know when the day before is the day before, prepare for tomorrow.

Thank you all!

FOREWORD BY DR. HARPER RANDOLPH

Spring 2020 - The year we discovered the SARS-CoV-2, COVID-19 global pandemic.

In the story of humanity, communicable diseases play a starring role. From the bubonic plague to cholera to HIV, we have been locked in a struggle for supremacy with deadly maladies for millennia. They attack our bodies with impunity and without prejudice. They're a merciless enemy, just one-billionth our size, and they've existed on Earth longer than man.

In 2020, we were a world under siege. In America, with the whole of the nation in the midst of a declared national state of emergency, most communities were ordered to abide by a mandated lockdown. Infections totaled over a million and deaths were recorded in the tens of thousands. The efforts to protect public health from this novel coronavirus was a striking example of this continuing war. As governments and health authorities battled to stop the spread of the new virus, they considered lessons from history.

As epidemiologists, we strive to understand the exact effects and nature of any strain of virus, a relative of the common cold. Our greatest concern is accepting that this information can remain unknown for months as scientists gather evidence as to its origin, spread, and immunology.

Experts are concerned about the speed at which the disease can mutate. Oftentimes, its presumed that animals may have been the original source—as was the case with severe acute respiratory syndrome, SARS, another virus in the same family as coronavirus—reflecting the proximity that millions in China share with livestock and wild animals.

Once an outbreak occurs and is identified, governments must grapple with a response. Today's strategy of containment—one of the key measures deployed against endemic diseases—would be familiar to civil authorities and medical personnel as far back as the ancient world. The concept of a quarantine has its roots in the Venetian Republic's fourteenth-century efforts to keep out the plague by blocking boat travel.

But the maritime power would have been hard-pressed to institute a *cordon sanitaire* on a scale required in China, where many of these infectious diseases originate. Using the early outbreak of COVID-19 by way of example, the ability to lock down the presumed place of origin, Wuhan, a city equal in size and population to the entirety of Los Angeles County, was a reflection of the power of China's Communist-authoritarian rule. To stop the spread of the disease, every citizen of Wuhan was ordered to stay in their homes. No exceptions for essentials. No excuses to visit a friend. No walks in the park. No mowing of grass. It was a severe measure, strictly enforced.

In 2020, mistrust and politics played a role as well. The Centers for Disease Control and Prevention has always been dedicated to identifying, containing, and eradicating diseases of all types. Too often, however, the CDC had become a political football, but not one handed off or passed from one side of the aisle to the other. Rather, the CDC was often punted, kicked, and fumbled as a result of never-ending budget battles or desires to use the agency's efforts to exploit its findings for political gain.

Misinformation and disinformation are also still prevalent, as they have been in the past. During the outbreak of Spanish flu in 1918–19, conspiracy theories of enemy bioweapons circulated. During an 1853 outbreak of yellow fever in New Orleans, immigrants were to blame. On social media during the COVID-19 pandemic, wild claims were circulating that the coronavirus was exacerbated by 5G cell phone towers. Fear and mistrust may be one of the greatest challenges we face in eliminating infectious diseases.

Technological changes have proved to be a double-edged sword. Modern diagnostic techniques have sped up identification, while data science has made it easier to track the spread of a contagion. But some advances, such as improved modes of transportation, have contributed to the rapid proliferation of infectious diseases around the globe.

Even global health cooperation has been less than straightforward. The conversation has far improved from 1851 when European nations sought to standardize maritime quarantines. Yet the World Health Organization, despite its message of worldwide solidarity and cooperation, continues to exclude Taiwan from key meetings and information sharing, under Chinese pressure. China, one of the most secretive nations on Earth, continues to closely guard information and delay announcements concerning outbreaks for economic and geopolitical reasons. Both of these examples are the kinds of unnecessary risks that create windows of opportunity for infectious diseases to proliferate. Frankly, pandemics and politics do not mix well.

However, perspective is needed. SARS, a disease that spread worldwide within a few months in 2002, gripped the nation's headlines, but killed fewer than 800. The perennial scourge of influenza concerns most pandemic watchers. An estimated fifty to one hundred million died from the Spanish flu during a time when commercial air, rail, and auto travel didn't exist. Even with modern medicine, the CDC estimates an average of 34,000 Americans die from influenza each flu season.

Outbreaks of unidentified diseases demand our vigilance and

study. Novelty does not necessarily make them inherently more dangerous than older foes, only more difficult to establish testing, treatment, and vaccination protocols.

I will leave you with this. Deadly outbreaks of infectious diseases make headlines, but not at the start. Every pandemic begins small, subtle, and in faraway places. When it arrives, it spreads across oceans and continents, like the sweep of nightfall, killing millions, or possibly billions.

Know this. Throughout the millennia, extinction has been the norm, and survival, the exception. This is why the Virus Hunters, the disease detectives on the front lines, work tirelessly to keep these deadly infectious diseases from killing us all.

I am Dr. Harper Randolph and this is our story.

REAL WORLD NEWS EXCERPTS

MYSTERY PNEUMONIA INFECTS DOZENS IN CHINA'S WUHAN CITY
~ South China Morning Post, *December 31, 2019*

Hong Kong health authorities are taking no chances with a mysterious outbreak of viral pneumonia in the central Chinese city of Wuhan, warning of symptoms similar to SARS and bird flu as they step up border screening and put hospitals on alert.

With Wuhan reporting 27 infections so far, Chan said the Department of Health would increase vigilance and temperature screenings at every border checkpoint, including the city's international airport and high-speed railway stations.

News of the outbreak in Wuhan came to light after an urgent notice from the city's health department, which told hospitals to report further cases of "pneumonia of unknown origin", started circulating on social media.

Thus far, no deaths have been reported.

CHINA REPORTS FIRST DEATH FROM NEWLY IDENTIFIED VIRUS

~ *KAISER FAMILY FOUNDATION Global Health Policy Report,* *January 13, 2020*

The Chinese state media on Saturday reported the first known death from a new virus that has infected dozens of people in China and set off worries across Asia. The Xinhua news agency cited the health commission in the central Chinese city of Wuhan, where the illness first appeared, in reporting the death.

A Chinese woman has been quarantined in Thailand with a mystery strain of coronavirus, authorities said on Monday, the first time it has been detected outside China.

The novel coronavirus resembles known bat viruses, but not the coronaviruses that cause severe acute respiratory syndrome (SARS) and Middle East respiratory syndrome (MERS).

Dr. Kwok Yung Yuen, a physician and chair of infectious diseases at the University of Hong Kong, said that finding the new strain within a month of the first case was impressive. The finding also drew praise from the World Health Organization, whose China office said the country now has strong public-health resources and a comprehensive system for monitoring illness outbreaks.

Wuhan has China's first Biosafety Level 4 laboratory, a specialized research laboratory that deals with potentially deadly infectious agents like Ebola.

FIRST TRAVEL-RELATED CASE OF 2019 NOVEL CORONAVIRUS DETECTED IN UNITED STATES
~ *CDC Newsroom, January 21, 2020*

The Centers for Disease Control and Prevention (CDC) today confirmed the first case of 2019 Novel Coronavirus (2019-nCoV) in the United States in the state of Washington. The patient recently returned from Wuhan, China, where an outbreak of pneumonia caused by this novel coronavirus has been ongoing since December 2019.

While originally thought to be spreading from animal-to-person, there are growing indications that limited person-to-person spread is happening. It's unclear how easily this virus is spreading between people.

The patient from Washington with confirmed 2019-nCoV infection returned to the United States from Wuhan on January 15, 2020. The patient sought care at a medical facility in the state of Washington, where the patient was treated for the illness. Based on the patient's travel history and symptoms, healthcare professionals suspected this new coronavirus. A clinical specimen was collected and sent to CDC overnight, where laboratory testing yesterday confirmed the diagnosis.

CDC CONFIRMS FIRST POSSIBLE COMMUNITY TRANSMISSION OF CORONAVIRUS IN U.S.
~ CNBC, February 26, 2020

U.S. health officials confirmed the first possible community transmission of the coronavirus in America, a troubling sign that the virus could be spreading in local cities and towns.

The Centers for Disease Control and Prevention doesn't know exactly how the California patient contracted the virus. The individual is a resident of Solano County and is receiving medical care in Sacramento County. The patient didn't have a relevant travel history or exposure to another patient with the virus, the CDC said Wednesday.

"At this time, the patient's exposure is unknown," the CDC said in a statement. "It's possible this could be an instance of community spread of COVID-19, which would be the first time this has happened in the United States."

WASHINGTON STATE REPORTS FIRST CORONAVIRUS DEATH IN U.S.
~ CBS News, February 29, 2020

Washington state health officials said Saturday a person has died of

COVID-19, the disease caused by the new coronavirus. It is the first reported coronavirus death in the United States.

The World Health Organization said earlier this week the risk of the new coronavirus expanding worldwide is "very high." There are now more than 85,000 cases worldwide — most of them in China, where the virus originated — and more than 2,900 deaths. As health officials try to learn more about the virus, it continues to put millions of people in the U.S. on edge and rattle the markets.

22 PATIENTS IN U.S. HAVE CORONAVIRUS, PRESIDENT SAYS
~ CNN, March 1, 2020

The president said at a press conference Saturday that 22 patients in the United States have coronavirus. He said more cases are "likely" and that people who are "healthy" should be able to fully recover, citing CDC briefings.

He described a Washington woman who died as a result of the virus – the first death reported in the United States – as "a wonderful woman", a medically high-risk patient in her late 50s.

EPIGRAPH

"As to diseases, make a habit of two things—to help, or at least, to do no harm."
~ Hippocrates, Greek physician, father of medicine, in Epidemics, Book I, Ch. 2

And there came unto me one of the seven angels which had the seven vials full of the seven last plagues ...
~ Revelation 21:9

Newcomers, place built without defense,
Place occupied then uninhabitable:
Meadows, houses, fields, towns to take at pleasure,
Famine, plague, war.
~ Nostradamus. Century II, Quatrain 19

As awful as this (Ebola) epidemic has been, the next one could be much worse. The world is simply not prepared to deal with a disease, an especially virulent flu, for example, that infects large numbers of people very quickly. Of all the things that could kill ten million people or more, by far the most likely is a pandemic.
~ Bill Gates, CEO and Microsoft founder, at the TED Conference, Vancouver, March, 2015

"Precautions are always blamed. When they are successful, they are deemed to have been unnecessary."
~ Benjamin Jowett, British theologian and Master of Balliol College, Oxford

VIRUS HUNTERS

A Medical Thriller | Part One

by
Bobby Akart

PROLOGUE

The Guliya Ice Cap
Northwestern Tibetan Plateau
Central Asia

Fifteen thousand years ago ...

Man created dog or dog created man thirty thousand years ago in Asia. Canines encountered modern man when we were still very much a part of the animal kingdom. Fifteen thousand years ago, we foraged for a living. It was a time before we had tools or had mastered agriculture. There was no money, no cities or meaningful societies. Like our fellow mammals, our sole existence was to survive.

Wolves, the predecessors to the domesticated dog that we know and love, dominated the landscape of the Northwestern Tibetan Plateau that later became a part of China. These fierce carnivores were the kings of their proverbial jungle at the time. They were adept at navigating the dangerous cliffs and snow-covered rocks as they spent their day hunting prey.

One such wolf, which would come to be known affectionately as Doggo, was having an uneventful day. He wandered along the plateau, exploring his favorite feeding grounds in search of any manner of delicacies. He was an expert scavenger and also a stealthy hunter, learning over time, and via his DNA, that certain creatures were more difficult to conquer than others, but certainly worth the tasty effort.

Doggo made his way in a lackadaisical manner one fateful afternoon. He'd noticed the temperatures gradually dropping over the last year, as were his meal opportunities. The small animals he usually fed upon were making their way off the plateau to lower elevations or even migrating toward the south. This made his task all the more difficult.

As darkness set in, he remained on the hunt. His insatiable hunger hadn't been satisfied in days, and his body was beginning to feel the weakness from his immune system failing. He made his way along the forest edge where the creek ran. He'd been successful there in the past, and he was on that evening, too. Sort of.

He spied the pangolin from a distance just as the sun set over the mountains to his west. Pangolins were mammals that could best be described as scaly anteaters. At the time, they grew to a length of three armor-covered feet. This protective coating enabled the pangolin to curl up into a tight ball, securing its pointed snoot from an attacker.

Many a wolf in Asia, or a lioness, in sub-Saharan Africa, had swatted, pawed, and pushed the ball of keratin scales around in frustration until they gave up in search of an easier mark.

The female pangolin meandered along a swollen creek in search of her favorite delicacies—insects. Solitary creatures, the pangolins were known to mate and the male would leave the female to fend for herself. This particular female had just given birth to three young.

Doggo crept up on the new mother, taking advantage of her poor eyesight. As she walked along the creek, nose to the ground and long tongue searching for ants and termites, Doggo snuck up, preparing to make his move.

The female pangolin's keen sense of smell and hearing didn't fail her. As Doggo approached, she wasted no time rolling into a ball and protecting herself with her natural armor. Doggo used all the methods of intimidation in his arsenal. He growled, snarled, barked and howled. All to no avail. The pangolin could settle into this protective posture for as long as necessary to avoid becoming the wolf's meal.

Doggo, however, had his own keen sense of smell. After an hour of toying with the creature, he sat back and raised his nose to the air. The wind had suddenly shifted from the north, and a cold breeze swept over his beautiful coat of fur. As did an insatiable aroma of baby pangolins.

Without hesitation, he raced in the direction of the female pangolin's nest. The mother was helpless to stop the inevitable assault on her young babies. The three newborns had not developed sufficient scales at their young age to protect themselves against the powerful jaws of Doggo.

He ran through the trees along the creek bed, sniffing at the base of each, in search of a hollowed-out tree where the pangolins liked to nest.

There! Doggo found it. The nest was a combination of a void between two massive roots and a hole dug by the mother pangolin. A hole that wasn't dug quite deep enough.

Doggo furiously pawed at the ground, slinging dirt under his belly and through his legs. Bits and pieces of the soft tree roots were shredded by his powerful claws in the process. The baby pangolins were trapped, and after fifteen minutes, they were exposed to Doggo's drooling jaws.

Wolves didn't settle in for a snack. They don't set the table and pull up a chair. Especially one like Doggo who was ravenous, both from not being able to eat for days and as a result of the frenzied hunt. In less than sixty seconds, the three baby pangolins were devoured and filled Doggo's stomach.

Fatigued from the hunt, Doggo slowly wandered off into the woods and found a rock outcropping to settle in for the night. Ordinarily, the nocturnal animal would continue to hunt, but his exhaustion dictated a change of routine. He slept soundly, his body oblivious to what was about to transpire.

During the night, his body digested his meal. It also digested the microscopic virus that was endemic to the region and that resided in the pangolin mother and her young.

The infecting virus swirled throughout Doggo's digestive system as if it were being flushed down a toilet. In a blink of an eye, several million microorganisms filled the wolf's body like a miniature marauding army.

Most were clumped together, enjoying the comfort of their brethren, before attaching themselves to Doggo's intestinal mucosa —the membranes of a mammal's body lining the many passages, tracts, and structures that sustain life.

Growing comfortable in the moist folds of Doggo's insides, the virus began to feed. It absorbed the nutrients available to it and, in return, excreted the poisons that would make their way throughout Doggo overnight.

The deadly, silent killer was on the warpath now. It was a form of karma for Doggo, who'd viciously attacked the pangolin young only to be infiltrated by an enemy one-billionth his size.

While the wolf slept, his body fought back. The excrements from the virus were caustic, burning throughout his internal organs and invading his bloodstream and respiratory system. His body defended itself as it normally did against the onset of an illness. Doggo's diminished immune system recognized the threat as the virus invaded his healthy cells. Chemicals were released that triggered virus-fighting organisms. The war was on against this unseen enemy.

The immune system was hard at work fighting off the offending virus. But Doggo was losing the battle. The virus invaded the epithelial cells that line and protect his respiratory tract. Soon, the virus had broken through the peripheral branches of the respiratory tree and then the lung tissue.

This was the beginning of the end for Doggo, but it would not be the proverbial cause of death.

He woke up the next morning to a heavy snowfall. His body was made for the cold, and he'd endured blizzards in the high elevations of the Tibetan Plateau in the past. But somehow this was different.

His survival instincts kicked in, and logic told him to follow the others off the plateau and to the south, where warmer climates could be found. Instinctively, he followed the creek and the flow of its water. He stopped frequently to gulp down the cold water and catch his breath. The struggle for air was a feeling foreign to him.

While he rested on his journey, the battle inside him was coming to an end. His immune system was no match for the invading viral army. While his body was struggling to repair the damage to his lungs through white blood cells that consume pathogens, the virus was attacking his other vital organs.

As one day turned to the next, Doggo struggled mightily to keep his footing. He refused to sleep as he desperately fought through the blizzard, which had overtaken the plateau.

After twenty-four hours, his body, fighting for its life, was too robust in its attempts to heal itself. It was successful in destroying some of the virus-infected cells, but it killed healthy tissue in the process. Doggo had suffered significant damage to the lining of his trachea and bronchi, resulting in the loss of the tiny hairs, or cilia, that sweep dirt and other respiratory foreign objects out of the lungs.

Now bacteria from his surroundings joined in the fight. His respiratory system was unable to prevent the deadly germs from entering his lower respiratory tract. His damaged lungs began to starve vital organs of oxygen, impairing his kidneys, liver, brain and heart.

Yet the mighty wolf had a heart and a will to live. He kept moving, hoping to find his way to a safe place where he could rest his tired body. He walked along a rocky bluff, tiptoeing to avoid falling. It was the kind of trek he'd made a thousand times in his life, but this time, it did not end well.

Doggo slipped. He frantically pawed at the rocks in an attempt to gain traction, but his weakened body failed him. He slid, tumbled, and fell into the swiftly moving icy waters of the creek.

He tried to swim to safety, but the torrent of water was too strong. He began to accept his fate, allowing the creek to carry him in an icy cold grip. And then, without warning, the water dropped into a crevasse, carrying Doggo's disease-ridden body a hundred feet to the bottom, where he drowned in an icy grave.

Doggo's tasty meal started a chain of events that threatened to change the face of a planet. And it all began fifteen thousand years ago.

PART I

LET ME INTRODUCE MYSELF

Please allow me to introduce myself,
I'm a man of wealth and taste.
Been around for a long, long year
Stole many a man's soul to waste.
I was 'round when Jesus Christ
Had his moment of doubt and pain.
Made damn sure that Pilate
Washed his hands and sealed his fate.
Pleased to meet you,
Hope you guess my name.
'Cause what's puzzling you is the
Nature of my game.
~ Sympathy for the Devil, The Rolling Stones, 1968

CHAPTER ONE

Burungu
Democratic Republic of the Congo
Africa

And so it begins ...

Dr. Harper Randolph bounded down a stench-filled hallway of a makeshift hospital that was once the village of Burungu's school and social center. This building was sturdy, made of masonry blocks and a metal roof. It stood in stark contrast to the earthen structures made of cattle dung and mud, then covered with a thatch of palm fronds.

The cots were filled with villagers of all ages. The old were wrinkled and lifeless, emitting moans of pain and pleas for mercy. The children, as young as infants, lay silent and listless. One baby's skin was gray and splotchy. All suffered from malnutrition.

It would break the heart of anyone who'd not experienced what this dedicated epidemiologist had seen while battling Ebola. For Harper, it was just another day at the office while she tried to stop the spread of the disease in the Democratic Republic of the Congo before it invaded the major port city of Goma.

Ebola outbreaks in the country were nothing new. The first, in 1976, ravaged Central Africa, as did the ten outbreaks that followed it. Battle lines had been drawn by the World Health Organization and the Congolese government. Ebola would be kept out of Goma. Otherwise, it would become a world problem once again.

Harper understood the importance of containment and preventing the disease from spreading to a highly populated area like Goma. But it was hard to focus on the big picture when the challenges she faced were barely alive all around her. At times, it was a struggle, but then she'd be reminded of her successes.

The villagers called her the *young miracle*—a baby girl who'd contracted the Ebola virus from her mother just six days after birth. With the treatment and attentive care of Harper, the baby had recovered from the deadly killer.

As she made her way through the *sick ward*, as it was called, she passed into the recovery room, where the infant was swaddled in a cotton blanket, her tiny mouth open in a big yawn. The baby's aunt had become a constant presence at the village's hospital following the death of her sister, the mother of the *young miracle* who'd died during childbirth. Her last breath was a wail and a push, giving her life for that of her newborn's. The newborn was given the name *Benedicte*, the Latin word for *blessed*. She truly was.

Harper reached down and lifted Benedicte out of her woven crib.

"How's my big girl today?" she asked with a smile, one that couldn't be seen behind her protective mask. Harper wore personal protective equipment at all times, including gloves, gowns, shoe covers, head covers, and a surgical mask. Ebola was not transmitted through the air, but she had to protect herself against an infected patient suddenly coughing or sneezing on her.

Benedicte, full of curiosity, reached for Harper's mask. "No, honey. You can't have that. But I love seeing you show off your strength." After a moment of snuggling the infant and swinging her around in her arms, Harper returned her to the dutiful aunt.

"She is eating well," the mother of seven offered. "And she gained two more ounces!"

The woman had been trained at a pediatric medical center in her early twenties. She enjoyed children so much, she had several, something that was not uncommon in Central Africa.

"Well, that's great news," said Harper as she provided both aunt and baby a thumbs-up.

Harper glanced around the room at the other recovering patients. She'd produced many miracles while treating the locals. After arrival, the first challenge she faced, along with her small contingent of epidemiologists and health care providers assigned by the United Nations, was gaining the trust of the villagers. Many were standoffish, suspicious that the outsiders were there for a nefarious purpose.

Harper gradually won them over, and those holdouts who refused to perform basic functions like washing their hands or allowing their temperatures to be taken changed their minds when Harper saved tiny Benedicte.

She took a deep breath and steeled her nerves. As part of her daily routine, she checked in on the saved before she rolled up her sleeves, figuratively speaking, to help the infected fight the deadly disease. To be sure, there were failures. Well, not so much failures, but losses. Not everyone could be saved, and Harper had accepted that. Nonetheless, she had to try.

Her coworkers at the Centers for Disease Control in Atlanta, Georgia, often questioned her as to why she felt compelled to fight the disease in the trenches. As a senior epidemiologist, her background and experience were far more valuable in detecting new infectious diseases and determining ways to battle them.

She didn't disagree, but she reminded them that seeing the results of a disease's spread helped her prepare to fight the next unknown killer. She was battle-tested and it would serve her well over time.

CHAPTER TWO

Burungu
DR Congo
Africa

Harper had packed her bags and taken off for African destinations several times in the last two years during the most recent outbreak. She'd joined nearly four hundred WHO volunteers who requested to be deployed to the DR Congo and neighboring countries to battle Ebola. Most had deployed three or four times. Not Harper, who was on her twelfth trip, making her the global response team's most frequent flyer.

She walked back into the sick ward and surveyed the health care workers who'd been deployed with her. The physicians and nurses from nearby Goma were working side by side with the UN-sponsored team. Goma, a city of two million, had felt the effects of war in the past. From Ebola to political conflict dating back to the Rwandan genocide of 1994, the Congolese people in Goma were used to strife.

Oddly, it was the onset of infectious diseases in their city that caused them the greatest consternation. During the period of genocide in neighboring Rwanda in the nineties, nearly a million refugees flooded the city and brought a deadly cholera outbreak with them. Thousands of lives were claimed in the refugee camps outside the city, and the residents of Goma fought the refugees to keep the disease off their streets.

The same was happening now. As Ebola once again spread through Central Africa, the people of DR Congo took up arms against one another. The tiny village of Burungu had been spared the fighting, thus far.

Harper had a good working relationship with the Congolese health care workers. The locals preferred to be attended to by familiar faces. Harper's tall, slender frame coupled with radiant brunette hair and blue eyes was clearly foreign to those residing in Burungu. Saving the young miracle from a certain death went a long way to breaking down these barriers.

Her goal was to install preventive vaccination campaigns in the villages surrounding Goma. For weeks, she'd strived to convince the villagers she wasn't a threat and the vaccination was safe. Over time, she built relationships with the physicians and assembled a team who'd join her at each of the villages, who would then lend her credibility with the locals. This also ensured continuity of the vaccination program after she returned to the States and her home in Atlanta.

"Good morning, Dr. Randolph!" The eldest nurse in the Goma contingent was in good spirits. "We're making some progress with this one."

"Is that so? I thought you were too stubborn to give in to the Ebola, Nkadaru."

Harper towered over the young man as she spoke. He'd sat up on his medical cot for the first time in days and was slowly feeding himself a small portion of moambe, a dish consisting of chicken made with cassava leaves, bananas, rice, and palm nuts. Harper had warned the villagers against serving the patients the recipe that included pepper sauce to avoid intestinal complications.

The young man looked up to Harper with sullen eyes. He was

still weak but not on the brink of death, as he had been several days ago.

"My family needs me," he whispered loud enough for all to hear. "They do not understand the goats."

Harper laughed. "Nor do I, right?"

Nkadaru managed a smile and nodded as he took another bite of moambe. When Harper first arrived at the village, she had been escorted into the village by two Ford Ranger pickup trucks that had been retrofitted by the DRC military with machine guns on the roof. The drivers did not respect the villagers' need to use the roadway to move their goats from one feeding pen to another.

Although Harper didn't understand French, the official language of the country, she understood tone of voice. She sensed that the soldiers intended to clear the road of the goats one way or another. Against strict orders she'd received before they left Goma's airport, she jumped out of the pickup and placed herself between Nkadaru's goats and the threatening soldiers.

Despite being raised in rural Georgia, she had no experience with the animals that had a tendency to be as stubborn as mules if they wanted to be. She tried to push their backsides in an effort to move them out of the way. Most goats are friendly and social by nature, but some, especially Nkadaru's, didn't appreciate being told what to do.

One of them began to kick its rear legs at Harper, forcing her to fall backwards into the muddy ruts of the jungle road. While she was unsuccessful in moving the small herd out of the way, she was able to diffuse the standoff by creating a reason for all of the locals to get a good laugh at her expense.

Once the hilarity subsided, Nkadaru stood defiantly in the middle of the road. Like the goat who took a swipe at Harper, he too had a stubborn streak. After a moment, he succumbed and shooed his herd onto a jungle trail and out of the way.

After that, Harper and the young man developed a friendly relationship, which resulted in a mutual accord. She promised to protect his mother from the disease, and he promised to protect her from the *mutineers*. It was a promise he shouldn't have made.

CHAPTER THREE

Burungu
DR Congo
Africa

There were many times Harper thought about the way of living in these remote African villages compared to her life in Atlanta. When she was younger and began her career at the CDC, it sounded very elegant to be traveling the world, saving lives. Her Catholic upbringing instilled compassion in her, and her Georgetown University medical degree gave her the tools. It was her desire to save lives, not only for those who'd been afflicted with an infectious disease, but future generations who'd confront deadly contagions.

Her work was physically demanding as well as mentally and emotionally draining. In the DR Congo, it was made all the more difficult by the constant threat of violence courtesy of the *mutineers*.

The conflict initially took root in 2009 when the second in charge of the Tutsi rebel group entered into a peace agreement with the Congolese government. The agreement allowed for a ceasefire in exchange for Tutsi fighters being incorporated into the DR Congo's armed forces and high levels of the country's government.

It was a coupling destined for failure, as a parallel government was operating in the shadows by the rebels, who awaited their opportunity to strike. When the former Tutsi rebels rose up in armed conflict against the established, recognized government, war broke out. The rebels were labeled mutineers and chased out of Kinshasa.

For years, the mutineers fought a guerilla war against the people of the DR Congo. Armed by ISIS in an effort to create instability, they spent the better part of two decades conducting raids on villages and the outskirts of the cities.

For a while, the Americans moved into help the government, but changes in administrations lessened the U.S. appetite for intervention. As a result, the government was depleted of military resources. The mutineers resumed their massacres and abductions.

Despite the political instability the African nation had endured for decades, health care workers and epidemiologists like Dr. Harper Randolph were committed to fighting the disease. In the DR Congo, frequently the epicenter of the Ebola epidemic, creating informal clinics like the one in Burungu that were capable of treating viruses as dangerous as Ebola, as well as malaria and other common illnesses, was dangerous.

In other villages, the disruptions caused by the mutineers' raids made it impossible to contain the outbreaks. Easily two-thirds of new infections could not be linked to existing cases because villagers would disappear and reemerge in another location.

That left Harper and the other epidemiologists in the conflict-stricken country racing to identify overlooked routes of infection. With each raid, the locals dispersed and the trust that had been built between the UN-sanctioned medical teams and the villages was lost. People became afraid of being associated with the foreign contingent as the mutineers blamed the outsiders for the raids. Some people with Ebola died without seeking medical help as a result, and those family members who cared for the dying contracted the disease. It was a vicious cycle that could only be resolved with the speed of their vaccination programs or peace between the Kinshasa government and the mutineers.

Thus far, neither Burungu or Harper had been placed in the line of fire between the mutineers and the Congolese army. Therefore, they were not assigned a contingent of blue helmets, the commonly used term referring to the UN peacekeeping forces.

Their sole armed protector was a seventy-year-old former soldier who sat vigilantly outside the hospital holding a Russian-made AKM automatic rifle in his right arm—the only one he had left since the mutineers had chopped off his left one.

Bedaya Jacques could not flee the village in the event the mutineers conducted a raid, as he was almost crippled. He'd been afflicted with malaria and recovered. He'd also contracted Ebola and recovered. He'd nearly bled to death after a mutineer chopped off his arm with a sword, but survived. His bony malnourished body revealed the wounds, but his mind kept the emotional scars hidden. He was a warrior in every sense of the word.

He'd adopted Burungu as his home when the villagers banded together to treat his wounds. He pledged his life to Harper when she saved him from Ebola. When a young villager found the AK-47 variant in the jungle miles away, Jacques agreed to be the sheriff of Burungu and Harper's protector.

He sat stoically on top of a barrel, with his back leaning against the hospital wall. He rarely showed emotion. He didn't speak English, nor did he care to. He did seem to understand basic commands given to him by Harper. The former bushman believed he had a solemn duty: protect the village that had adopted him and the American who saved him from the fever.

This was the world that Dr. Harper Randolph lived in when she was away from the vibrant metropolis of Atlanta, the quaintness of rural Georgia where she was raised, and the geopolitical dynamics of the most powerful city on the planet—Washington, DC.

CHAPTER FOUR

North Base Camp
Mount Everest
Tibet Autonomous Region
People's Republic of China

Adam Mooy was growing impatient with his friend. "C'mon, mate! We can't spend all arvo sitting in the parking lot. We still have some work to do, ya bludger."

The two men had traveled to Tibet from Australia for their employer, but also to visit unusual places. One of the highest priorities on their trip to the *Roof of the World*, the Tibetan Plateau, was to climb Mount Everest.

"Bugger off!" replied Trent Maclaren, a former soccer player and avid climber. He'd scaled K2 in the Himalayas and had planned on ascending the peak at Everest years ago, but the South Base Camp had been closed due to an avalanche. This was his first opportunity to approach from the north face, but he had to settle some business with his girlfriend first. He was frantically texting her, but the wireless internet brought to the region by Everest Link was failing him. "Two minutes!"

"No minutes, ya flamin' galah. They'll lock these gates and we'll sleep in the car."

Mooy and Maclaren only had limited time away from their jobs, so they were unable to climb Everest from most climbers' preferred trek, the south face via South Base Camp in Nepal. Many consider the south side slightly less challenging because the north face was often windier and chillier.

A debate had raged since the avalanche that took the lives of several climbers and almost engulfed the South Base Camp years prior. Long considered the safer route to the summit, South Base Camp required a lot of time and effort to get there. The Chinese government had built a road to the North Base Camp, making it quicker to get to the climb. This upgrade became so popular that tourists flooded the area just to get a view of the tallest mountain in the world's north face. As a result, the visitors' area was soon restricted, and access to the North Base Camp was closed early in the afternoon.

"Fine!" Maclaren exited the rented vehicle and immediately pulled the zipper up on his jacket. It was early April and spring had come early that year, a trend that had taken place over the last decade. Average temperatures in Eurasia had risen by a couple of degrees, and weather patterns responded accordingly. Winters had been cut short and springtime arrived sooner.

The two men worked together to gather their gear, which included a couple of bottles of Baijiu, China's national drink, a spirit distilled from wheat and sometimes rice, with a hint of soy sauce. While they waited in base camp to start their climb to the summit, they intended to enjoy the time off and hopefully the company of some female climbers. Maclaren's girlfriend suspected as much, hence the flurry of text message activity.

Despite the early spring, temperatures were still frigid. It was a sunny day, but the high temps hovered around freezing. At night, five degrees was the norm. Despite the chill, beads of sweat poured off Mooy's forehead. He'd complained of feeling achy on the drive to Everest, and both men shrugged it off as being related to the physical labor they'd been performing. Maclaren, who was the more physically fit of the two, was used to the manual labor aspect of their jobs and therefore was feeling fine.

Maclaren had quizzed his friend on multiple occasions as to whether he had the stamina and expertise to climb the north face. Statistically speaking, the north side was more daunting. Thirty-six people had died climbing the North Ridge over the past decade, while fifteen had died while attempting the South Col route, as the gap between two ridges was known.

The biggest issue on the north face was altitude. The ascent from the south was more gradual, and climbers were given plenty of time to adapt to the altitude as they traveled through Nepal to the South Base Camp. For those choosing the northern route, once they exited their vehicle, they immediately noticed the elevation due to their shortness of breath.

"Whoa, I feel strangled," said Mooy as he followed Maclaren up the trail toward the North Base Camp.

"It's just the altitude, mate," said Maclaren. "We'll have a few nights to get used to it while we enjoy some time with our fellow climbers, if you know what I mean."

"What about your girl back home?" asked Mooy.

"She'll be fine. Listen, I'm an international bloke. I need variety. Plus, we're gonna be at the top of the world. Can you think of a better place to get laid?"

Mooy laughed. "I can't think of a bad place to get laid."

The two men continued to the advance base camp situated on the north side at seventeen thousand feet. Both were sufficiently experienced to handle the technical rock climbing that was prevalent on the north side of Everest. However, Mooy continued to have trouble adjusting to the altitude, and his breathing became more labored.

"You gonna be all right, mate?" asked Maclaren. "Do we need to chuck a U-ey?"

"No, ya mope. Keep moving. It's just the bloody altitude, is all."

"Okay, mate. No problem. Just don't fall out on me. The Chinese don't allow helicopters on the north face, so any rescue means you're gonna be carried down on the back of a yak. That'll make for a good Insta-story."

"Bugger off, mate, or I'll take the lead!" Mooy shot back in between heaving breaths.

Both men were fully aware of the danger their choice imposed upon their dream of climbing Mount Everest. Because they were short on time, they took the most expeditious route through Tibet rather than using the aid of the Sherpas, the experienced Himalayan tour guides renowned for their skill in mountaineering. They'd been running hundreds of people up and down the south face for decades, so there was very little unknown to them about the route. Knowing your route was a really big deal in mountain climbing.

The north side always had the potential for things to go terribly wrong. Mount Everest was known as a beast with a very sharp tail.

CHAPTER FIVE

North Base Camp
Mount Everest
Tibet Autonomous Region
People's Republic of China

Every spring, a pop-up city was built at the foot of the world's tallest mountain. Hundreds of international mountaineers journey to Mount Everest each spring, hoping to make a successful ascent of the world's highest peak. The vast majority of their time, however, isn't spent climbing up the mountain. It's spent resting, acclimating their bodies to the altitude, and socializing with their fellow climbers.

Life at base camp was an odd mix of everyday, mundane domestic chores, discussing logistical challenges as the climbers traded stories of their experiences, and the occasional opportunity to relax.

The North Base Camp was snuggled below the Rongbuk Glacier. Like its south base counterpart, the camp was situated below seventeen thousand five hundred feet for good reason. Somewhere between eighteen thousand and nineteen thousand feet, the human body enters a state of decay above which life is not permanently sustainable.

Water loss increases, resulting in dehydration. The significant altitude causes the climbers' metabolism to speed up significantly while suppressing their appetite, forcing them to eat more than they feel like to maintain a neutral energy balance. Their lungs try to keep up with the low levels of oxygen, causing them to breathe faster. Their heart starts beating faster to increase the quantity of oxygenated blood in the body—red blood cells that are now more prevalent, making their blood thicker.

All of this activity weakens the body and its immune system. However, these are normal responses to altitude gain, and if they are occurring, it means the human body is coping well with the higher elevation. High-altitude sickness, the symptoms of which can manifest themselves within hours after arrival at a high elevation, can be resolved with acclimation, or not. Sometimes, the symptoms of headache, nausea, shortness of breath and overall weakness was shrugged off as part of the price to pay for successfully climbing the tallest mountain on the planet.

By the time Mooy and Maclaren got settled in at North Base Camp, they were experiencing all of the symptoms of high-altitude sickness, as well as the natural high generated by their excitement to be there. Upon their arrival, they found their way to the locally licensed logistics company, which had been assigned to them when they obtained their foreign climber's permit. The logistics company provided the base camp with accommodations, meals, and basic bathroom facilities.

A small army of support personnel occupied North Base Camp during the climbing season. For every climber, there were three to four workers living at base camp who handled these logistical duties.

Like all towns, North Base Camp was divided into neighborhoods, some of which were considered better than others. The larger tents capable of housing a dozen climbers had hot showers, projectors for after-dinner movies, and electricity powered by gasoline generators. These creature comforts didn't come cheap, and they certainly were not within the budgets of Mooy and Maclaren.

But today was their lucky day.

Upon arrival, they learned that two of the climbers scheduled to arrive had been delayed by a few days. Therefore, they were assigned one of the luxury tents with ten other climbers who'd arrived earlier. The twelve climbers would be awaiting their turn together and ascend Everest as a group.

The Aussies' new acquaintances were an eclectic group from all over the world. They worked for IBM and had been awarded this trip as part of a company-wide incentive program. The only stipulation was they had to be experienced climbers. In a company of nearly four hundred thousand employees, that was not difficult to find.

The men got settled in to their new environs and made a few lady friends both inside their temporary home and in the nearby tents. Within hours, the men learned that their fellow climbers either loved base camp or they hated it.

For some, base camp was a form of purgatory. A temporary asylum where they were forced to wait for days in exchange for the chance to climb Everest. For others, like Mooy and Maclaren, it was the ultimate adult summer camp. Mooy immediately became infatuated with an Irish programmer from IBM. Maclaren broke up with his girlfriend, as he immediately fell in love with a Swedish woman who was hiking with her family.

There was partying to do. Women to engage. And Instagram photos to take and upload via Everest Link. If it were up to the Aussies, the climb to the summit could be delayed and they'd be just fine with that.

The two men became so popular at North Base Camp that most of the international contingent acquired their own version of Australian accents and greeted one another with *G'day, howzit*. *Good day* and *how's it going* became mashed into one distinct yet uniquely Australian drawl.

Meanwhile, despite their good times, both men were frustrated they weren't recovering from the altitude sickness that was supposed to be temporary. They stopped into Everest ER, a walk-in medical tent able to dispense basic medications for a variety of ailments. Both men were deemed to have a cold and given antihistamines and anti-inflammatory drugs. They were also provided Diamox, a drug designed to reduce the symptoms of tiredness and shortness of breath.

The guys took the drugs as prescribed and self-medicated with wine, women, and song. It took their mind off their ailments as they prepared for their big day climbing the ridge leading to the summit.

CHAPTER SIX

Burungu
DR Congo
Africa

The rumble of engines, any engines, was the signal for the villagers here to flee. They would leave behind smoldering pots of wild roots, palm nuts, and leaves, a meager afternoon meal but valued nonetheless. Motorized vehicles brought threats with them. Whether it be the mutineers on a raid or the government soldiers who held little regard for the villagers, once the sound was heard in the distance, they would run into the jungle until the threat passed.

Dr. Harper Randolph was in the sick ward going over the patients' charts when the doors flung open. It was a woman from the neighboring village, carrying a sick girl in her arms. She was closely followed by the ever-dutiful Jacques, hobbling in on a crutch under his left stump and waving his AKM in his only arm.

"Les mutins! Les mutins!"

Harper didn't need to understand the French language to discern that trouble was coming. The doctors immediately began to

29

gather their most prized medicines and tools by cramming them into satchels and totes. They were preparing to flee.

"My baby! She is sick!" the new arrival plead with the doctors, tugging at their arms and medical gowns to get their attention.

One of them paused long enough to issue a stern warning. "You must leave here! It is not safe!"

As she finished her warning, the child let out a projectile vomit that coated the dusty concrete floor of the building. Harper reached into her pocket and retrieved her forehead thermometer.

"One-oh-two-point-three," she mumbled to herself. After she let out a sigh, she exclaimed to the medical personnel. "She's burning up! Can't we at least get her fever down?"

A member of the WHO contingent burst through the doors and answered her question. "Dr. Randolph, they've called in an extraction. We need to leave for the rendezvous point now!"

"Extraction? Why? Are they sending a vehicle?" The questions flew out of her mouth as her mind raced.

The WHO nurse replied, "We must go! There's no time!"

Harper ran to the window and listened. The sounds of the truck engines were growing louder, but they weren't there yet. She turned to the woman holding her ill child and was nearly knocked over by a heavyset woman racing out the door.

The world became a blur as she had to choose between saving herself and treating the child whose fever spelled a death sentence anyway. Harper took a deep breath and gathered herself.

"Will you stay with the child? No matter what?"

"Yes! She is the only baby I have left. The Ebola has taken the others."

Harper led the woman by the arm to an empty cot nearest the recovery room entrance. Another adult carrying a toddler brushed past her, causing her to spin around and lose her balance. She crashed her shoulder against the concrete wall separating the recovery room from the sick ward. Pain shot into her neck, but she ignored it.

"Here! Place her here!" She motioned for the woman to bring her daughter to a cot.

Harper had never moved so swiftly in treating a patient. During her residency at Georgetown before joining the CDC, she'd spent a considerable amount of time in the emergency room. On one occasion, a gang-related shoot-out had scattered wounded patients throughout the District in need of treatment. The scene that day had been as hectic as any concocted on the nighttime television dramas.

Harper immediately started an intravenous drip of fluids and electrolytes. She lovingly placed an oxygen respirator over the young girl's nose and mouth, talking to her reassuringly as she worked.

Outside, the shouts of the villagers reminded her that danger was coming. She injected intravenous ibuprofen to address the child's fever, as well as a dose of Zofran for her vomiting.

Harper thought for a moment. Reportedly, the mutineers were afraid of the Ebola virus. In fact, she'd been told by the villagers that the mutineers were known to weaponize the disease by kidnapping infected and taking them into Goma under cover of darkness. She considered these things as she decided whether it was safe to leave the patients and the new arrivals alone in the village. She sighed and then she turned to the mother.

"You are going to be alone for a while, but the doctors will be back for you," she began as she pulled over a three-legged stool and a bucket of water. "Use this towel to keep her cool. Wring it out and gently place it on her forehead and neck. The medicine will help soon, but you being with her makes a difference. Now, are you sure you will be okay?"

"Yes. I have nothing to live for except my baby. Thank you, Doctor."

Harper checked her patient one last time and made a slight adjustment to the IV line. The roar of the motors and the sounds of the low-hanging palm fronds being pushed out of the way by the trucks signaled that she, too, had to go.

She raced toward the doors leading into the center of the compound, and then she heard it. The sound was faint at first, and then it grew to a wail. There was a baby crying in the recovery room.

Harper took a deep breath and ran back through the sick ward, past the surprised mother caring for her Ebola-ravaged daughter, and between the curtains separating the two rooms. In the far corner of the room was a toddler wearing nothing but diapers, crying alone as tears streamed down his dusty, cherub-like cheeks.

The sight of the young boy was not what concerned Harper the most. The dutiful aunt had abandoned Benedicte, her *young miracle*. Harper shook her head in disbelief. She looked around the room in search of any of the adults. She was certain one was left behind to care for these two children and had simply frozen from stress.

She was wrong. She was alone.

The two babies had survived the deadly disease only to be left to the devices of these so-called mutineers, a group of criminals who spent their days murdering, raping, and burning villages to the ground. Harper had already made the decision to possibly sentence a mother and her infected daughter to a possible death, but they were most likely facing that anyway due to the disease. She would not allow the monsters on the loose to harm these babies.

She scooped the toddler into her right arm and then gently lifted Benedicte into her left. Clutching them both firmly against her chest, she ran into the compound and squinted her eyes as they adjusted to the bright sun. It took several seconds that felt like hours for her vision to be restored and for her to get her bearings.

Her eyes darted around the compound and toward the huts in the village. She looked for help. Only one person stood stoically in the face of danger. It was Bedaya Jacques and his rifle.

CHAPTER SEVEN

Burungu
DR Congo
Africa

Jacques hobbled next to her, spinning his head around from time to time to look for the oncoming mutineers. He spoke very little English, but when coupled with hand gestures, his comprehension improved. He'd pledged his life to Harper, and now he was going to be tested. Thus far, he hadn't abandoned his post.

Harper looked past him as the roar of the engines grew louder. The sounds of the vehicles bouncing through the rut-filled roads increased her sense of urgency. She turned to Jacques as the two babies began to cry in unison. The old bushman couldn't run like the others. This was going to be his last stand and they both knew it.

"Hide your gun, Jacques. You cannot fight them."

"Fight!" he replied, thrusting the AKM into the air.

"You will die," begged Harper as the reality of her statement caused her to well up in tears.

"Fight! Win!"

He was adamant. Harper didn't have time to argue. She fought back the tears and smiled at the decrepit bushman.

"Jacques, you are a hero!"

"Hero!" he parroted her words, once again waving his weapon high and almost toppling over in the process.

Harper leaned down and kissed the old man on the cheek. Her soft lips made contact with the leathery skin of his face that had known nothing but scorching hot sun and sadness its entire life.

"Hero," she whispered in his ear as she turned to run away from the approaching trucks.

As she entered the jungle on the trail the villagers had made to connect the village with the new helicopter landing zone utilized by the United Nations, the sound of gunfire could be heard behind her.

"Fight!" Jacques's voice followed her down the trail above the melee taking place in the village.

Suddenly, she noticed the gunfire was getting closer. Harper began to race through the jungle, using her years of running competitive track events and later marathons to gain on the villagers who'd fled already.

The young boy was draped over her shoulder like a proverbial sack of potatoes. He barely weighed twenty pounds, two-thirds the size of a boy his age in the States. Benedicte weighed less than the medical gear stuffed in her lab coat.

Both babies had stopped crying, fortunately, as the mutineers had apparently arrived in the village and were now on the hunt. The shooting had stopped, which meant only one thing—Jacques had died a hero.

Harper didn't have time to second-guess her advice to the old man or mourn his loss. She had to save these babies and herself.

The trail widened and soon she was running alongside some of the elderly and overweight villagers. Their chests were heaving as they tried to flee the mutineers.

Gunshots rang out again, this time dangerously close and aimed in her direction. The bullets whizzed by, shredding the rubber trees and embedding into the tall, majestic trunks of the mahogany trees that bordered the trail.

She passed one of the women. Seconds later, a shot found its mark, passing through the woman's shoulder and spraying blood all over Harper's back and the baby's face.

More villagers came into view. All of them were running for the perceived safety of the UN helicopter at the landing zone. Harper hoped there were armed Blue Helmets present to repel the attack of the mutineers. Even if they didn't engage the approaching killers, they would at least act as a deterrent. Surely the rebels wouldn't fire upon a United Nations contingent on a humanitarian mission.

More bullets whizzed by her, killing another villager. Harper instinctively ducked, lowering her body to become a smaller target. When she noticed her pace had slowed, she realized she had to take her chances; otherwise they'd catch up to her.

Automatic gunfire raked the tree limbs over her head. Harper gasped and gripped the children tighter. "Hold on, babies!" she whispered loudly and she broke into a sprint. She'd lost track of her whereabouts in relation to the clearing, but all she knew was that the menacing gunfire was gaining on her.

She passed more villagers and tried to warn them. "Run into the jungle and hide. Hurry! Into the jungle!"

Several followed Harper's advice and peeled off into the thick foliage. Some of the bullets followed them, but most of them were directed toward her. A staccato outburst sent a dozen rounds along the trail near her feet, raking the dirt and fallen palm fronds for twenty yards in front of her.

She looked up and saw the sky for the first time since she left the village. The clearing was not much farther. The sounds of the chopper gave her hope.

With newfound energy, she pressed ahead, passing even the young men of the village who were used to running barefoot through the jungle. Her increased pace put a little distance between her and the shooters, and within seconds she burst into the clearing where the bright white helicopter came into view.

The helo's rotor blade were spinning furiously as it awaited Harper's arrival. Three UN security personnel spread out around the chopper with their weapons raised. As soon as Harper entered the clearing, they moved toward her and began to fire their automatic weapons high into the trees. These warning shots proved effective, as the gunfire from the mutineers ceased almost immediately.

Several villagers rushed into the clearing and immediately fell to the ground to avoid getting shot by the Blue Helmets. One of them was a nurse's assistant who'd helped Harper in the sick ward on occasion.

"Dr. Randolph!" a man with a British accent shouted to her from the helicopter. "I must insist that you hurry." *They are always so very proper*, she thought to herself.

With her head lowered, Harper jogged toward the helicopter, using her hands to protect the babies from the winds that whipped up palm fronds and debris from the surrounding jungle.

"Doctor, you must leave the children here!" he shouted as she approached.

"What? I can't." Harper stopped and hesitated before getting closer.

"You must, Doctor. It's protocol. Taking the babies will create an incident."

"They're gonna die! How's that for an incident?"

"I'm sorry, Dr. Randolph. Our hands are tied."

Harper turned away from the helicopter and looked around at the few villagers who'd managed to make it to the clearing.

"Aw, shit," she mumbled as she realized her choices sucked. She dropped to a knee and gently set the young toddler in diapers onto the ground. He stared at her with tear-filled eyes and shoved his hand into his mouth.

Harper was heartbroken for the child. *What kind of life would he have? He'd survived this deadly disease, but would he survive the next one? Or the next raid?*

The nurse's aide from the village ran past the UN security team, who kept their rifles trained on the jungle. She slid to her knees next to Harper and the babies.

"I will care for them, Doctor. I make you this promise."

The little boy ran into her arms and she spoke softly to him in French. He turned and gave Harper a slight smile. He'd stopped crying, or he'd simply run out of tears. Harper knew he'd have more.

She turned her attention to Benedicte. The baby was swaddled in the blanket to protect her from the debris and the noise caused by the rotors. Harper pushed the blanket aside just enough to get her face inside the protective layers of cotton. She whispered to her *young miracle*.

"I can only imagine what life holds for you, Benedicte. I want you to know I will pray for you every day. I will pray that you grow up to be a healthy young woman who will help your village as they have helped you. God will be with you, always."

Harper reached in through the top of her shirt and pulled out the rosary given to her by her grandmother. It had been blessed by the Pope and meant the world to Harper. She'd had a lengthy conversation with her priest about wearing the rosary daily. Harper lived in a world full of disease and death. She frequently prayed it. For her, it was far from a piece of beautiful jewelry or a symbol of her Catholic faith. She prayed her rosary daily at home and, while in Africa, multiple times a day.

She closed her eyes, said a silent prayer, and gently pressed it against Benedicte's forehead. She gently kissed the rosary and the baby simultaneously.

"I will always remember you, blessed baby. God bless you, young miracle."

CHAPTER EIGHT

Somewhere over West Africa

The United Nations aid worker from Great Britain had helped
Harper inside the helicopter, and the security team boarded on both
sides, leaving the doors open as they monitored the ground for
sporadic gunfire. After the pilot expertly lifted the chopper into the
sky and sped off toward the west, Harper let out her emotions. At
first, she was filled with sadness at having left behind a village that
needed her. Then she voiced her frustrations, to the consternation
of the UN personnel who were forced to listen to her.

"They're terrorists!" she exclaimed, breaking the awkward
silence. "They'll wave their damn guns around and act like a bunch
of badasses, and then they'll leave to prey on other innocent
villages."

"Yes, ma'am," said the head of the three-man security team, an
American.

Harper continued her rant. "Why can't we let them do what they
do and take me back down there?"

"We have orders, ma'am."

"From whom?" Now Harper demanded answers.

The security personnel clammed up, looking toward the Brit, who was dressed in navy blue UN fatigues. He was not, however, part of the security forces. It was protocol when entering a hot zone that administrative personnel wore uniforms similar to the security contingent so they wouldn't stand out as a potential target for gunmen.

"From the top, Dr. Randolph. We were en route to extract you anyway, our efforts hastened by the oncoming rebels."

"What? Why wasn't I notified that I was being recalled? When you say the top, are you referring to World Health? Or my bosses at the CDC?"

The middle-aged gentleman gulped and carefully thought out his response. "This came directly from the administration."

Harper took a deep breath and exhaled. She was trying not to take out her frustration on these men who saved her life. However, she was tired of them beating around the bush.

"Dammit, man! Which administration?"

"The White House. The extraction orders came directly from the president himself. Please understand, this wasn't just directed at you in Burungu. All Americans are being recalled."

Harper was puzzled. "Why? Did something happen?"

"No. During the presser, the White House Press Secretary simply said the decision was made to protect Americans. As he put it, *we're not going to incur any casualties helping people who don't want to be helped.*"

"Aw, shit," said Harper as she rolled her eyes. "Do those people not think the villagers want our help? Of course they do. The sick are not the problem. These thugs. These so-called mutineers are the problem. If they'd just provide us protection ..." Her voice trailed off.

"We can't," offered the UN representative. "Our ability to provide humanitarian aid around the globe is dependent upon all sides of the geopolitical spectrum understanding that we don't take sides. We're there to help those who can't help themselves."

Harper brusquely interrupted. "And to eradicate diseases before they reach our precious Western soil. I simply don't understand why protection measures can't be put into place so aid workers—whether they're from the UN, Doctors Without Borders, or the Red Cross—can do their jobs without fear of losing their lives to criminals."

The conversation ended as Harper leaned against the window of the helicopter. The pilot banked slightly, providing the passengers a bird's-eye view of Gabon, the location of a Level 4 biolab that had been compromised years before. The breach had been the result of a complex terrorist plot, a grim reminder that infectious disease can be spread naturally as well as an instrument of biowarfare.

A United Nations naval vessel was anchored off in the distance, rocking gently from the slight waves in the Gulf of Guinea. As the chopper raced past Libreville, Gabon, and prepared to land on the ship's heliport, Harper promised herself that she'd return to Africa someday when the opportunity presented itself and there was an administration in Washington with the political courage to take the necessary risks.

The pilot began to lower the chopper onto the ship's deck when a loud ding interrupted Harper's thoughts. It was a notification to the phone of the UN representative. Curious, she glanced in his direction.

He read the message and then looked up at her. "Dr. Randolph, you'll be ferried from here to Dakar in Senegal. From there, you'll join other American relief personnel and flown to Atlanta. You should be home by tomorrow afternoon."

Harper managed a smile and nodded. It would be nice to sleep in her own bed for a change. She began to peel off her white scrubs. The UN peacekeepers watched as she partially disrobed.

"Gentlemen! Give the doctor some privacy, please," ordered the Brit, who then looked down himself. "I'm sorry, Doctor. I don't have a change of clothes for you."

Harper pulled off her scrub pants, leaving her in a pair of cut-off jean shorts and a gray tee shirt that read *I was social distancing before it was cool.*

"It's fine, really," she said as she crossed her tan, toned legs. The soldiers continued to avoid eye contact with the attractive doctor.

The UN representative faced Harper once again and continued with the best news although it came across as an afterthought. "Oh, and there's one more thing. Your husband would like to know if you'd be up for dinner and drinks tomorrow night."

"Wait, Joe sent you a text?"

"Um." He hesitated before responding, "Not directly, of course. Through channels. Shall I respond?"

Harper shook her head and smiled. "Yes. I mean, tell him absolutely, and if isn't too mushy for your *channels*, let him know that I love him and miss him, too."

"Of course, Doctor. I'll pass it along."

Harper leaned back in her seat and allowed the rotors of the chopper to slow to a halt before unbuckling her harness. She missed her husband terribly. Any text, any phone message—even the most miniscule of a reminder of his existence still made her heart flutter after ten years of marriage.

Then she furrowed her brow and thought to herself, *How did he know I was coming home?*

CHAPTER NINE

North Base Camp
Mount Everest
Tibet Autonomous Region
People's Republic of China

The Aussies and the rest of those assigned to their tent were delayed a day due to adverse weather conditions on the north face of Mount Everest. This simply enabled them to extend their socializing and carousing. It also allowed their unexplained illness to take a hold of their respiratory systems. As their symptoms worsened, they gradually pulled back from the other climbers, but it was too late. Throughout North Base Camp, people were coming down with the early effects of what was presumed to be the flu.

Spring was not the typical flu season. Those who went into the infirmary of North Base Camp speculated with the medical staff that perhaps the pack animals, the yaks, were extending the flu's life that year and spreading it to others.

Word quickly spread through base camp that those exhibiting flu-like symptoms were being refused access to the mountain. The

Sherpas claimed the trek was simply too dangerous for any climber of diminished capacity.

Mooy and Maclaren, like most of the others, were there for a once-in-a-lifetime experience. They'd never have this opportunity again, and they were damned if they'd let something like a silly flu bug stop them from achieving their dream.

Morning came and the climbers, many of whom were overdosed on Theraflu, gathered their gear and began the ascent from base camp to the advance base camp, a rugged twelve-mile hike on boulders, ice and snow. The route follows the Rongbuk Glacier under the slopes of the Changtse Mountain to an elevation just over twenty-one thousand feet.

This two-day hike, while challenging, was easily achieved by experienced climbers in good condition. The group stopped at High Camp to rest for the final leg of their journey. Everyone broke out their own tents and were mostly divided up into groups of two.

Exhausted, Mooy and Maclaren stuck together, abandoning any notion of one final fling with their newfound girlfriends. Both sensed that something was seriously wrong as they discussed their final ascent to the summit.

"Mate, I don't know," began Mooy, who was the sicker of the two. "I thought I could soldier through this, you know?"

Maclaren, who seemed to enjoy bustin' his friend's chops, was more subdued in his response than normal. He, too, was feeling progressively worse. In fact, during the entire climb to High Camp, he considered approaching one of the guides to lead them back down the mountain as everyone else continued. Then he seemed to get a second wind and pushed failure out of his mind.

"Tomorrow is our day, mate. We've been boogerin' women. We've been drinkin' like the bottle-o is closin' for good. But now, it's time to get serious. Can you make it one more day to the next level?"

Mooy laughed and then had a coughing fit. He stuck his head into his sleeping bag so the other climbers wouldn't hear him. He'd noticed that those who seemed to be getting sick were doing everything they could to hide their symptoms, just like he and Maclaren were doing.

He wiped his mouth and felt the moist sputum, the mixture of saliva and mucus coughed up from his respiratory tract. Had there been more light in the tent other than the faint illumination provided by his cell phone flashlight, he would have noticed the droplets of blood mixed in with the mucus.

"Yeah, I got another day in me and another one after that. No U-ey for Mooy."

Maclaren clapped spontaneously and patted his best mate on the back. He tried to change the subject and put on his professional climber face.

"Okay, let's talk about tomorrow. We start a series of climbs to interim camps. The next phase takes us another two thousand feet into the sky along the North Col to an elevation of twenty-three thousand feet."

Maclaren paused as the reality of the daunting task ahead began to settle in. Here, the effects of the higher altitude would begin to take a maximum toll on the climbers' bodies. In addition, the winds would pick up, making concentration of utmost importance. Then he continued.

"After we get to twenty-five thousand feet, we'll be at High Camp 3. This is where the going will get rough and, mate, it'll be our last chance to turn back. We'll have to use supplemental oxygen to breathe, and we'll make the rest of the way using our crampons." Crampons were a traction attachment to the climbers' boots that improve grip and mobility on snow, ice and rocks.

Mooy sat upright in his sleeping bag. "Hey, I forgot about the bloody oxygen tank. I should start sucking on it now. It'll probably make me feel better."

"Not gonna happen, mate. You won't have enough to reach the summit and back if you burn through it now. You just gotta fight the cold. Here, take some more vitamin C."

Mooy shook his head vigorously and held both hands up to his friend. "No way, mate. You want me to get the bloody shits up here?"

Maclaren laughed. "You're not gonna get diarrhea from a few thousand milligrams of vitamin C. Take it."

Mooy reluctantly accepted the capsules and swallowed them without taking water. Then Maclaren continued outlining their day.

"Once we get started on the final stretch up the summit, we'll hook up."

"With the girls?" asked Mooy, who perked up at the thought of one last go in the sack before the hard work began.

"No, you mope. We'll clip into the fixed rope and use our ascenders. Now, if you want, we can position ourselves to buddy up with them, but it'll have to be boy-girl, boy-girl, to avoid a weak link in the human chain."

Mooy leaned back into his sleeping bag, wincing as a twinge of pain shot through his chest. He silently cursed the vitamin C Maclaren forced him to take. Then he coughed again. After he was finished, he wiped his mouth and chin before snuggling into the sleeping bag.

"Okay. You know, I can do this. Tomorrow." His voice trailed off as he passed out.

CHAPTER TEN

Mount Everest
Tibet Autonomous Region
People's Republic of China

The Sherpas gathered the group together and led them up the North Col toward the summit. Everyone was filled with nervous excitement as they began the day. Mooy and Maclaren managed to locate the women they'd befriended, and the group agreed to make their way up together.

As instructed, they'd affixed their crampons to their footwear and clipped onto the fixed rope.

One of the Sherpas, a well-spoken Himalayan who was fluent in English, explained the importance of this. "This is a safety measure for this stretch of the climb. Every route and every pitch requires something different. There are times when it is safer to be clipped together, and other places, as in traveling over a crevasse with the use of ladders, it is better to go it alone.

"It is very important for you to notify us if you are enervated. It is not uncommon to get fatigued and wear out at this altitude. During the ascent to the summit, if you become exhausted, you simply must unclip for the protection of others. The fixed rope is strong, but it cannot handle the weight of many climbers slipping off the edge into the deep crevasses. If you slip or your legs give out, you might find yourself cartwheeling all the way down to base camp and taking the rest of us with you."

His final statement, although deadly serious, was said with a chuckle. It was better that each climber take his own chances. It was unlikely, at that altitude, anyone had the strength or the speed to effectively arrest a falling member of the group. Nonetheless, his lighthearted approach to the serious subject helped lighten the mood as the climbers psyched themselves up for the difficult task ahead.

Maclaren patted Mooy on the back, which caused his friend to stumble slightly from being startled. "Hey, mate. Ya all right? I was just gonna ask—"

"Fine. I'm fine. You just caught me thinkin'. That's all."

"Are you sure about this?"

Mooy tried to convince himself, and his partner. "No doubt about it, mate. I'm ready."

It was a bright, sunny day although somewhat windy, creating a windchill below zero throughout the ascent. Despite their illnesses, Mooy and Maclaren kept pace with the others and refused to ask for a rest period. The group worked together until the first crevasse.

At Mount Everest, like the other tall peaks of the world, under the top layers of snow and ice are deep cracks that climbers fall into on occasion. With the safety precautions in place, the second, third, and fourth climbers can keep from being dragged down with the first guy.

Crevasses regularly open up and close in glaciers as they shift ever so slightly. This movement can't be predicted although warming springtime temperatures was a catalyst. The danger comes when a crevasse created by the shift can't be seen because the top layer of snow doesn't always collapse and fall into them. These thin layers of snow cover can create a deadly trap for a misstep or improper distribution of weight.

After hours of trudging through ice and snow, it was time for a respite. At twenty-seven thousand feet, the Sherpas advised the group that their break would be a brief one. Everyone settled in for a snack and some water. The Aussies spent time talking with their new friends.

The young woman from Ireland spoke in hushed tones. "I've been feeling crappy all day. I think I caught your cold," she said as she playfully slugged Mooy.

Maclaren couldn't resist. "Be lucky if that's all you caught from me, best mate!"

The group of four laughed and then immediately started coughing in unison, drawing a curious look from the other climbers. They regained their composure and stifled their coughs.

"We're almost there, right?" asked the Swedish woman. "I'm excited, but I feel dreadful."

"There will be plenty of time to sleep and recover later," offered Maclaren, who, despite his own illness, was always there to encourage the others.

One of the Sherpas approached the group. "Are we all good here? If not, I can place you at the end of the line after we cross the gully."

"No, we're fine," Maclaren announced on behalf of the group. Then he thought for a moment before asking, "But would it be best for us to be at the rear in the event we need to unclip?"

"Yes. The next step is to cross the North Col equivalent of the Yellow Band. Then it's a series of ramps and we'll be on the northeast ridge. This is the most difficult climb of the route." The Yellow Band was well known to climbers utilizing the route on the Nepal side of Everest. It was the first rock a climber touches on the route up Everest. When their crampons hit hard rock, they've reached twenty-five thousand feet.

"We've got this," mumbled Mooy, who choked back a cough.

Maclaren, who was now having difficulty taking a full, deep breath, wasn't so sure. He rolled his head on his neck and shoulders while blinking his eyes. The sun was causing an excruciating headache, so he searched for some ibuprofen in his pack. He watched as the Sherpa hesitantly left them to locate the other guides. They began to assemble the group for the next stage of the climb.

Maclaren stood and looked back down the north face of the mountain. He considered whether it was time to give up the dream. While he was deep in thought, their new girlfriends had donned their gear and shouted to him, "Now or never!"

Maclaren sighed. *I guess it is.*

CHAPTER ELEVEN

Residence of Dr. Harper Randolph
Brookhaven
Northeast Atlanta, Georgia

Harper's home in Brookhaven, a suburb just northeast of downtown Atlanta, Georgia, met the social requirements of all career-minded couples who might enjoy shopping, night life, and entertainment. The town provided the conveniences of living in close proximity to high-end shopping at Phipps Plaza and the entertainment venues found in Buckhead and Midtown. Restaurants were plentiful, as were nearly a dozen parks providing plenty of recreational greenspace for avid runners like Harper and her husband. For all intents and purposes, Brookhaven lived up to its moniker as the *City in the Forest*.

Their all-brick home was modest compared to others in the community. Bordering the affluent enclave of Buckhead to the west, Brookhaven was replete with new single-family construction, as well as townhomes and lofts. The two-story, four-bedroom house was full of wasted space, namely the upstairs. The guest bedrooms had never been furnished and were used for storage of Christmas decorations, clothing, and a room for the couple's Peloton exercise bikes.

Downstairs was built for entertaining, which the two did from time to time when their schedules allowed. Large spacious living areas coupled with contemporary design created a place for gatherings of up to thirty people comfortably. It was every couple's dream home, yet they rarely used it for their intended purpose.

The CDC had sent a car to pick Harper up from the Dobbins Air Reserve Base in Marietta, northwest of Atlanta. She'd slept well on the military transport that carried her from Dakar to Atlanta. She was accompanied by several epidemiologists who'd been evacuated from Africa or who were at the end of their tour of duty. They made small talk and exchanged information before the droning of the C-130 engines put them all to sleep like exhausted children.

Harper didn't have any luggage. She still wore the same pair of jean shorts and the social distancing tee shirt from three days ago. As the car drove away, she lifted her arm to stretch and immediately lowered it.

"Shower time for you, Dr. Randolph," she said aloud with a laugh. "You're a little gamey."

Harper didn't have any keys either, which was often the case when she returned home from doing fieldwork. She bounded up the brick steps and punched in the house's security code into the biometric lock attached to the solid oak front door. The green light illuminated and the bolt lock disengaged.

Seconds later, she was inside the marble foyer and taking in the cool, fresh air of her home. Harper let out a sigh of relief. She loved her job, but her home was truly her sanctuary. After she took a moment to let her two worlds meet, she stripped off her tee shirt and shorts, along with her shoes, and left them in a pile in the foyer.

"Doc! Hey, Doc, I'm home!" she called out into the spacious home.

Initially, there was no response. Harper walked barefoot across the cool floor toward the kitchen and looked around.

"C'mon, Doc. Stop messing around!"

That was when she heard the unmistakable sound of feet digging as fast as they could on the marble floors. The pitter-patter of puppy feet filled the air as her longtime bestest pal, Doctor Dog, came scampering out of the master bedroom. Harper crouched to the floor and braced for impact.

The lovable beagle was all legs and paws as he crashed into her. He let out a series of howls, barks, and happy yaps that was befitting of his breed's origin—*begueule*, a French word meaning open throat. Harper let him have his moment, not even thinking about admonishing him to use his so-called inside voice. In that moment, she was so happy to be smothered with his kisses that she wanted to hoot and holler, too.

In fact, her beagle pup was so talented at vocalizing his emotions that Harper could easily identify his moods. Of course, there was the standard bark for everyday things like the doorbell ringing or when he demanded a treat for a perceived job well done. Then there was the *I'm-bored-come-play-with-me* forlorn howl that he'd use to hound her, pardon the pun, until she complied with his demands.

Most importantly, however, was the baying sound she'd taught him as a puppy and trained him to use only under certain circumstances. Beagles were bred as hunting dogs. It's believed that their origins dated back to ancient Rome when their ancestors hunted rabbits. Then, over the centuries, in Europe, they were trained as the ultimate fox-catching hounds. Many homes in the suburbs of England and America had a painting of the dapperly dressed Brits riding white horses as their devoted beagles gave chase of a fox.

Beagles were renowned for their sense of smell. Their short legs kept them close to the ground, which allowed them to take in scents without having to stop. Their big floppy ears also helped them notice smells by wafting them toward their powerful noses.

Beagles are not necessarily the best sniffers of all dog breeds. Basset hounds can scent just as well as beagles, but they lack the giddy-up-and-go of beagles. Bloodhounds can actually scent better, but they're big and slobbery and howl a lot. Harper chose Doctor

Dog, the trim, tidy, lovable beagle, for a specific task—to sniff out infectious diseases.

Harper had trained him since he was a puppy to sniff out patients who'd contracted a disease. His first task was to learn the superbug *Clostridium difficile*, or *C. diff*, an infection that plagued hospital patients, especially the elderly, causing lethal outbreaks within health care facilities.

Because existing laboratory tests to diagnose *C. diff* were expensive and slow, potentially delaying the start of treatment for the disease by up to a week, the concept of disease-sniffing dogs was bantered about. Harper taught Doctor Dog to detect *C. diff*, and during her residency at Georgetown, the two were frequently seen walking the hospital corridors on the hunt for infected patients.

Doctor Dog became known throughout Washington for his abilities. In initial tests, he'd correctly identified twenty-five out of thirty patients with *C. diff* after just two months of training.

She'd taught him to sniff the patients until he came to one who was infected. He would sit down and then begin baying, which sounded a lot like yodeling. This throaty yowl was used by the beagle breed to alert fellow dogs on the hunt that they'd picked up an interesting scent. Harper had taught Doctor Dog to use it only when he'd discovered someone with a disease.

Over the years, she'd upped his game, so to speak, to go after even the hint of a disease. She started with using a vial of diseased blood to teach him the scent. Then she'd hide it in the house along with a couple of dozen other clean blood samples. Soon he was able to identify a number of common viruses.

"Hey, buddy. Have you calmed down enough to say hello now?" She teased Doctor Dog and then jutted out her chin to accept some normal, subdued kisses. "Did Miss Sally take good care of you while I was gone? She didn't overfeed you Canine Carry Outs, did she?"

Sally Oglethorpe was a retired nurse from nearby Piedmont-Atlanta Hospital. She'd been an ER nurse for thirty years before her health forced her into retirement. Harper had placed the apartment over their three-car garage for rent, sort of. She and her husband were looking for a caretaker, someone who'd watch over the house and Doctor Dog, as well as do some light housekeeping. It wasn't hard to keep a house neat and tidy when the two primary occupants were frequently gone. Sally jumped at the opportunity to receive free room and board in exchange for taking care of the delightful and lovable beagle pup while, in a way, adopting Harper and her husband.

Doctor Dog put on his best poker face, but his wagging tail didn't lie. Harper laughed as she rubbed his tummy. "Yeah, that's what I figured. Tomorrow, you and I are back on the program. We'll start running before it gets Georgia-hot outside. Deal?"

He began to salivate to the point of creating a pool of drool on the marble floor. Harper shook her head and laughed.

"Doc, what did you do to deserve a treat?"

He responded with a single bark.

"Sorry, buddy, being cute and adorable doesn't earn you a treat."

He immediately flopped to the floor and gave her that sad beagle look she couldn't resist.

"Doc, you're such a manipulator, much like your father," she said with a chuckle. She moseyed over to the pantry closet and dug into the bag of Canine Carry Outs. "I'd better get in the shower, or instead of taking me out for dinner and drinks, he might tie me to a tree like the other mommy hounds."

Woof! Woof!

"I agree, he wouldn't do that, but I do need a shower. Do me a favor and stay. When he comes home, let me know, okay?"

Doc grinned and wagged his tail as if he understood. He probably did.

CHAPTER TWELVE

Residence of Dr. Harper Randolph
Brookhaven
Northeast Atlanta, Georgia

Harper stood in the hot shower for twenty minutes until the water began to turn lukewarm. Then, with a new sense of urgency, she scrambled to wash up and conduct some ladyscaping, a long overdue necessity after being in the jungles of Africa for more than two weeks.

After blow-drying her hair, she checked the time. She had an hour or more before her hubs would return, so she picked out her dress for the evening and lay on the bed in her plush robe. She spent a few minutes on her iPad, scanning emails and the news headlines. Without intending to do so, she fell asleep.

She was awakened by her husband nuzzling her neck and biting her earlobes. She slowly awoke to his kisses and then stretched her neck to make his task easier.

Harper giggled. "Get off me, lover. My husband will be home soon. You know how he can be. Sooo jealous."

Joe Mills responded in a low, manly voice. "I ain't scared, ma'am.

I'm bigger and badder and smarter and, um, I have a beard and he doesn't."

Harper reached up to touch his face. "You don't have a beard," she said in a gentle, sexy tone.

"Um, oh yeah." Joe laughed as he rose onto his knees. "I'm still smarter."

"What about bigger and badder?" she asked as she sat up to embrace him.

"Yeah, that too. All of the above." He held her tight as the two reunited properly.

"God, I've missed you, Joe."

"I've missed you, too. I'm glad you were able to come home early."

Joe Mills was big, but not bad, on the eyes that is. He was eight years older than Harper and had aged well into his mid-forties. He stayed physically fit, as he practically lived in a gym when away from home. His rugged handsomeness and pleasant demeanor made him well liked by everyone and adored by his wife. He began to take off his suit, prompting Harper to reach out for his hand.

"Now you're talkin'. Come here, sir, and ravage me proper."

"Oh, don't you know I want to. But I need a shower, and we've got a car coming to pick us up in an hour."

"We're not driving?" she asked as she hopped out of bed. An hour was a mighty short period of time for a woman who needed to get ready for a dinner date with her husband, especially one that required someone else to drive them.

"No, this evening there will be wine and adult beverages and possibly a late night, so we'll be chauffeured."

"Do tell, a limo?"

Joe started laughing as he teased her. "No, silly girl. Uber."

"What?" she asked in protest. "I'd rather Miss Sally drive us."

"No way! She's half-blind!"

"No, she isn't. She just has trouble with night vision."

"Still. Plus, it'll be dark when we come home."

Joe stripped off his boxers and headed for the shower. Harper took a moment to admire his physique and still-taut derriere.

"Mister, you're lucky I've already blown out my hair or I'd be hot on your heels."

"Save up that pent-up energy, Harper. I'm feelin' it, too. They may have to call the cops on us tonight when we get home."

"Promises, promises," she said as Doctor Dog entered the bedroom. Harper stood over him with her hands on her hips. "Hey, you insubordinate hound, you were supposed to give me a warning when Daddy got home."

The beagle sat down and licked his chops.

"Don't blame him!" Joe shouted from the bedroom. "I bribed him with one of those peanut-butter-filled bones."

Harper knelt down and sniffed Doc's snout. "Sure enough," she whispered. "Bribery works every time. I'm gonna have to figure out a way to step up my game."

The couple busied themselves getting ready and exchanged anecdotes from their time apart. Harper elected not to give Joe the details of her extraction from Burungu, but she did intend to query how he knew about it. For now, she looked forward to a nice quiet evening with the love of her life. Much to her surprise, that wasn't the plan.

CHAPTER THIRTEEN

Home of Herbert Brittain
Buckhead
North Atlanta, Georgia

They weren't picked up by an Uber driver or even a taxi. Instead, an executive car service arrived with a modified Cadillac Escalade outfitted with a wet bar and a television. The two had a glass of wine and talked about the evening as Harper became curious as to where he was taking her.

"Honey, I'm sorry, but I'm guilty of some serious subterfuge here," Joe began to explain before Harper interrupted.

"You're taking me to the Varsity, aren't you?" The Varsity was a downtown Atlanta institution that was known as the world's largest drive-in restaurant. It was also one of Harper and Joe's favorites, but they were a little overdressed.

The sun was beginning to set as the driver continued west on Paces Ferry Road through the heart of Buckhead and toward Pleasant Hill, a small affluent neighborhood in North Atlanta.

"No, we're going to the home of Herbert Brittain," he confessed.

"Wait. Isn't he the—"

Joe finished her sentence. "CEO of Coca-Cola and one of the richest men on the planet? One and the same."

"But he lives in Tyler Perry's house when he's in town, right?" Tyler Perry was a world-renowned actor and producer who once lived in Atlanta in a home worthy of an episode of *Lifestyles of the Rich and Famous*.

"That's correct. Seventeen acres of pristine Chattahoochee River frontage. A whopping thirty-five thousand square feet. Home theater. Spa. Wine cellar. A kitchen just for catering and, drum-roll please, a ballroom."

Harper chuckled. "Big whoop. Ma has a ballroom."

"Not like this one," Joe countered.

"Ma's is older."

Joe laughed and lovingly squeezed his wife's hand. "Okay, you've got me there."

"So we're going to have dinner and drinks, and maybe even dancing, with Mr. Monopoly?"

"Maybe not the dancing part. We'll save that for later if all goes well," quipped Joe.

"Joe, what's this all about?"

He patted her on the leg. "Trust me. You'll see."

The car arrived at the security gate, and after a moment, they were waved inside. Joe and Harper marveled at the massive home as they drove past a courtyard fountain and were greeted by several security personnel, who opened their door.

Harper took a deep breath and waited as Joe exited the vehicle. He assisted her out by extending his hand. Harper elegantly exited, being careful to hold the front of her black evening dress together so the slit didn't reveal too much. She took his arm and walked to the front door, where they were greeted by members of the Brittains' staff.

As if they had arrived at a nineteenth-century party, the butler formerly announced their arrival.

"Ladies and gentlemen, presenting Congressman Joe Mills and his wife, Dr. Harper Randolph."

A smattering of polite applause could be heard through the foyer and into the parlors that flanked the entry. Harper was in awe of the magnificent home. She leaned into Joe and whispered, "Joe, I'm underdressed."

Joe furrowed his brow and admired his wife's beauty. "No, you're not. You're stunning."

She smiled and whispered in his ear as an older man and his wife approached, "I forgot my tiara."

Joe couldn't contain himself as he burst out laughing, relieving some of the nervous jitters. It turned out to be the perfect introduction to their host and hostess.

"Well, I see our little soiree has already become a roaring success!" exclaimed Herbert Brittain, a self-made billionaire, philanthropist and political activist. "Welcome, Congressman! Please let me introduce you to my wife, Beatrice."

"Congressman, it's such a pleasure to finally meet our guest of honor," she said as she extended her hand to shake Joe's.

Harper raised her eyebrows and shot Joe a glance. *Guest of honor? What?*

"It's my pleasure, Mrs. Brittain. Please, both of you, let me introduce you to the woman who keeps me grounded and saves the world in her spare time."

The host and hostess laughed at Joe's introduction as Harper shook hands with them both, a practice she'd abandoned long ago, but the circumstances caused her to let down her guard.

"Oh, please." She laughed. "Grounding Joe would be like tethering a rocket to a hunk of Styrofoam. Up, up and away!"

The two couples hit it off right from the start, which was exactly what Congressman Joe Mills needed. Within seconds, Beatrice Brittain had whisked Harper away in one direction while Herbert Brittain had led Joe in another to make more introductions to wealthy individuals, all of whom looked forward to pumping the hand of the up-and-coming congressman from the Sixth Congressional District of Georgia.

You see, an election was coming, and these wealthy business

owners had plans for Joe.

Harper was a tomboy at heart, having grown up in a small town in rural Georgia a couple of hours east of Atlanta. Fancy dinners or rubbing elbows with the rich and powerful was not something she was accustomed to. It certainly was a far cry from living in a tiny hut in the African jungle as she did a few days ago. Yet here she was, the wife of a dynamic, powerful congressman who'd made a name for himself around the country as an honest straight shooter. Certainly a rare trait for Washington politicians.

"You have such a lovely home, Mrs. Brittain," began Harper as she was taken through the parlors and into the wine cellar.

"Thank you, dear," the matronly hostess said. "I'm told you were raised in quite a magnificent home yourself."

At first Harper was surprised at the woman's statement, but then she remembered the many conversations with Joe about how no part of their lives would ever remain a secret.

Harper laughed, doing her best to be a dutiful, attuned wife. "Oh, that old place."

Mrs. Brittain playfully swatted at the air with her free hand as her other arm wrapped through Harper's arm. The Southern born and raised woman said, "Aren't you the sweetest doughnut in the dozen. I would hardly call a home built in 1795 *that old place*. I hear it's quite special."

Harper smiled and nodded as she admired the wine selection. She was surprised she hadn't been offered a glass yet and vowed to sneak back to the cellar later for a complimentary bottle to go.

"Yes, ma'am." She poured on her Southern charm. "It is more than just home to me, my grandmother and great-grandmother. It's a part of history they vowed to preserve many years ago. However, at the end of the day, it's a comforting home, full of love and a home-cooked meal whenever we have the opportunity to visit."

"Did you say great-grandmother?"

"Yes, ma'am. Mimi, as I call her, is ninety-eight. My grandmother, whom I call Ma, is seventy-four."

"My goodness, child, you have some phenomenal genes."

Harper shrugged as a wave of sadness came over her that she quickly pushed back into the dark recesses of her memory. "I suppose I do."

Mrs. Brittain suddenly stopped as if she knew what Harper was thinking. She quickly changed the subject.

"Before we join the others, I'm going to ask you a pointed, personal question. May I?"

Harper tried not to think about her answer, as she didn't want the woman to consider her response to be contrived. *Besides*, Harper thought, *she most likely knows everything about us anyway.*

"Absolutely."

"Harper, politics is a dirty business. It's full of a criminal element that is never held accountable for their dastardly deeds. However, it is a necessary evil. A game practiced by people who actually enjoy it."

"Yes, ma'am." Harper knew there was a question coming, although she had no idea why it was being asked.

"Are you, and your husband, for that matter, prepared to withstand the kind of scrutiny that few people have the intestinal fortitude to volunteer for?"

Harper turned to her. "We've been through five congressional campaigns, and Joe has never lost."

Mrs. Brittain scowled. "I'm not talking about winning and losing. I'm talking about brutal assaults on your character. The questioning of every decision you've made while at the CDC. Blatant lies that take weeks to refute."

"Ma'am, I fight diseases that can't be seen. Of unknown origin. And kill with brutal efficiency. Nothing scares me off anymore."

Without another word, her hostess escorted her into the ballroom, where Mr. Brittain and Joe met them halfway. "Herbert, I love this young woman. I wish I had a daughter just like her."

Harper glanced from Mr. Brittain to her husband. Joe was beaming with pride. Harper winked, assuming that she'd passed the test. Now, she looked forward to pulling Joe aside and demanding to know what the hell this was all about.

CHAPTER FOURTEEN

Mount Everest
Tibet Autonomous Region
People's Republic of China

The north face of Mount Everest was steeped in history, starting with multiple attempts by climbers to conquer it through the 1920s and 1930s. It wasn't until 1953 that Sir Edmund Hillary, a New Zealander, became the first climber confirmed to have reached the summit of the tallest mountain in the world. It was a Chinese team who made the first summit from Tibet some seven years later. It took ladders and herculean efforts on the part of the climbers to make it to the top.

When the skies began to darken and the wind began to whip up, Mooy and Maclaren thought their day would be coming to an abrupt end. There was only one problem. The group had been divided.

The challenging climb up the northeast ridge was still ahead. There were three steps of rock climbs to the summit. The first of the three features required the climber to pull hand-over-hand on the fixed ropes along a lengthy gully to the top of the ridge. Once that was accomplished, the climbers would take a deep inhalation of their oxygen to prepare for the second step. It was the crux of their climb, utilizing what had become known as the Chinese Ladder, an upgraded version of the one used by Sir Edmund Hillary.

The climbers were required to scale a ten-foot slab of rock and then ascend a near vertical, thirty-foot-tall ladder. During this maneuver, the climber was exposed to a certain death. A slip of the foot or a momentary lapse of concentration resulted in the climber falling ten thousand feet down the mountain.

The group had made their way up the ladder except for Mooy and Maclaren, the two women, and the trailing Sherpa. The group had already spent eight hours on their climb to the summit and were one step away from the final five-hundred-foot ascent to the top.

The combination of high altitude, heavy breathing, and an unknown sickness had taken its toll on the group. They encouraged one another, and the Sherpas, no longer oblivious to the poor health of some of their group, Mooy and Maclaren in particular, were carefully monitoring the climbers and assisting them as much as possible.

The decision had been made to disconnect the last four climbers, as they were showing signs of fatigue. At this stage of the climb, it was not possible to stop and make camp for the simple reason there was no place to pitch a tent and secure it.

Returning with only part of the climbers was not an option either. It was more difficult to navigate on the descent, especially on the Chinese Ladder, as the climbers were unable to see their feet placement on the ladder rungs. Because Mooy and Maclaren were able to convince the last Sherpa they were capable of continuing, they slowly started up the ladder.

One by one, summoning all their strength and concentration, and in the face of an unknown illness that had overtaken their bodies, the four remaining climbers made it up the ladder to the Third Step.

Their pace was much slower than the one set by the group of

healthy climbers. As the first half of their group reached the final, steep snowy slope to the summit, a second trailing group of climbers was approaching the stragglers—Mooy, Maclaren and the women.

Causing another group of climbers to wait on the side of a treacherous mountain was extremely dangerous. This wasn't like golf, where a slow foursome pulled over to let a faster group play through. Or even auto racing, where the driver would steer his slower car out of the racing groove to make way for the speedier leaders to pass.

Climbing Everest was a single-file, one-way-up and one-way-down endeavor. The slow pace made by the Aussie's group was resulting in a traffic jam of two dozen climbers and their Sherpas along the steep snowy slope leading to the pyramid-shaped summit.

The final five hundred feet was narrow with ten-thousand-foot drop-offs on both sides. The sloped angle ranged from thirty to sixty degrees. The climbers were throttled by the wind and extremely cold temperatures. Despite the challenges and the danger, their goal, their dream was in reach.

At this point, it was well after midnight, but there was still daylight. At this elevation, on top of the world, the curvature of the Earth plays a different role than what most are accustomed to around sea level. The sunset of many hours ago at lower elevations had not occurred at the summit due to the fact that nothing obstructed the climbers' view. From this perspective, the planet looked flat. Until you looked down.

Just above the Third Step, as they prepared to climb the final five hundred feet, Mooy was the first to see the two dead bodies, which lay a hundred feet below him on the side of the ridge. He squinted his eyes and tried to wipe the hallucinatory effects of the disease inside his body out of his mind.

It wasn't always possible to retrieve the dead from Everest. Sometimes, there was no path for the Sherpas to reach them. Other times, they'd fallen so far that only a helicopter was able to retrieve the dead, and helicopter rescues had been forbidden by the Chinese government.

Mooy shook the thoughts out of his head. In his confused state of mind, the down suits worn by the dead climbers resembled the same colors he and Maclaren were wearing. He looked around for his mate, but Maclaren had already started up the rope with the two women. Mooy gathered himself and pulled on the fixed rope.

A little too hard, in fact.

CHAPTER FIFTEEN

Mount Everest
Tibet Autonomous Region
People's Republic of China

An ancient exercise that had gained popularity around the world was rope training, commonly referred to as *battle rope* exercises. Rope training consisted of vigorously undulating a rope with the upper body to create a kinetic wave effect. The process of shaking the ropes into continuous waves that rollicked from the exerciser to the post where it was affixed had proven to be an excellent tool for cardiovascular training and body toning. It required stamina and coordination to control the rope so that it didn't pop out of your hands.

Mooy didn't intend to grasp the fixed rope so hard, nor did he anticipate losing his balance as he did so. But nothing about his actions could ever be explained because those who witnessed it wouldn't live to tell about it.

As he grasped the fixed line, it shook in a violent wave thirty feet up the final slope to the summit. The kinetic effect impacted the next three climbers in line—Maclaren and the two women. They lost their grip on the fixed rope and then their footing.

Like several dominos that had been toppled, Maclaren crashed into the woman from Ireland, who in turn rolled into the feet of the woman from Sweden. All three of them desperately tried to grasp the fixed rope to slow their descent toward Mooy and the trailing Sherpa.

The Swede was the first to let go of the rope. She slid off the side of the narrow ridge, desperately grasping the lifeline until she let go. She sailed off the edge, her body crashing against the granite and tumbling thousands of feet to her death.

The fixed rope whipped back into its normal position, but the force of its snapping into place caused a ripple effect up the line. Several other climbers, fatigued by the arduous climb and their bodies weakened from the onset of the illness contracted from the Aussies, fell to the snow.

A train wreck was unfolding, and only a handful of people had the best view—the second group of climbers who'd just completed the climb up the Third Step.

Body after body came tumbling down the snowfield leading to the summit. The gravity, the slippery conditions, and the sixty-degree slope all prevented the climbers from arresting their fall.

Some climbers in the second group wisely scrambled out of the way from the people rocketing toward them. Others, valiantly, but foolishly, tried to break the climbers' fall in an attempt to save lives. They lost their own in the process.

Below the Third Step, the remaining members of the second group stood in surreal silence, mouths agape as they looked upward. Body after body flew over their heads, crashing into the top rungs of the Chinese Ladder. Their bones could be heard breaking as they were smashed against the steel before disappearing to the midpoint of Mount Everest. The impact of these bodies broke the ladder loose from its supports in the rock and bent it backwards until the entire structure crashed to the rocks below.

It was a brutal death for all who were caught up in the horrific chain of events. It was even more so for Mooy. He survived the initial fall, landing in the snow just above where the top of the Chinese Ladder was attached. Some members of the second group pulled him to the side as more bodies tumbled in their direction, including a screaming Maclaren, who bounced once on the snow before flying over the cliff.

"He's barely breathing!" shouted one of the climbers.

"Give him your oxygen!" instructed another.

When Mooy was unable to recover with the assistance of oxygen, another climber suggested mouth-to-mouth resuscitation to force air into his lungs. One of the climbers, a nurse practitioner, stepped in to help. She followed the protocols she'd learned since nursing school.

"Hurry! He's turning blue!" yelled one of the climbers hovering over his body.

"It looks like he's drowning!" shouted another.

She began to clear his airways, and suddenly, a frothy foam of bubbly saliva began to come out the sides of Mooy's mouth. Then he had a seizure. His body shook violently as the convulsions overtook it. His chest heaved as if it was gasping for air. Finally, as fast as the onset of these symptoms occurred, Mooy's body collapsed. He was dead.

The nurse practitioner closed his eyelids and knelt on her knees over him for several minutes, crying. She wiped the foam off her gloves onto the snow. Because of the extreme cold, her tears began to freeze on her cheeks and caused her eyes to sting. She furiously rubbed them to alleviate the pain until the others who'd witnessed the gruesome death huddled around her to create some warmth.

The bodies stopped flying over their heads. Mooy's corpse lay lifeless in the snow. And they prayed that this nightmare would be over. Unfortunately, it was only beginning.

PART II

EMERGENCE OF A MONSTER

We stop looking for monsters under the bed when we realize they're inside of us.
~ The Joker

CHAPTER SIXTEEN

Centers for Disease Control and Prevention
CDC Headquarters
Atlanta, Georgia

Harper wheeled her black Porsche 911 onto North Druid Hills Road and headed south toward the CDC Headquarters in the Druid Hills community of Atlanta. She cued up her favorite Apple playlist and allowed the speakers to fill the interior of the sports car with music. She was in a great mood that morning. Spending forty-eight consecutive hours alone with her husband was a cure for all that ailed her.

The bombshells dropped on her Friday night caught her off guard, but she didn't chastise Joe for his surprises. He was proud of the opportunity to rub elbows with some of the largest political donors to his party in America. They liked him. No, they wanted him to aspire to bigger and better things.

Politics was a process that involved lots of elbow-rubbing, ass-kissing, and money-raising. For reasons that Harper fully understood because she married the man, the entrepreneurs and political leaders at the Brittain home Friday night had taken a keen interest in Joe. It made her proud, but it also reminded her that their lives could change considerably if he sought a Senate seat, residency at the governor's mansion, or something even higher.

Harper shook her head in an attempt to get politics out of her mind, and she focused on her upcoming day. She never bothered asking Joe how he knew she'd been pulled out of Africa. In his position, he had powerful allies within the government, and it wouldn't surprise her one bit that he had someone keeping tabs on her.

Furthermore, Joe and her boss at the CDC knew each other well, as the two of them frequently had to consult on budgetary matters. Especially now. The federal government faced yet another shutdown as the two political parties played tug-of-war with taxpayer dollars.

Dr. Berger Reitherman was the director of the Center for Surveillance, Epidemiology, and Laboratory Services, CSELS, a mouthful no matter how it was enunciated. Prior to coming on board with the CDC, he was a program manager in the infectious disease office at DARPA, the Defense Advanced Research Projects Agency, an agency of the U.S. Department of Defense known for its secrecy and innovative breakthroughs on behalf of the nation's military. His expertise as a physician, scientist, and dedicated laboratorian provided a strong foundation to lead the CDC's efforts to track infectious disease. It also commanded the respect of his peers, coworkers, and international counterparts.

Dr. Reitherman appreciated Harper's desire to work abroad. In his early years with the CDC, he'd spent a considerable amount of time as an attaché at the U.S. Mission in Vietnam, where he coordinated work in the fight against HIV/AIDS.

Now, as the chief administrator of CSELS, and Harper's direct supervisor, he had to consider the larger picture when he dealt with his staff. He'd warned on more than one occasion that Harper's capabilities and experience were far too valuable to risk her on humanitarian missions to Africa or any other nation abroad.

Harper took a deep breath and sighed as she pulled into the

parking garage at the CDC campus located adjacent to Emory University. She walked with purpose, as she always did, to the secured entrance when she stopped. She checked her watch and remembered that nobody was expecting her to be in today despite the fact it was the start of a workweek for most. She was allowed as many days as she wanted to decompress from her tour of duty in Africa.

Before checking in with security and swiping her badge, she chose to walk across the Emory campus to fetch a caramel latte with extra caramel and extra foam, a delicacy she'd craved above all others while away. Besides, she felt certain some type of notification or red light would flash in Dr. Reitherman's office the moment she entered the building, prompting a page or a phone call or even an armed security escort to his office. She needed to make the rounds before being told she was being sidelined from international work, an order she was certainly expecting.

Emory was nestled in the midst of Druid Hills, which was often referred to as Atlanta's second suburb. It was located just a few miles to the east of the downtown business district but was in a world of its own. Designed by the famed city planner Frederick Olmsted, who laid out the Capitol Grounds in Washington and Central Park in New York, Druid Hills was a quaint neighborhood of multimillion-dollar homes, serene parks, and tree-lined lakes.

Emory University and the CDC were grouped together in the center of Druid Hills, creating a campus-like atmosphere. Harper enjoyed the one-mile stroll to the Emory Bookstore, where Starbucks was located. Seeing the college kids congregating under the trees, sharing notes about upcoming classes, or discussing the events of the day reminded Harper of her undergraduate days at the University of Notre Dame just outside South Bend, Indiana. She'd hustled through undergrad in just three years but still managed to enjoy college life. Once she moved on to post-graduate studies and medical school at Georgetown, she was all business, focusing on her coursework and medical training.

Thirty minutes later, with the rush of caffeine from the latte coursing through her body, Harper stood in line to enter the CDC. Like all public buildings, visitors and employees alike were required to enter through a metal detector and agree to a random pat-down. Having CDC credentials and being familiar to the security personnel didn't grant you a waiver.

Another security protocol was having every entrant's temperature taken with a noncontact digital thermometer. While the lack of a fever didn't mean you were free from an infectious disease, having a fever meant you might be ill. The CDC, the protector of Americans against contagions, could ill afford its headquarters to be the site of an outbreak.

Harper passed through and then looked skyward as if she awaited alarms to be sounded or the voice of the CDC gods to page her to Dr. Reitherman's office.

Neither of those things happened, so she smiled as she headed to her office—the long way. As much as she loved fieldwork, she enjoyed suiting up to go into the lab. Nestled in the center of the building was the brain of disease detective work. Built like a spaceship, the biosafety level 4 laboratory, BSL-4, was over ten thousand square feet of airtight, pressurized space that was closely monitored by multiple computer systems and a dozen sets of human eyes.

This was where as many as thirty doctorate-level epidemiologists and scientists tried to determine how deadly infectious diseases live, infect, and kill their hosts. Just outside the BSL-4, there were a series of computer workstations giving the CDC personnel immediate access to research and data, if needed. It wasn't unusual for Harper, when she was in the BSL-4, to communicate directly with her assistant to relay information back and forth.

Harper waved and smiled to a few familiar faces who happened to look up as she passed by. She never grew tired or bored with her job because she was given the latitude to perform multiple functions. Harper was too extroverted to be a lab rat, hunkered down for hours upon hours in a laboratory. Yet she still loved the thrill of the hunt from a disease's natural environment to the vials of the BSL-4.

She made her way to her assistant's office. Elizabeth Becker was one of a kind. You simply couldn't replicate the enthusiasm, drive, desire, and downright-perky demeanor she exuded. When she was assigned to Harper as an assistant, the two created a dynamo of a team.

"Becker, did you miss me?" Harper never referred to her assistant by her first name. In fact, Becker had more nicknames than anyone at the CDC, perhaps combined. And, to be sure, there was a story behind each and every one of them.

"Dr. Randolph!" she shouted exuberantly. She waved for Harper to enter her office. "I heard you were back this morning."

"You did? How?"

"The *Bergermeister*'s been looking for you," she responded with a grin. One of the reason Becker had accumulated so many nicknames for herself was the fact she'd assigned so many to others, except Harper. She chose to take a poke at Dr. Reitherman's ancestry by modifying the German word for mayor —*Bürgermeister*.

"Already?" asked Harper, unsurprised at the revelation.

"Actually, he stopped in personally right after my arrival this morning to see if you'd checked in with me. He didn't want to bother you at home since Joe is in town."

Harper scowled. *Why is everybody keeping tabs on me?* She glanced down at her desk and saw a coffee mug bearing the crimson-colored B of Bradley University, Becker's alma mater. It was full of multicolored jelly beans. As they chatted, Becker seemed to have a method to eating the sugary candy.

"Becker, I have to know something."

"What?"

"When you reach into the mug and pluck out a few jellybeans, do you just randomly grab a few, or are you intentionally picking the same color?"

Becker cocked her head to the side and studied Harper, curious as to why her boss would ask such a silly question. "Intentionally pick the same color, of course. I'm not some wild animal!"

Harper started laughing, but Becker's face remained emotionless. Harper caught herself and stifled the laugh by covering her mouth for fear she'd offended her assistant. That caused Becker to burst out laughing as well.

"Okay, okay. You know me," she began. Becker held her thumb and forefinger against one another, allowing barely enough space to see through. "I've got just a twinge of OCD. It could be worse, right?"

"That's true. In our job, not being a little obsessive-compulsive could get us killed."

Becker was about to add something when her eyes grew wide at the sight of Dr. Reitherman, who'd arrived outside her office with another CDC staffer. He finished up his instructions to the man and then poked his head inside the office.

"Good, I found you," he said brusquely.

"Me, I've been here all morning," said the petite blonde, ever the jokester, whose adorable nature allowed her to get away with more than most. Becker was also very protective of Harper. She wanted to give her boss time to prepare for Dr. Reitherman's unexpected arrival.

Dr. Reitherman seemed to enjoy the effort to buy time. "Yes, I know. We spoke earlier. I was referring to Dr. Randolph. Would you join me in my office? We have some catching up to do."

Harper shrugged and agreed. She followed the director out but managed a sly wave and a thumbs-up to Becker, who immediately picked out three green jelly beans.

CHAPTER SEVENTEEN

CDC Headquarters
Atlanta

Dr. Reitherman was a busy man, so he wasted no time in getting to the point. "I'm glad the UN was monitoring the mutineers' activity and got you out of there safely."

"Of course, sir, I'm very appreciative of what they did. I hate that the country has to battle a virulent disease like Ebola and their fellow countrymen at the same time. Frankly, I'm not sure which war is more difficult to fight."

"Well, it appears you appreciate the need to remove you from the situation. The administration sees you, and others at the CDC, as valuable assets that shouldn't lose their lives in the middle of a civil war."

"Sir, those people need me. All of us. They truly want our help."

"And one day, they'll have Americans there again. For now, the situation is too hot on the ground and, just as important, politically. I know you're aware of the potential budget impasse looming over our heads."

Harper sighed. She might have been on the front line of fighting diseases, but her husband was navigating the shark-infested waters of Washington like a rear admiral in command of an expeditionary strike group. It was a multitrillion-dollar chess match with people's jobs and lives caught in the middle.

"I remember two years ago before the election. Hundreds of thousands of federal employees didn't know if they'd be going to work from one day to the next. Around here, it was like *The Walking Dead*. A bunch of zombies consumed by the budget impasse. I was one of them."

Dr. Reitherman nodded. "It was a terrible time. In my fourteen years at the CDC, it was the only time I felt I couldn't do my job. We had to prepare to furlough eighty-eight hundred staff members. They were people at all levels of our operation who had been protecting Americans from deadly diseases one day and would be sitting at home the next."

Harper shook her head in disgust. "Diseases don't care if we're here or not."

Dr. Reitherman raised his eyebrows and sighed. "Truer words, Harper. Truer words. It's a good thing we have a real friend in Washington like your husband. I've been able to work closely with his staff to outline must-haves versus wish-list items in our budget."

"Are they gonna cut us?" asked Harper, who was somewhat in the dark. Much of the budget negotiations had taken place over the last couple of weeks while she was in Africa. She and Joe had agreed not to waste any of their precious time over the weekend discussing the budget or anything else that might aggravate them.

"Not if Joe has his way. You know the game. Ask for too much, settle for what you need. Spend your allocation plus a few percent for inflation. Blah-blah-blah."

Harper chuckled and smiled. She dreaded the day Dr. Reitherman was elevated to a higher position within the CDC. He was a fairly young man at fifty-four. It was only a matter of time before he was moved up the chain of leadership to principal deputy director and then, depending on the party affiliation of future administrations, the top position of director of the CDC. She felt fortunate to have his ear and confidence. From a career standpoint, she'd hitched her wagon to the right horse.

She started to push herself out of the chair in an effort to avoid the real reason she was probably called into his office. Dr. Reitherman, however, hadn't forgotten.

"Harper, Africa's field operations have been shut down indefinitely. Face it, they'll be fighting the current strain of Ebola for years to come. The vaccine, Ervebo, was fully approved by the FDA, and Merck has been distributing it throughout Central Africa. The trials in Zaire were exceptionally successful, and your work, along with others', in the DR Congo has stemmed the tide of cases."

"I'd like to continue that work, sir. Isn't there a way around the president's decision? You know, loan me to the UN and we could claim ignorance that they sent me back in."

Dr. Reitherman laughed. "Not gonna happen, Harper. For one thing, fair or not, you're too high-profile as it is. A congressman's wife garners more attention from the media snoops than the rest of our people. Besides, you're a disease detective. Let's leave the treatment aspect of what we do to local physicians on the ground."

"I know, sir. I get it. It's just that I want to help wipe out the diseases, not just find them."

"Listen, Ebola will never fully be under control in Africa. It's endemic just like pneumonic plague is to Madagascar and parts of our American Southwest. As you know, there is a never-ending supply of infectious diseases to deal with. We're called the nation's health protection agency for a reason.

"The military may protect the nation from terrorists or countries that hate us, but at least their enemy can be seen and, at times, negotiated with. We're at war with organisms one-billionth our size that can suddenly emerge from any number of unexpected origins. It's up to us to look for clues and figure out what we're battling."

"Yes, sir. I understand. The fact is, I guess," she began before hesitating to gather her thoughts. "I like the challenge. I like saving lives and seeing the appreciation on the faces of the villagers when I do. It's almost an instant gratification thing."

"The work you do here saves lives, Harper. You may not get to meet them face-to-face in the kind of intimate setting you've experienced in Africa. But they are lives saved nonetheless."

Harper nodded in agreement as Dr. Reitherman continued. "We've got plenty on our platter right now. West Nile virus is on course to break records in the Gulf States. Hantavirus has exploded in Colorado. When these outbreaks occur, the EIS is the first on the scene. We're the Sherlock Holmeses of medicine. You're one of a hundred sixty physicians, scientists, and veterinarians who are ready to fly around the world on a moment's notice to investigate these newly discovered infectious diseases, help the CDC manage a response, and contain a burgeoning outbreak."

Harper sat a little taller in her chair. She was proud to be one of the chosen few who made up the Epidemic Intelligence Service. Perhaps she needed a reminder from Dr. Reitherman as to how important her role was in the overall scheme of things. She managed a smile and nodded her understanding of what he was trying to do.

"I'm on board, sir. One hundred percent. I won't ask again."

Dr. Reitherman pushed his chair back and studied Harper for a moment. "We're very lucky to have you. On a professional level as well as a personal level. I would be devastated if something happened to you out there."

"Thank you, sir."

CHAPTER EIGHTEEN

Mount Everest
Tibet Autonomous Region
People's Republic of China

Dead bodies were a common sight on top of Mount Everest. Each spring, eleven people die on average in their attempts to climb the world's tallest mountain. One year, a sudden avalanche roared through Everest, killing nineteen.

When people die on Everest, it can be impossible to retrieve and remove bodies. Over time, they lay exposed to the elements, decomposing a little slower due to the cold temperatures. Eventually turning to dust before the strong winds carry away the climbers' gear, and the remains with it.

For those loved ones seeking repatriation of the remains, they have to pay tens of thousands of dollars to Sherpas willing to risk their own lives to recover the dead. After two Nepalese climbers perished trying to recover a dead climber decades ago, most bodies were left lying on the mountain. The lawyers got involved and began to offer grim *body disposal* forms to be signed by climbers before they began their trek to the top. The document had the same force and effect as a *Do Not Resuscitate* order, except it provided that the dead climber's corpse would remain on the mountain.

The Sherpas operating from the South Base Camp on the Nepal side of Everest were more compassionate and willing to accommodate family members in their quest to recover the dead. On the North Col, the Chinese military had to get involved, and the answer to recovery requests was always the same—no.

After the collapse of the Chinese Ladder, Beijing got involved in the evacuation of the stranded climbers nearest the summit. Military specialists were sent in, which angered the Sherpas, who were very protective of their turf in the Himalayans. It was part of an ongoing feud between the Sherpas and both the Nepalese army and, to a lesser extent, the Chinese military. One doesn't feud with the People's Liberation Army, only complain inwardly.

Sadly, Everest and its nearby peaks were also the home of nearly forty tons of waste and refuse left behind by years of climbers. Everything from empty oxygen canisters and climbing gear to food waste and decomposing bodies littered the cliffs and crevasses.

When a cleanup effort was mobilized by both nations, they chose military personnel over the local Sherpas and porters to do the work. Sherpa guides complained they were best equipped and should be paid accordingly. The military disagreed.

After the disaster at Mount Everest involving the climbing party that included the two men from Australia, Mooy and Maclaren, the Beijing government closed the North Col route to the summit and sent in their highly skilled special forces to scale the mountain, repair the Chinese Ladder, and rescue the stranded climbers.

After the new ladder was reinstalled, they had to deal with the stranded climbers and the dead bodies. Of the eleven who perished in the accident, only one, Mooy, was easily accessible. He would be removed by a team of four soldiers from the famed Shenyang Military Region Special Forces Unit known as the *Siberian Tiger*. This unit was trained to complete missions that involved wilderness survival in extreme conditions. Training included forcing soldiers to spend as long as four months in the mountain environments with no shelter or food. They were, by trade, experienced climbers, and the four members of the body-retrieval team had scaled Everest multiple times.

The four men were on loan that spring as part of the mountain cleanup to the Chengdu Military Region, which included Tibet. The men were granted great latitude in their jobs, as they were given discretion as to whether an aspect of the cleanup was too dangerous to undertake. As a reward for their bravery, they were extended extraordinary social privileges, which included long periods of time off and expedited travel permits abroad.

Their team leader, Yao Qi, orchestrated the recovery effort. He was also a trained medic. He and his men free-climbed up the vertical face of the rock where the Chinese Ladder hung precariously to its lower-half bolts. Once his team was in place at the top, he assisted in the rescue of the stranded climbers. It would take another team of PLA engineers from the Siberian Tiger unit to repair the ladder later.

After the climbers at the top were evacuated with the assistance of the PLA soldiers, and safely dropped to the bottom of the thirty-foot rock face, Yao turned his attention to the dead. Ordinarily, the bodies are put into some type of rigging, whether it be a lightweight sled or simply wrapped in fabric. Ropes were secured to the body to avoid a sudden slip or weight shift as they descended the mountain.

He commanded a unit of twelve overall, some with greater skills than others. There were several bodies who'd crashed into the Chinese Ladder and fallen to the rocks just below it. They were easily retrievable by the less experienced members of the unit.

Other bodies, such as Maclaren's, had fallen too far into the crevasse and couldn't be recovered without taking great risk. Because his orders were limited to repairing the ladder, rescuing the stranded, and removing the dead who were on the route, Yao assigned those duties based on experience and capabilities.

Along with his three most experienced climbers, Yao scaled the Chinese Ladder to prepare the body of Mooy for transportation. Descending the near vertical Chinese Ladder with a dead body would prove difficult. Yao worked with the men to prepare a sled to transfer the body in.

As they made their preparations, the death of Mooy began to strike him as odd. He had seen the badly broken bodies of fallen climbers in the past. Most died instantaneously from the head trauma and broken spines. Mooy's body was different.

According to the climbers they spoke to who witnessed his death, Mooy's fall, while certainly painful, didn't kill him. He seemed to die from some type of internal injury that caused his mouth to foam and his body to drown, for lack of a better description.

At this point, after more than twenty-four hours lying in the shaded cold ice and snow, Mooy's corpse was beginning to freeze. His body weighed nearly twice its actual weight, and it would be extremely difficult to take him down the Chinese Ladder, much less the North Col.

Yao made the extraordinary decision to call in an air ambulance, of sorts. At nearly twenty-five thousand feet, operating a helicopter was considered borderline insane. However, the PLA was prepared. So the four men gathered around Mooy's body and chatted about their upcoming furlough while they wiggled their toes and fingers to avoid frostbite.

CHAPTER NINETEEN

Mount Everest
Tibet Autonomous Region
People's Republic of China

Most helicopters were not made for high-altitude flying, much less performing hovering maneuvers at over twenty thousand feet. The cold temperatures and gusty winds provided a challenge for both man and machine.

Flying airplanes at thirty-five thousand feet was routine. However, helicopters with their relatively small rotary wings struggle in the thin air of higher altitudes. The record altitude for helicopter flight was forty thousand feet in a highly modified French-made chopper. Most helicopters were only capable of hovering in ground effect. HIGE, in helicopter jargon, was around fourteen thousand feet.

Much depended upon the design of the engine. In the thinner air, it becomes more important for the engine to breathe than the rotor's ability to provide lift. If the machine's design allows it to achieve the high altitude in flight, then it's up to the pilot to hover close to the high ground to maximize its capability.

The Chinese-made Changhe Z-11W was based upon the Eurocopter AS350 that had performed a high-altitude rescue at Alaska's Mount McKinley years ago. Primarily used by the PLA's ground forces as a utility helicopter, this variant was designed and retrofitted for medical-evacuation roles.

This rescue was dangerous on many levels. The effort would take place in two phases. First, two members of Yao's team would be lifted into the chopper to assist in hoisting the body upward. With strong winds prevalent near the summit, the dead weight could begin to swing wildly, making the pilot's ability to maintain control of the helicopter difficult. Second, Yao and the fourth member of the team would be lifted skyward to extract them off the mountain.

The pilot hovered roughly a hundred feet off the north face of Everest, steadily allowing the winch to drop a steel cable toward Yao. The wind was strong and blowing in gusts, causing the helicopter to twist and roll as the cable swung wildly below it.

The powerful rotors wreaked havoc below them. Between the gusty winds, the cold temperatures, and the blowing debris, Yao and his team were pummeled by the elements. They persevered, however, as the first two members of the team, strapped into their rescue harnesses, rode up the face of the mountain, using their legs to prevent them from being smacked against the side.

Next, it was Mooy's turn. His corpse was placed into an inflatable rescue stretcher. Yao and his men stripped off Mooy's excess gear and parkas so he could fit in the slender sled. As the chopper, with the aid of the soldiers, lifted the stretcher upward, the body experienced a brutal ascent. Smashing wildly out of control at times, the exposed face and body parts were crushed against the granite, causing gashes in his flesh to appear. However, because of Mooy's frozen state, he didn't bleed.

Lastly, Yao and his immediate subordinate gave one final look around the accident scene and then joined their team in the chopper. The pilot ensured everyone was secure, and then he asked the team if they were interested in a little heat throughout the cabin of the helicopter. They all got a good laugh as they exchanged barbs with the pilot, who slowly descended to a lower altitude before banking north toward Lhasa, Tibet, the region's capital.

As they flew at a more comfortable altitude, all four men breathed a sigh of relief and enjoyed the warm air generated by the chopper's ventilation and heat system. They began to remove the extra layers of clothing and gear designed to protect them from the frigid temperatures and cold winds of Everest's north face. After an hour in flight, they began to thaw out.

So did Mooy.

CHAPTER TWENTY

Office of Congressman Joe Mills
Longworth House Office Building
Washington, DC

Joe Mills was a Georgian. Born and raised in Atlanta, he grew up as a kid playing baseball, adoring the Atlanta Braves, and learning politics from his father, who'd been a well-known figure in Georgia politics for twenty-six years. His dad started as a Gwinnett County commissioner, moved on to become a state representative, and then a state senator. Eventually, he was elevated to the position of majority leader of the Georgia State Senate.

Joe's father had been the congressman from Georgia's Sixth Congressional District for twelve years until his untimely demise. The official cause of his death was listed as pneumonia, but the disease that precipitated it was a mysterious respiratory virus that plagued the Middle East. Similar to MERS, Middle East respiratory syndrome, the disease was spread from an infected person's respiratory secretions such as coughing and sneezing.

His dad had traveled to the Middle East as part of a congressional delegation to meet with U.S. troops deployed in the

Central Command Area of Operations. The delegation to CENTCOM, known as CODEL, was a bipartisan group who understood that spending Christmas away from their families wasn't easy, especially for servicemen and women in an area known for hostilities.

They delivered thousands of packages of Tate's cookies to the troops and spent time chatting with them about their families and their important role in maintaining peace in the region. At some point during the delegation's visit, several of the congressmen came in contact with someone who was contagious. Joe's father, who'd been diagnosed as having type 2 diabetes due to his weight issues, was especially susceptible to the MERS-like ailment. The other members of Congress recovered; the former congressman Mills did not.

Joe had graduated from Georgetown law school and had landed a coveted position with the world-renowned firm of Alston & Bird. After working as an associate in their government and public policy division in the Washington office, a period when he met Harper, Joe transferred to Atlanta so he and his new bride could start a life together.

Then his father died, and he was appointed by the governor of Georgia to fill his seat in Congress.

Joe had considered politics in the past and had learned a lot from his father. However, he was truly thrown to the wolves with the appointment. First, he had to make the decision to choose public service, and the scrutiny it entailed, as a career choice. Second, he had to get Harper on board, and she supported him one hundred percent. Finally, he had to win over the voters, which, as it turned out, he was a natural at doing.

Joe was considered a retail politician. He enjoyed rolling up his sleeves, driving down to the local restaurants of Brookhaven on a Saturday afternoon, and chatting up the patrons to hear their concerns.

Because he had nominal competition in his first primary race due to the fact he'd been temporarily appointed to the position by the governor, and since he'd won the hearts of the residents of the nearby communities of Alpharetta, Roswell, Sandy Springs, Chamblee-Dunwoody, and Doraville, Joe became a heavy favorite to win the seat permanently after a three-month stint as a placeholder.

This was the beginning of his career in Congress, and unlike so many who were sent to Washington, the city and its political machines hadn't changed him. He was seen as somewhat of a maverick. He didn't always toe the party line. He was an independent thinker who considered the wishes of his constituents first, his personal beliefs second, and then, if those two things aligned with what was best for the country, he'd support new legislation.

Joe believed, or wanted to believe, anyway, that if it was good for the country as a whole, then both sides of the aisle would agree. Secretly, admitted only to Harper, he was an advocate of gridlock. The nation was equally divided along highly partisan lines. If one side or the other took extraordinary control of this delicate pendulum, then unfairness to the other side was sure to come. However, as he believed, if both sides could agree along bipartisan lines, then legislation should pass, as it would be good for the country as a whole.

Congressman Joe Mills was a rarity in Washington, the kind of politician, it seemed, that could only occur in the movies or a novel. Yet he existed and was highly respected outside the Beltway and especially back home, where it mattered.

Today, he was ready to pull out his thick black hair. It was time to reconvene the House Appropriations' subcommittee on Labor, Health and Human Services, Education, which included funding the CDC and related agencies.

Reporters had gathered outside his office, requiring him to shut his doors and call the Capitol Police to move them out of the corridors. The White House had just thrown him a huge curveball under the guise of compromise. In reality, he knew it would have a negative impact on the CDC and quite possibly his wife.

Which was where the press came into play. Rather than focusing on the administration's move to slash the CDC budget, they wanted to focus on whether he could remain impartial during the negotiations because Harper was employed by the CDC. It wouldn't matter that her job wouldn't be affected by budget cutbacks because of her position and senior status. It was the mere appearance of favoritism that put him in the political crosshairs.

Joe's chief of staff, a longtime Washington operative who was as politically savvy as anyone in DC, was livid over the administration's ploy.

"Joe, this is directed at you personally," Andy Spangler began in between huffs and puffs of outrage. "This town has been abuzz ever since word of your meet and greet at the Brittains'. They see your potential and, face it, Joe, your popularity is through the roof."

Joe stood from his desk and wandered over to a credenza that held photographs of his father, mother, as well as one with Harper and Doctor Dog sitting in the middle of sand dunes on Tybee Beach near Savannah.

He was a principled man who believed in the work his wife did and the value of the CDC overall. In addition, he had his father to consider.

"You know what, Andy. Let's go to the committee room. I've got my personal story to tell. It's the one of a good man whose life and legacy was cut short by the types of diseases the folks at the CDC combat every day."

"Your father's."

"You betcha! Come on." Joe set his chiseled jaw, grabbed a stack of notes handwritten on legal pads, and stormed out of his office, loaded for bear.

CHAPTER TWENTY-ONE

CDC Headquarters
Atlanta

Infectious disease epidemics have been the scourge of mankind for generations, and epidemiologists consult with health care providers and public officials to identify and control any new outbreaks of a potentially deadly disease. Many epidemiologists work for governmental agencies and universities conducting research, but some are hired in the private sector by hospitals, health insurance companies, and pharmaceutical concerns.

Harper had been approached on multiple occasions by the top hospitals in America for infectious diseases, like the Mayo Clinic, Johns Hopkins, and Massachusetts General. Even Merck and GlaxoSmithKline, two of the world's premier pharmaceutical companies that help fight diseases, had come calling in the past.

She'd always turned them down despite the large sums of money she'd been offered. Deep down, Harper felt that public service had been her calling in much the same way Joe had been called into the political arena. Clearly, both of them could've made huge salaries had Joe stayed in private practice and Harper joined Merck, but they wouldn't have been happy. Both of them were right where they belonged, or so they thought.

Harper, like most epidemiologists, focused on the collection and analysis of data related to contagious diseases. The gathering of data was cumbersome at times. It required more than just observing an outbreak and its victims. It required interviews, surveys, and the gathering of blood and tissue samples from all who came in contact with an infected patient.

At the CDC, Harper's team gathered evidence from outside sources as well, but most came from their own efforts. It was important for them to be accurate in their conclusions and research, as they had a profound influence on the public health policies affecting millions of people who might be exposed to these communicable diseases.

With years of experience, and a nose for the unexpected, Harper had become especially adept at disease surveillance—the process of keeping tabs on mutating viruses such as the various strains of influenza. Viral diseases can mutate rapidly and are therefore a major cause of pandemics. Identifying new influenza variants, their virulence and potential risk was one of the key responsibilities of the CDC.

Harper had been elevated to a supervisory role over the years and was, in the eyes of most, one step away from taking Dr. Reitherman's position as director of the CSELS. Her boss had proposed in his department's budget that a new position be created within his department's organization chart. The newly created director level position, associate director of Infectious Disease Response, would be tailor-made for someone of Harper's credentials and desires.

Whoever filled this new position would not only oversee the surveillance of emerging diseases, but they would also be one of the first on the scene of a potential outbreak. Much like the way a senior crime scene investigator coordinates the operations of an evidence team and then assists detectives in determining the who, what, and why of a crime, Harper would be the first to arrive when a potential diseased victim is identified. She would coordinate containment, assignment of investigative duties, and then supervise the data collection, which would then advise public policy makers.

Dr. Reitherman had discussed this with Harper in the past, and the two of them put their heads together to create a detailed job description and department organizational chart. Now the only obstacle was obtaining the necessary funding from Congress. *Ay, there's the rub*, as Shakespeare's Hamlet once said.

The problem was that the CDC budget was always threatened to be slashed, not expanded. Somehow, those in Washington found more important uses for taxpayer dollars, like millions of dollars to study how hamsters fight; a couple of billion dollars a year for maintenance of empty, abandoned government buildings; and several million dollars for a Super Bowl advertisement encouraging people to fill out the government-mandated census forms.

When Dr. Reitherman and Harper discussed the misguided Congressional spending, one of their favorites to complain about was the $172 million spent over five years for vacuum erection systems. They could barely get the words out of their mouths before they burst out in uproarious laughter. Only, it wasn't funny.

On a more serious note, they both often wondered what it would take in this country for people to realize how close America was to enduring a deadly pandemic and how wholly unprepared both the government and the health care system were to deal with it. It seemed the warnings from the CDC usually fell on deaf ears, especially in Washington.

Harper was almost finished with her work for the day. Before she headed home, she stopped by to speak with Becker and found her office empty. In fact, many of the offices along the corridor where the epidemiologists hung their hats were vacated. Harper foolishly looked at the watch and chuckled. It wasn't quittin' time, as they say, because at the CDC, disease detection and mitigation was a twenty-four-seven job. But it was barely after five o'clock that afternoon, and it was odd everybody had bugged out so soon.

She wandered toward the elevator when she heard noises coming from the common area and break room near the center of her floor. The television had been turned up louder than usual. Just as she approached the doorway, she noticed a sea of white lab coats staring at the wall-mounted television monitor. Many of them were sniffling and wiping their tears off their faces with tissues. Others choked back their emotions as they spoke in soft tones to one another.

They appeared to be watching a news report that suddenly shifted to a commercial break before she could determine what was causing the angst among the group. Several shuffled out past her and smiled. A few spoke to her as they walked by.

"Your husband is a hero."

"We're lucky to have him."

"I just love Joe. Please thank him for me."

Harper was puzzled as she replied, "Um, I love him, too. Can you tell me what's happened?"

They slowly exited past her, leaving only a handful of epidemiologists and Becker, who was blowing her nose into a Kleenex like she was trying to eject a bad memory from the dark recesses of her overactive brain.

"Becker, will you please tell me what's going on? Is Joe all right? Why is everybody crying?"

Becker quickly moved to her boss and hugged her. "He's the best."

Harper was growing concerned and then slightly agitated. "I know this. Why?"

Becker took a deep breath, blew her nose one more time, and then explained, "I've never seen anything like it. The news was showing him during a budget hearing today. He was going toe to toe with this congresswoman, you know, one of the president's best pals. She kept trying to say the National Institute of Health and the CDC should spend more of their budget on what she called *public goods*. You know, research into infectious diseases and mobilization against pandemics."

"I can't disagree that both of those aspects of what we do are critical to the nation," interjected Harper.

"Yeah, but she went on to say we should have our budget cut back because of pet projects that have nothing to do with public goods. Your husband fought back, saying the cuts the president proposed went too far. They were arbitrary across-the-board decreases. He accused the administration and this congresswoman of not understanding and appreciating the great work we do at the CDC."

"They argued?" asked Harper. She rarely had time to watch her husband in action on networks like C-Span. When she did, although she was proud of what he did, it seemed tedious and mundane.

"Fireworks, at first. And then everything changed."

"Oh no, what happened? Did he knock her out or something?"

Becker chuckled. "No, but it was a knockout punch. He told the story of his father and how he died. It brought many in the committee to tears, and most of us watching were crying, too."

Harper dropped her chin to her chest. It wasn't like Joe to use personal anecdotes to get an advantage in the public arena. He was truly fighting for their budget needs. Harper also knew that after the administration and the media had time to digest the emotional exchange, they'd begin to question his sincerity, which would necessarily lead right to her.

CHAPTER TWENTY-TWO

Las Vegas, Nevada

Famous for being America's adult playground, Las Vegas was seen as the place to go for glitzy showbiz events, cavernous state-of-the-art casinos, luxury hotels featuring endless buffets, and every manner of shopping the heart, and wallet, could desire. It's a place where tourists come to forget their troubles—not add to them.

Clark County, Nevada, where Las Vegas was located, had a population of over two million people. Every day, that number swelled with temporary visitors to the tune of forty-two million travelers a year. More than half were there on vacation, and millions came to attend conventions. One thing most visitors enjoyed doing while there was gamble.

There's a reason why Las Vegas was also known as Sin City, and it wasn't just the strip clubs or the discreet prostitution activity that bills your credit card with unique company names like Five Aces Luxury Car Rental or Bon-Bon Delights, Inc. This city in the desert was born from the gambling industry.

From the first luxury hotel-casino on the infamous Las Vegas Strip, the Pink Flamingo, built by notorious gangster Bugsy Siegel, to the one hundred seventy located throughout the county, the gambling mecca of the world provided visitors and locals with thrills and chills.

In recent years, in an effort to attract non-gambling millennials whose pulses didn't race from the sounds of slot machines raising a ruckus with every big win, the Vegas tourism industry created a new strategy. The *mega-weekends*, as they were called, were designed to string together sports events, musical acts, or international conferences to push the numbers of non-gaming visitors higher.

However, the name of the game in Vegas was gambling, and the hard-core players loved poker. Many gamblers see poker as different from the games of chance. It's one thing to plunk your quarters in the slot machine and hope for a win. It's much different to sit around the table against challenging opponents, matching your intelligence, skills, and strategies to win.

With gaming machines, the spin of the ball around the roulette wheel and, to an extent, at the craps table, a person places their bets and hopes for the best. Mostly, the house wins in these games. Have you ever marveled at the massive hotels and millions of lights that line the Las Vegas Strip or encompass the Fremont Street Experience? Somebody has to pay for that. The gamblers do. It's not uncommon to sit on a flight into McCarran International Airport and listen to a conversation between any random couple. *I'm only going to lose five hundred dollars and that's it.* Of course, it always ends up being more, but assuming the number was accurate, that comes to over twenty billion dollars a year. Those billions buy a lot of light bulbs for the fancy signage and free drinks for the players.

With poker, the gambler feels he has an element of control over who wins and loses. Their skills are matched against others. Their emotions are challenged as the luck of the draw ebbs and flows. There are moments during the game when their levels of sensation rise and a roller coaster of emotions becomes almost impossible to control. The poker face, worn so well by some, invariably cannot be maintained, as even the greatest players have a hard time managing their bodily expressions throughout the game.

Poker tournaments became wildly popular in the late 1990s, and Vegas answered the call for more venues to host players. With the advent of online poker, more and more players became experts and pros drawing them in to bet big money. The allure of winning that big pot or gaining the respect of their fellow players sucked them in even more.

McCarran International had been bustling with activity that Thursday as tourists from around the world crammed the airport for a long weekend in Las Vegas. The Formula One racing circuit had returned to Las Vegas after a long layoff. Taylor Swift was performing at Allegiant Stadium, home of the Las Vegas Raiders. The Fremont Street Experience was hosting the Poker Stars International tournament.

The venues would include all of the downtown Las Vegas hotels at Fremont Street and was going to be televised internationally on ESPN. It was hands down the largest, and most lucrative, poker tournament in history.

Four weary travelers had flown halfway across the world to participate in the event. They'd flown twenty-eight hours via China Southern Air and Delta Airlines from Xinjiang, China to the gambling mecca.

They were led by their commander in the field and their undisputed leader of the pack when entering a casino—Yao Qi, who was sweating. Not from nervous anticipation of the big poker tournament but, rather, from a low-grade fever caused by the mysterious disease coursing through his body.

CHAPTER TWENTY-THREE

Fremont Street Experience
Downtown Las Vegas, Nevada

Yao and the other three members of the team who had retrieved Mooy's body from Mount Everest had more than earned their junket to the Poker Stars tournament held at the casinos of the Fremont Street Experience. Not only had they pulled off the daring rescue without losing any of the Chinese soldiers under his command, but he and his personnel had kept quiet about the unusual cause of death that had befallen the Aussie.

As part of their training, Yao and his countrymen from the famed Siberian Tigers unit had learned conversational English. It was always anticipated that China would go to war with the United States, and therefore having the ability to speak English would be a benefit when it came time to interrogate prisoners.

For Yao, it was extremely useful when they came to Las Vegas to participate in poker tournaments. The presumption of most Americans, which the group of four never attempted to dissuade, was that they did not speak English. The men used that to their advantage on many occasions, feigning a lack of understanding when the Americans spoke to them.

They were staying at the iconic Gold Palace hotel located in the heart of Fremont Street's never-ending party. One of the oldest casinos in Las Vegas, the Nugget had undergone numerous transformations since its opening in 1946. Like the Pink Flamingo, the founder, Guy McAfee, was a kingpin of Los Angeles gambling, who'd fled the City of Angels after a crackdown on organized crime.

McAfee set the standard for casino construction for decades to come. The Gold Palace Saloon, as it was first known, was lavished with care, attention, and a whole lot of McAfee's ill-gotten gains to create shiny gold, vintage décor reminiscent of the gold-rush days in San Francisco. His hotel was adorned with polished brass and imported marble from Italy. But its most important feature, which set it apart from others, was a huge air-conditioning system to keep gamblers cool while the desert temperatures routinely soared above a hundred degrees.

As the granddaddy of the downtown casinos, the Gold Palace was the anchor for the Fremont Street Experience and the host venue for the poker tournament. Its twenty-four hundred rooms and suites were filled to capacity. The casino was packed with poker players and their guests anxious for the first cards to be dealt later the next day.

Meanwhile, Yao and his companions were ready to get settled into their rooms to rest. They wanted their minds sharp for the tournament that started on Friday night. Plus, each of them was feeling the early symptoms of the illness. They made their way through the casino and into a small sundries shop, where they purchased Tylenol, non-drowsy DayQuil, and Halls throat lozenges to ease the sore throats they were experiencing.

After checking in at the Rush Tower, they stopped by the Hideout bar for a drink. There were other bars more readily accessible, but all of the guys wanted to get a view of the third-story infinity pool and its late afternoon occupants. The setting sun provided the attractive female sunbathers all of the rays they needed to bake their bodies. The bright light provided the four poker players all the illumination required to enjoy the view of said sunbathers.

One drink turned into two as the male bartender slid the men their cocktails and retrieved their glasses. After drink number three, Yao provided a second bartender, a cute female, his room keycard to pay the tab and then handed her a twenty-dollar-bill as a tip. She was appreciative of the large tip, kissed the twenty, and shoved it into her shirt.

Feeling good, they debated whether they should take a shower and hit the casino floor or simply rest as planned. The slow-moving elevator rode up to the twenty-third floor, where it seemed to stop a dozen times to allow passengers in and out of the cramped cab, dampening their desires to party.

Yao made the call to rest and prepare for the big day. The men did, but the microorganisms invading their body simply ramped up their efforts.

CHAPTER TWENTY-FOUR

Residence of Dr. Harper Randolph
Brookhaven
Northeast Atlanta, Georgia

"Hi, Harper!" Sally Oglethorpe greeted her happily as Harper emerged through the door leading to the garage. She stopped in the utility room and slipped off her shoes. It was another one of her things. Shoes were left at the door. It wasn't because of a Japanese tradition or a religious expectation at a mosque. It was because there were germs on the ground, and she didn't want to track them through the house. She knew what germs were capable of.

"Hi, Miss Sally!" Harper shouted back. "What is that glorious smell?"

"Well, Doc and I talked about it. We decided on a touch of England for dinner."

"You did, did you? Doc weighed in as well?" Harper entered the kitchen and kissed the matronly woman on the cheek. Then she dropped to a knee and proceeded to exchange kisses with the exuberant beagle pup.

"It's a special occasion in the old country for Doc, you know."

"What's the special occasion?"

"Prince George is making his first official visit to the States since his father became king. There's going to be a ball at the White House in his honor, and we're gonna watch it on TV."

"We are?" asked Harper with a chuckle. She recalled when the young prince was born. He was cute as a button growing up and had turned out to be one heckuva lady killer. The president also had an eighteen-year-old daughter, and the tabloids in the United Kingdom were thrilled at the possibility of a betrothal between the two political dynasties.

"Yes, and to enjoy the occasion, I made bangers and mash with a side of red kidney beans."

Harper shook her head in amazement. She reached into the refrigerator and searched for a Bass Ale or some other form of British beer to celebrate the big event, but settled for the usual Samuel Adams Boston Lager. *Oh, the irony.* She popped the top and took a healthy swig.

"You are such a Southern gal. I didn't think you'd ever prepare any recipe that didn't have Southern roots."

"It's simple, really. I just needed to hit Fresh Market for these banger things."

She picked up the sausages with a pair of tongs as she stirred the brown gravy with her other hand. She was momentarily distracted and turned the heat down on the gravy, lowering the arm holding the sausage in the process. Doctor Dog took a leap for the plump yummy, but Sally's reflexes were too fast.

"Not so fast, young man. You mind your manners or you'll go to bed without supper."

Harper started laughing and found her way to the bedroom to change clothes. She pulled on a pair of cotton shorts from The Gap and then searched her closet for the appropriate tee shirt for the occasion. After a moment, she settled for one she'd purchased from Lucky Brand with *The Tongue* emblazoned across the front, the unofficial logo of the Rolling Stones. It was designed by a student at the Royal College of Arts to represent the famous band's anti-authoritarian attitude and Mick Jagger's habit of sticking his tongue out during his concert performances.

Harper drank some more of her beer, whipped her hair into a ponytail, and checked herself in the mirror. Comfy casual was her favorite attire.

The two enjoyed supper in the breakfast room with one eye on the television and the other on Doctor Dog, who was having fun slinging a stuffed fox across the marble floor before retrieving it.

"I was watching the news today," she said hesitantly. "Um, did you know Joe was going to have an important hearing?"

Harper quickly chewed her mouth full of mash before replying, "Honestly, I knew he was in the middle of this budget thing, but I understand it turned into a big hoo-rah-rah."

"He is very passionate and principled," said Sally. "It made me cry."

"You're not the only one."

"I just wanted you to know, not that it matters, that your public phone line rang off the hook today."

Harper chuckled as she continued eating the delicious food. Both of them were in the public eye, and as a result, they were frequently sought after for comments or statements. Rather than go through professional channels like Joe's chief of staff or Harper's communications director at the CDC, some reporters, and citizens, felt compelled or even entitled to search for the family's personal phone number. The two both carried iPhones with carefully guarded numbers.

In order to give up something to mislead the nosy bodies, they published their landline number at several places online. The research gatherers of the world thought they'd scored a major find when they discovered it. It was disseminated across the web but simply led to a telephone in Joe's study that rang off the hook and was never answered.

"A lot of good that did 'em."

"Ain't that the truth. It's a good thing your place is in a gated community. At least it keeps the lazy looky-loos out."

Harper watched as Prince George was introduced to the president and first lady. She tried not to look upon the leader of the free world with contempt just because he was on the opposite side of the political spectrum as her husband. Nonetheless, she certainly disagreed with his policies of funding cuts to the CDC.

"Did Joe sway any minds today?" she asked Sally as she finished her meal and helped gather the dishes.

"It depends on who you listen to. I wasn't sure if you'd know about what happened, so I bounced around the cable news networks to see what the talking heads had to say. Overall, they said he was effective, but they doubted it would convince the president."

Harper grimaced and sighed. Politics was a royal pain in the ass, she thought to herself. The news coverage of the royal visit broke for a commercial, and she glanced at images of a Las Vegas tourism commercial encouraging people to come visit, let their hair down, and throw dem bones at the craps table. It closed with their new slogan adopted a decade ago—*What happens here, only happens here.* She liked the old one better.

Harper muttered to herself, "Really? I kinda doubt that."

CHAPTER TWENTY-FIVE

Fremont Street Experience
Downtown Las Vegas, Nevada

The men didn't wake up invigorated. If anything, it was just the opposite. Their bodies were weakened and sore as if they'd been performing strenuous physical labor. As a result, they found themselves unable to focus and concentrate. As part of their routine to get their minds right for the start of a poker tournament, they descended upon the casino floor after a light breakfast at Starbucks. Yao suggested they load up on stimulants.

Another trip to the sundries shop at the hotel yielded several bottles of Brain Booster, a dietary supplement designed to reduce mental fogginess while stimulating the logical processing power of the mind. The herbal supplements were combined with vitamin B12 to pack a powerful punch to the human body's nervous system. It might seem like an odd item to sell in a casino's sundry shop, but not when a casino considers a sleeping gambler a nonproducing asset. The longer they play, the more they pay.

The guys got jacked up on espresso coffee from Starbucks and the Brain Booster tablets before hitting the floor. The false high

created by the stimulants immediately made them feel better although their symptoms were getting worse.

They spent the early afternoon playing various table games for small stakes, intending to save their large gambling reserve for the buy-in at the poker tournament that evening.

Yao was having some success at the slot machines, and he bounced from one high-roller machine to another, inserting his 24 Karat Players Club card, hoping to earn a free meal at the Red Asian Cuisine Japanese restaurant.

One of his companions got his attention as the four men gathered around the craps table with a group of attractive South Korean women who spoke some Chinese. Yao wiped the sweat off his brow and pulled his players card out of the Mad Max: Fury Road slot machine, but his coordination was off. He tilted sideways as he slid off the stool, and in his haste to join his friends, he inadvertently dropped his card without knowing.

"Sir! Sir!" an elderly woman shouted at Yao. She knelt down and retrieved the players card and was waving it in the air as she tried to get Yao's attention.

"Ma'am, may I help in some way?" asked a casino floor supervisor who happened to be wandering by.

"That Asian man dropped his players card. I tried to get his attention, but he didn't hear me. He's one of those guys at the craps table over there."

The woman handed the casino host the card, who assured her he'd deliver it to the man. Anxious to get started again, she reached into her bag, pulled out a wad of one-dollar bills, and licked her fingers to peel off several to insert into the machine Yao had been playing.

Meanwhile, at the craps table, the party was going strong. The attractive South Korean women had lured Yao and his friends into buying them drinks as well as providing them chips to play with. Yao, after taking the players card from the casino supervisor, took his turn throwing the dice.

"Comin' out!" shouted the stickman of the craps table, announcing that Yao would begin the roll.

He smiled at his friends, shook the dice, and blew on them for good luck as he rolled.

"Seven! Winner!" announced the stickman.

Everyone at the table hopped up and down with joy, exchanged high fives, hugs, and Yao even earned a kiss on his sweaty cheek from one of the others.

"Same dice!" he yelled in English to the stickman, forgetting their vow to avoid letting others know of their command of the language. It was the first of many mental lapses he'd make during the day.

Yao rolled for over ten minutes, a considerable length of time at a craps table, before yielding his turn by crapping out. All of the chips he'd used to place his bets were pulled in by the casino personnel and neatly stacked by the dealer to be used for the next round.

After the stickman shuffled the five dice, he shoved them across the felt tabletop to the next shooter, who picked up two of them, including by chance, one of the ones used by Yao. This process of exchanging dice, chips, high fives, and hugs went on for an hour or more at GN 111, the internal designation for this particular craps table.

When the guys were finished playing and ready for the tournament, they came away from GN 111 winners while all of the casino personnel and other players left big-time losers.

CHAPTER TWENTY-SIX

Fremont Street Experience
Downtown Las Vegas, Nevada

All of the seats in the thirteen-table poker room were filled with players as the first night of the tournament got under way. As was typical, the players started out betting conservatively unless, of course, they had a sure winner. Poker was like a game of chess. The idea for the player was not to telegraph their strategy, but when the opportunity to strike and win a big pot presented itself, they shouldn't hesitate.

By agreement, Yao and his companions always played different tables. The first obvious reason was they didn't want to play against one another. Second, there had been occasions in the past where poker players came into a tournament with a preplanned alliance and team strategy. One of the players would be designated to win, and the others would do their best to drive up the pot by using strategy to goad the other participants. To be sure, there were plenty of Asian participants in the tournament, but very few of them were physically imposing like Yao's group of four. Others would've noticed they were together, and called foul.

The tournament got under way and the men played for hours. They were successful players in the past, spending most of their spare time from their military duties practicing against one another and discussing strategies.

They rarely took a break from the table except to wander outside the poker room to Claude's Bar to check on their newfound South Korean girlfriends. The guys had provided them money to gamble, and duplicate room keys should they wish to join them later.

Yao, like his friends, wore a black Poker Stars ballcap on his head together with sunglasses despite being in a dimly lit room. *Eyes are the windows to your soul*, as the saying goes, and Yao knew they also betrayed a poker player. They revealed too much information about the player's mood, intentions, and excitement.

He was an expert at recognizing his opponents' *tells*— unconscious behaviors that potentially revealed the true strength of their poker hand. Oftentimes, these tells involved eye movement. This innate ability to study human behavior was often used during those occasions he had to interrogate a prisoner. Knowing how to manipulate the mind was essential to his job.

The sunglasses also enabled him to hide his bloodshot eyes. As he became more ill, and with the help of the many stimulants he'd been ingesting throughout the afternoon, his pulse rate had quickened and his blood pressure had shot up dangerously high for a man of his physicality.

Yao, like his friends, also began to sweat profusely as their bodies began to fight the fever that consumed them. During a high-stakes poker tournament, it was not unusual for anxiety to cause the players to sweat. However, this wasn't normal for the four special forces operators. They were continually wiping their foreheads with their hands and then transferring the sweat inadvertently to the cards and chips. They guzzled bottles of water, exchanging them readily with the cocktail servers working the packed poker room.

Yet, despite feeling ill, feverish, fatigued, and at the end, somewhat disoriented, they played until nearly the last hands were dealt. Then, as a group, exhausted for many reasons, they retired for the night.

Outside the poker room, the Friday night crowd in the casino was boisterous, exuberant and mostly inebriated. The guys stopped by Claude's bar in search of their new lady friends, who were nowhere to be found. They skipped getting a drink and headed straight for the elevators, where they had to wait in line, as many people were headed to their rooms for the evening.

Yao was fine with that as well. The disease that consumed him, plus his mind coming down from the stimulant-induced high, had taken its toll. He just wanted to fall into bed when he finally reached his hotel room.

He fumbled for his hotel keycard. He couldn't focus and had difficulty inserting it into the lock. Frustrated, he angrily tugged at the door handle in an effort to make it open, and then suddenly, it popped open on its own.

Yao appeared drunk. He was slurring his words, staggering, and having difficulty standing. Had it not been for the nude woman inside his room to help him to bed, he most likely would've collapsed in the hallway until someone called for medical help. Instead, he was undressed, pushed onto the bed, and was joined by the woman he'd met at the craps table.

She tried in vain to rouse him to have sex. Yao was awake, but incoherent. He was unable to put together a sentence, and his fever caused his body to shake uncontrollably. The woman became concerned and pulled additional blankets out of the closet to cover him. She joined him and tried to keep his body warm.

Yao was breathing heavily and soon it became more rapid.

"Are you okay?" she asked in Chinese.

Yao tried to reply in a mixture of Mandarin and English, but his words were garbled and overtaken by a violent coughing fit. Bubbly saliva began to come out of the side of his mouth as a foamy drool. He placed his hands near his throat and his eyes grew wide.

Then he had a seizure. His body shook violently as the

convulsions overtook it. His chest heaved as if it was gasping for air. Then a stench was emitted from his throat that repulsed the woman, causing her to convulse and vomit.

It was Yao's last dying breath.

CHAPTER TWENTY-SEVEN

Fremont Street Experience
Downtown Las Vegas, Nevada

Within fifteen minutes after Yao's death, hotel security and management had entered his hotel room and questioned the woman who watched him die. First, they contacted Las Vegas Metro Police and the Southern Nevada Health District because, in the opinion of the security team, it appeared Yao had been poisoned. They held the woman for questioning in the hotel administration's offices under armed guard, pending the arrival of detectives.

Within an hour, a crime scene investigation unit from the City of Las Vegas as well as the Clark County coroner were on the scene. Every one of the first responders agreed the seemingly fit young man had died of something out of the ordinary. Whether it was natural causes or the ingesting of some type of poison would be up to the coroner's office and pathologists to determine. Regardless, the twenty-third floor of the Gold Palace was now deemed to be a crime scene.

And the night was young.

The lead investigator for CSI ordered the floor to be evacuated and the hotel guests moved elsewhere, even if it was to another hotel within the Fremont Street Experience. Hotel administration set about locating the guests occupying the other nineteen rooms on the floor. Some had already turned in for the night and complained about the inconvenience, but when they were told a dead body was down the hall, they scrambled to comply with the request.

At several of the rooms, there was no answer from the guests, so it was presumed they were having dinner or on the casino floor. For now, those rooms remained locked, and LVMPD officers were stationed at the elevator in case those occupants returned.

An hour passed as the forensics team prepared to secure the crime scene and began processing the hotel room. It was approaching midnight now, and the floor was crawling with law enforcement personnel and forensics.

More hotel guests returned and were quickly ushered off the floor to other accommodations. Eventually, three hours after Yao's death, the head of hotel security, together with the front desk manager of the Rush Tower, reviewed the hotel records to see which rooms had not yet been vacated. That was when they discovered the names of the occupants.

With the approval of hotel management, at three in the morning, hotel security entered the three remaining rooms they thought were unoccupied at the time. They were shocked to find the occupants inside and dead in a manner similar to Yao.

The Clark County medical examiner and his chief pathologist were called out of bed at four o'clock that morning, over six hours since Yao had succumbed to the disease. For several hours, they documented the deaths of the four men and took samples of the excrements as well as the deceased men's blood.

While CSI continued to process the four deaths as possible homicides or even a suicide pact, the pathology labs at the Clark County Coroner's office got to work. They employed five full-time medical examiners with a team of forensic pathologists, their assistants and technicians to carefully examine the bodies. Everyone joined in the gathering of the blood and tissue samples. They photographed the corpses from every angle and placed samples of any excretions into vials to be brought back to the coroner's office.

By late afternoon, fifteen hours after Yao's death, they were all laser-focused on their microscopes, trying to make sense of what they'd discovered. After some final lab work, the Coroner's Office came to a consensus, and the phone call they all dreaded was made.

CHAPTER TWENTY-EIGHT

CDC Headquarters
Atlanta

Harper gathered in the small conference room with Becker and three epidemiologists who'd been working on an outbreak in the western United States. The first signals of a problem had begun several years prior, and it had been on the CDC's radar since.

Panthera, a global wildcat conservation organization, had been studying the movement of cougars in Yellowstone National Park for fifteen years. They'd successfully tranquilized and collared nearly a hundred of the fearsome cats over the years.

Two months ago, the researchers had received a ping from one of the collars of an older cougar. According to the collar's mortality sensors, the female hadn't moved in over twelve hours. This was considered an ominous sign for the researchers. Everyone on the team assumed she'd died of starvation, as the ping occurred in the dead of winter.

When a rescue team tracked the signal to the base of a large tree, they found the female and a younger cougar that had not yet been tagged. Although starvation was still the presumed cause of death, tissues were sent to Wyoming's Game and Fish Department for analysis. They, in turn, contacted the CDC.

It was determined the cats had died of pneumonic plague. This soil-living bacterium, *Yersinia pestis*, was a cousin to the bubonic plague, the so-called Black Death, a pandemic that killed between fifty and two hundred million people during the Middle Ages. *Y. pestis* was found throughout the western states, infecting small hosts such as fleas, which then jump to ground-burrowing rodents, and so on up the food chain.

The plague was rare in the U.S., infecting on average seven people a year in mostly rural areas of the American Southwest. In Africa, it was still endemic to Madagascar, where it kills two hundred locals yearly. *Y. pestis*, in its purest form, could be treated if diagnosed quickly. However, like so many other diseases, it presents symptoms similar to the common cold and was, therefore, often misdiagnosed by overworked health care providers.

Following the discovery of the dead cougars, the researchers and a team of zoology-trained epidemiologists from the CDC began to collect blood samples of three dozen cats. Just over half tested positive for plague antibodies in their blood.

Unfortunately, the spread of pneumonic plague didn't stop with the cougars. The greater Yellowstone ecosystem was huge, and it reminded the CDC that the plague was more prevalent there than they thought. This point was driven home when two of the researchers who were drawing blood from the cats contracted the disease and had to be hospitalized.

The reason for this urgently called meeting was that a teenager contracted the plague after visiting Yellowstone with his Boy Scout troop. The boy was recovering, but his physicians were at a loss as to how he contracted it.

Harper reviewed the information and was discussing whether they should send a larger team of field biologists, veterinarians, and epidemiologists to Yellowstone to institute containment protocols.

"This highlights the pneumonic plague's elusive nature," began Harper as she paced the floor in the conference room. "Think about it, for all the damage plague has done to mankind over the millennia, there's still a lot we don't know about this deadly pathogen. We don't know how it persists or even why it persists in certain soils longer in some areas over others."

Becker weighed in. "Bubonic plague has that additional segment of DNA that allows it to infect humans. *Y. pestis* is similar. Once these two killers made that leap, the pathogen spread easily in fleas, rats, and ground-dwelling mammals."

"Two hundred plus mammals," added another epidemiologist.

"Especially in the Southwest," continued Harper. "Plague is very much a part of the landscape, and as humans, or their pets, continue to interact with wild animals, they will continue to spread the disease, preventing its eradication."

"Should we put out an alert to the health care providers in the region?" asked Becker.

"Absolutely," replied Harper. She glanced at the door and noticed movement through the rectangular glass positioned near the handle. "Medical practitioners know how to treat patients with the disease if they correctly diagnose it from the beginning. We need to put it in their brain to be looking for symptoms of the plague—visibly swollen glands, fever, chills, and weakness. Even though we're dealing with pneumonic plague that attacked the respiratory symptoms of these cougars, have them look for blackened tissues on the fingers, toes, and nose, the signs of bubonic plague, as well."

"I'm on it," said Becker.

Dr. Reitherman opened the door slightly and stuck his head in to get Harper's attention. She held up her hand to acknowledge him and then finished her instructions.

"Also, notify all the appropriate agencies, hospitals, and health care facilities that if they get one more case, they'd better be on the phone to us first."

"Yes, ma'am," the group replied in unison.

Harper quickly exited the room to join Dr. Reitherman in the hallway. He wasted no time in getting to the point.

"We have a situation in Las Vegas."

Harper pointed back over her shoulder at the epidemiologists as they wound up the meeting. "Is it pneumonic plague? We were just discussing a case in Yellowstone—"

"No. Well, maybe not. I just got off the phone with an investigator with Clark County CSI. The coroner is on the scene as well."

"A pathogen?" asked Harper, her face awash with concern.

"Listen, it's unknown although it appears to be respiratory. You need to pull a small team together and get out there immediately. I'll have the jet ready in fifteen minutes."

"Dr. Reitherman, we get false alarms all the time. Why are we mobilizing so quickly?"

"I have a gut feeling about this, Harper. Besides, that's what we do."

PART III

SO MANY QUESTIONS, SO LITTLE TIME

Time is an illusion, death is not.
~ Unknown

CHAPTER TWENTY-NINE

Urumqi, Xinjiang, China

Few in the Western world had a true understanding of what life in China was like and the views most Chinese held. It was a nation of immense size and population. Geographically and economically, it was one of the most diverse on the planet. Many in the West visualized millions of peasants living on subsistence incomes, which was largely the case. However, there were just as many millions who were moving to urban centers and achieving lifestyles comparable to America's middle class.

China's economy had moved at warp speed from a primarily manufacturing nation focused on imports to Western consumers, to a more balanced, consumer-driven economy. Its education system for children and teenagers was remarkably disciplined and successful. The country still lagged behind in its college-level education, relying upon foreign universities for top-flight graduate schools.

American's dystopian view of life in China was largely unwarranted. Media visuals of smog-filled cities contrasted with peasants working the fields in the countryside were common.

Oftentimes, some of the three hundred thousand Chinese students studying in American universities were asked whether they'd ever used an iPad or been on Facebook and Instagram before. While those social media platforms were not found in China, alternatives like WeChat, a group-based platform commonly referred to as the *China Storytellers*, were hugely popular.

The scenes from Tiananmen Square of many years prior, in which a lone dissident stood up to a Chinese tank, was a reminder of the power of the Communist state in controlling its citizens. That part of Chinese life was certainly true.

Dr. Zeng Qi was a product of all aspects of Chinese life. One of his ancestors, and his namesake, had been the founder of the Chinese Youth Party over a century ago. It was the dream of a group of Chinese students studying in Paris to create a youth movement advocating the elimination of China's warlords and promote a nationalist agenda. The group became a viable anti-communist party for many decades until they were slowly forced out of Mainland China and into Taiwan.

By contrast, Dr. Zeng's grandparents were anything but political activists. They were illiterate farmers living in the Chinese autonomous region of Xinjiang, the westernmost in the country. They wanted the best for their children, but they were so poor that they had to force one of their kids to drop out of school so they could afford to let the other continue.

Years later, Dr. Zeng's father and his new bride became the only college graduates from their familial village. Their incomes rose during China's rise to the world's leader in manufacturing of consumer goods, and they were financially able to send their son to California to study medicine.

Afterwards, like so many Chinese students studying abroad, Dr. Zeng returned to China, specifically to Urumqi, the capital of Xinjiang. He took a position as a general practitioner at the First Affiliated Hospital of Xinjiang Medical University, and after paying his dues and earning the respect of his superiors, he was able to rise to a level of prominence in the medical community.

Physicians working in a Chinese hospital experienced a far different level of control by the government than their counterparts in the West. Influenced by the Communist Party's central-planning approach, many hospitals were managed as government agencies rather than how a traditional health care provider was in the States. Administrative personnel inserted by the government were far more powerful than the physicians in a hospital. The management team usually did not recognize individuals for their skills as much as they lauded physicians for doing as they were told.

As China evolved into a more Western-like economy, doctors were encouraged to enter into private practice. Beijing's economic policies were modified to assist physicians to open private clinics. Dr. Zeng was in a position to make this leap, one that would give him more freedom to treat his patients and earn a better income for his family.

Unfortunately, his plans were derailed.

"Good morning, everyone," he solemnly greeted his group of twenty undergraduate health technicians. First Affiliated was a teaching hospital, and Dr. Zeng handled both his regular duties as well as lectures.

"Good morning, Doctor," they eerily responded in unison. The structured relationship between lecturer and students was opposite of what classrooms were like in the West. In China, order was the norm, and playful banter or classroom interruption was the exception if not downright forbidden.

Dr. Zeng was the associate director of the Institute of Hydatid Disease at First Affiliated. Cystic echinococcosis, also known as hydatid disease, was often caused by long tapeworms found in dogs that acted as the disease definitive host, an organism that supports the sexually reproductive form of the parasite.

Hydatid disease could easily transfer to farm animals like sheep, cattle, goats, and pigs. It could also be found in humans through direct contact with an infected animal. The disease was dangerous because the infection was asymptomatic in humans, meaning there were no apparent or recognizable symptoms of the infectious disease. Slowly, the disease caused cysts, which enlarged in the liver, lungs and other vital organs, often growing unnoticed until they caused death. Most often, they were discovered post-mortem.

In the U.S., hydatid disease was extremely rare and accounted for barely a thousand deaths per year. In China, especially in rural Xinjiang, it was the most prevalent parasitic disease and was closely monitored because of its effect on livestock as well as humans.

Dr. Zeng began his lecture, outlining the importance of the institute to the day-to-day activities of rural Chinese peasants. Many of the students were from this region of China and appreciated the need to study and diagnose new cases so the infected livestock couldn't enter Xinjiang's many open-air markets.

"You will be working with veterinarians specializing in the detection and analysis of this disease. As you know, with the growing domestic pet population in China, veterinarians are overworked. They are looking to us for expertise in dealing with hydatid disease."

Dr. Zeng glanced at his watch. The hour was almost up, and he was anxious to get back to his laboratory to see the results of a culture he'd run on a recently deceased patient. "After our session, you will all be briefed by the specialists at First Affiliated Hospital to understand the combination of tools required to diagnose this disease. You will learn that imaging is the main method of detection. Computed tomography and magnetic resonance imaging are the starting point. This will be followed by serology testing using the blood of patients to identify whether they have been exposed to this infectious agent. Finally, the genetic specialists will discuss the use of antigens to study the structural molecules of the disease."

He glanced at his watch again. Perfect time to wrap it up.

"It will be a busy, informative day for you, and I will see you again in a week's time."

Or so he thought.

CHAPTER THIRTY

First Affiliated Hospital
Urumqi, Xinjiang, China

Dr. Zeng Qi would not yet be designated an infectious disease specialist by the Chinese government until he had one more year in his position. It would be a career boost for him, but it would not result in a significant pay boost. Following the administrative guidelines imposed upon physicians at First Affiliated meant years of repetitive work with no economic benefit. For that reason, he was preparing to take the leap into private practice.

Despite his abandonment of the career path expected of him by his superiors, Dr. Zeng was still passionately interested in studying infectious diseases. The hospital typically routed unknown cases of pathogens to the immunology department for study, but one was referred to Dr. Zeng under the assumption it was hydatid related.

The patient had been treated in a Tibetan hospital in the city of Lhasa. The Tibet Autonomous Region was the most unsophisticated and technologically backward in all of China. The few hospitals had basic health care facilities with access to Western pharmaceuticals.

However, the culture of the Tibetan people chose herbal remedies above all other forms of treatment.

The unusual geographic makeup of Tibet also complicated health care. The residents were exposed to climate as well as altitude extremes. Temperature variations between day and night were huge. Altitude sickness was common, as was exposure to hydatid disease, Dr. Zeng's specialty.

This patient lived in a village at the base of Mount Everest. The villagers, including the patient's family, were primarily goat and sheep herders. The patient, who worked on the family's farm, was found dead at the lower elevations of the mountain while tending to their herd of goats. The natural assumption was that he'd been afflicted with hydatid disease, but a cursory examination at the Lhasa hospital was inclusive. The body was transferred to the pathology department at First Affiliated with access granted to Dr. Zeng.

He followed the normal protocols in dealing with someone who was infected with hydatid. Like the physicians in Lhasa and the pathologists in his hospital, the official cause of death remained listed as unknown. Dr. Zeng, however, was intrigued, but he had to be careful.

The government administrators of the hospital had little tolerance for their physicians expending time and resources on medical investigations outside their purview. While he enjoyed detecting and analyzing infectious diseases, none of them ranked in the official list generated by the Communist government of the top ten causes of death in China. Hospital rules required Dr. Zeng to transfer the body out of his department once he concluded the cause of death to be something other than hydatid.

As part of his training, Dr. Zeng had studied all of the infectious diseases prevalent in China, including respiratory diseases like H1N1 (swine flu) and H5N1 (avian flu). The pathogens causing the fastest growing number of deaths was his specialty, hydatid, followed by hepatitis C, the needle-sharing disease, and then the two sexually transmitted killers—syphilis and HIV.

While he attended college at the University of Southern California, oftentimes conversations with his fellow medical students revolved around the topic of outbreaks of infectious diseases originating in China. China was known as a hotspot for novel diseases for several reasons.

Its cities were overpopulated and highly concentrated. China's culture was such that the public had intimate contact with lots of different species of animals, especially those that were potential reservoirs for infectious diseases. Ultimately, as Dr. Zeng readily admitted, China didn't have the hygiene standards found in the West.

South Central China, in particular, was a notable mixing bowl for new viruses. The provinces of Guangdong, Hunan, and Guangxi were often mentioned when an outbreak occurred. In the Western part of China, there was an abundance of livestock farming, particularly poultry, sheep, and pigs. Sanitation practices were limited and oversight was lax.

Farmers often brought their livestock to *wet markets* in these overcrowded urban environments. The term wet market simply referred to the types of perishable goods sold there, like fresh meat, poultry, fish, and produce. They were distinguished from the dry markets that sold durable goods such as nonperishable groceries, electronics, and fabrics.

In the last hundred years, some of the worst global pandemics in history had originated in China. The Asian flu pandemic of 1957 killed over a million people worldwide. The Hong Kong flu of 1968, the H3N2 strain of influenza A, killed fifteen percent of the city's population. The avian flu, H5N1, nearly destroyed the poultry population in China when the first known transmission to a human occurred in 1997. Millions of birds were destroyed as a result, as well as human lives. Severe acute respiratory syndrome, or SARS, encircled the globe in the early 2000s after the initial outbreak originated in horseshoe bats in South China. It was a related viral strain of SARS known as SARS-CoV-2, or coronavirus, that devasted the planet in 2020 into 2021.

Dr. Zeng nervously discussed these disease outbreaks with his classmates. After the coronavirus outbreak, an us-versus-them mentality had overtaken the medical world when it came to the prevention of infectious diseases. China was blamed for the outbreak, and those countries that suffered extreme death tolls or significant economic hardship were looking for a place to direct their ire. China was the logical target and reparations were demanded, none of which were paid.

After the coronavirus pandemic, Dr. Zeng vowed if the opportunity presented itself to protect the world from a novel virus like SARS-CoV-2, he would tacitly join in the effort. A novel virus referred to a pathogen, a virus, that had never been seen before. If steps were taken to isolate the virus to its natural reservoir, whether it be bats, swine, or poultry, then man could avoid contracting the disease.

It was against that backdrop that Dr. Zeng and those who assisted him risked their jobs as he began studying the death of the patient, a part-time goat herder and part-time Sherpa on Mount Everest who'd died of a mysterious illness.

CHAPTER THIRTY-ONE

First Affiliated Hospital
Urumqi, Xinjiang, China

Dr. Zeng settled into his office chair and perused his notes as well as the medical records he'd gathered from the hospital in Lhasa, Tibet and from the medical team at First Affiliated. The man's family said he'd complained of persistent fever, slight difficulty breathing, and body aches. Initially, he exhibited a dry cough resulting in a sore throat, which later included mucus.

Because of his work as a Sherpa at Mount Everest, which exposed him to people from around the world, prior attending physicians considered that he'd succumbed to atypical pneumonia, also known as walking pneumonia. The symptoms were considered milder than typical pneumonia and more akin to the common flu. Both the North and South Base Camps at Everest had experienced flu outbreaks in the past, and it was logical to assign this as a cause of death.

However, the pathology didn't reveal the presence of the bacteria *Mycoplasma*, nor was there evidence of the bacteria *Streptococcus*, prevalent in typical pneumonia.

Dr. Zeng was both puzzled and intrigued by the case. He'd studied the accounts of epidemiologists who'd worked tirelessly during the SARS outbreak and the related disease coronavirus. When dealing with a novel virus, it's often necessary to eliminate what's not possible before identifying what is. He'd been following this process for days despite being pressured to return the body to the man's family in Tibet, who'd insisted upon a sky burial.

Sky burials, in Tibetan Buddhism, were the most widespread way for peasants and commoners to dispose of the dead. While the ceremony itself was designed to create a peaceful environment to allow the passage of the dead person's soul into heaven, the act itself was far from peaceful.

The body was stripped naked and placed sitting upright in a fetal position, knees bent and the head above them. Then smoke was burned as part of the ceremony to attract vultures, seen as holy birds, which greedily ate the corpse.

Dr. Zeng had genuine concerns about releasing the body to the family for transportation across China. If the man had died of a novel virus that was still prevalent in his blood or tissue, it could be transmitted to others or to the vultures, which could then possibly spread the unknown disease.

He was stalling, looking for answers, but knew his time was running out. There was already a message from his direct administrator looking for answers. He could buy one more day, but then they'd be at his office door. After that, they'd take action on their own.

He sat at his computer and began to compose a summary of what he knew so far. He outlined the patient's background, his known personal history, and the details of his symptoms. Next, he shared all of the pathology at his disposal and made a checklist of what he still hoped to accomplish in the brief period of time he had with the body.

He printed two copies of the report, one for his personal files and the other for a young man whom he trusted with his life. He could because it was his nephew, a college student at Xinjiang

University. Dr. Zeng erased the record of the report he'd generated and deleted it from the hard drive on the office computer.

He checked his watch and thought for a moment about his nephew's class schedule. If he hurried, he could get there just as his nephew was exiting his final class of the day. Within minutes, he'd left the hospital and was on his bicycle, pedaling furiously along the short two and a half miles of city streets toward Xinjiang University.

His nephew, Zeng Fangyu, was a student at the College of Journalism and Mass Communications Broadcasting at the university. He was also cut out of the same mold as their mutual ancestor, the original dissident in the family, Zeng Qi's namesake.

Fangyu was a citizen journalist. After the Tiananmen Square incident in 1989, citizen journalism grew exponentially in China. The mainstream media was under tight control by the Beijing government. Citizen journalists played a role in shedding light on government oppression and provided an element of transparency on the most secretive Communist government in the world.

The goal of these underground journalists was to make it more difficult for the Communist Party to control online information flows within the country, and beyond. These journalists also risked their lives, and the well-being of their families, by being the vehicle for the expression of nationalistic sentiments that ran contrary to the hardline Beijing government. By so doing, their information was available to the Western world, who could then shed light on China's human rights abuses.

Like the West, alternative news and citizen journalists had to look outside mainstream media to disseminate information. In America, Facebook, Instagram, YouTube and Twitter had become ingrained in society to the point many citizens rarely turned on the television for news or entertainment.

In China the top social media site was WeChat, a messaging platform developed and owned by Chinese tech giant Tencent. It boasted more than a billion monthly users, just behind Facebook's Messenger and WhatsApp in popularity. It was also capable of being used as a payment vehicle for in-person or online purchases. Users could even book travel arrangements through its app.

The WeChat app's primary use was messaging. Users exchanged contact details by scanning a unique barcode on their phone to instantly add them to a chat group of mutual interest. In China, people were more likely to use WeChat with others than they would the telephone or email. Because services like Facebook were blocked in China by the government-controlled internet service providers, WeChat had become the preferred social media platform.

Dr. Zeng parked his bicycle outside the journalism building at the university and hustled across the grassy compound to search for his nephew. He didn't need to lock up his preferred means of transportation because people don't steal each other's bicycles in China. The government, however, could monitor any calls or messages to his nephew's phone, so Dr. Zeng opted instead for an in-person meeting.

To say he was paranoid would be an accurate statement. Virtually everyone in China was to an extent. While the government wasn't as ruthless and murderous as North Korea, they were certainly capable of making anyone disappear in the dark of night without explanation or accountability.

"There!" he exclaimed under his breath. He saw his nephew speaking with a group of students near a cluster of apricot trees. The rose-colored flowers were some of the first ornamental trees to bloom every spring.

He walked briskly toward his nephew until the young man noticed his uncle approaching. Immediately suspecting that something was amiss, he politely excused himself from his friends and casually walked toward Dr. Zeng to meet him halfway.

"Uncle, is everything good?"

"Yes, my nephew, or maybe not. I have a difficult project. A case, actually. One that is secretive but requires insight of others. Can you help me?"

"Of course, Uncle. I assume you are referring to an encrypted WeChat post?"

Sophisticated citizen journalists like Dr. Zeng's nephew evaded government censors by creating messages for others within their WeChat groups in complex and garbled text. Sometimes, they'd post the message by writing it backwards, intentionally filling it with typographical errors or replacing words with a string of emojis.

Sharing posts as pdfs flew under the radar of government computers that scanned WeChat for keywords identified as being associated with dissidents. Some groups were able to share information by writing the messages in Klingon, the language developed in the American Star Trek television and movie series.

"I think a pdf or image scan will be sufficient this time. Please use an untraceable account. I want you safe."

Fangyu began to laugh. "I am the master, my uncle. They know nothing of what I do, nor can they determine the source of the message. If they close down the account, I have thousands more to use for the next post."

"I worry for you, nephew."

Fangyu continued to chuckle, drawing the attention of passersby. He placed his arm on his shorter uncle's shoulder. "I worry for you, Uncle. Your viruses are more deadly than mine!"

CHAPTER THIRTY-TWO

CDC Learjet
Flyover Country, U.S.A.

The CDC leased several private jets to move its personnel and supplies to infectious disease outbreaks. Ordinarily, Harper would fly commercial, as would the other members of her team. Dr. Reitherman's concern elevated this response, and the Learjet was quickly readied for her departure from the Peachtree-Dekalb Airport in Chamblee, just northeast of Atlanta.

As the pilot announced they'd reached their cruising altitude, Harper unbuckled her seatbelt and got comfortable for the nearly five-hour flight. Joining her were two epidemiologists, who'd handle the bulk of the field evidence gathering. She also had her *right-hand man*, Elizabeth Becker, by her side, who was always ready to spring into action when called upon.

"This is a little different approach from what we're used to, Becker," Harper began as she leaned against the jet's fuselage and spread her long legs out across the row of three seats. Becker sat across from her on a backward-facing row. A fixed table separated the two, which Becker promptly covered with her laptop and several files. "Generally, we have pretty good evidence or confirmation of an infectious disease outbreak. We would've put together our team of state and local resources on the ground before we were wheels down."

"This is odd. Why do you think Reitherman sent us out here in a rush, especially if the locals think this may be some type of poisoning?"

"I don't know, but I've never seen him overreact. Something prompted it and we'll follow through."

"I've got time to make some calls. Should I reach out to the State of Nevada's emergency response team and their own epis? I imagine they have a PHRST at the ready." PHRST was an acronym often used by state governments referring to Public Health Rapid Support Team. Generally, a PHRST included an epidemiologist, an industrial hygienist, a nurse, a pharmacist, a veterinarian, and an administrative liaison to work with local first responders.

Harper shook her head and grimaced. "We don't even know if we have an outbreak yet. We have four dead guys so far. No pathology reports. No ME opining as to cause of death. No external evidence like some kind of cult-suicide pact or murder-for-hire arrangement. Zero. Zip. Nada."

Becker thumbed through the files. She was old school in many respects. All of the information contained in the files she'd created while they scrambled to leave Atlanta were also in her computer. Like modern-day novel readers, some folks liked their electronic devices, and others preferred the so-called *dead tree* formats. Becker was more dead-tree than digital, just like her boss.

"We also don't have any other cases. If an infectious disease was spreading, it would've shown up within the hotel or somewhere in our alerts. There's nothing comparable that I can find."

"Okay, based on what we know, can we at least form the basis of our case definition? What do we know about the victims?"

"Four males, late twenties to mid-thirties. Chinese nationals. Excellent physical condition."

"Until they all died," quipped Harper.

"Well, yeah, there's that. But, based on the notes sent over to us by the coroner's office, these guys were muscular. They weren't chain-smoking, alcohol-guzzling slot players looking for a free buffet to chow down on."

"Stereotype gamblers much?" asked Harper with a chuckle.

Becker furrowed her brow. "Okay, maybe a little. My husband plays poker. Several times a year, we'll make the drive up to Murphy, North Carolina, to Harrah's on the Cherokee reservation. He plays the tables. I lose my money in the video slots and then I go bowling."

"Bowling? Really? There's something I didn't know about you, Becker."

"Hey, a gal's gotta have an outlet, you know? This is a stressful job and my boss sucks balls. So I imagine her face on the ten white pins down the lane and I heave that thing at them."

"Aw, shit, Becker. Gimme a break."

"I'm just kiddin'. But, actually, bowling is fun. It's a noncontact sport."

Harper sighed and shook her head. Not surprisingly, the two of them went off on a tangent. "Okay, they were all in good physical shape. What else do we know about them?"

Becker thumbed through the coroner's notes. "They all died within an hour of each other, with Mr. Yao Qi being the first reported death. His registration and passport shows he was from Shenyang, Liaoning Province."

Harper frowned. "That's northeast China along the coast and adjoins North Korea. That's not exactly a hotbed of pathogen activity other than maybe HFRS." HFRS was an acronym for hantavirus hemorrhagic fever, an illness often found in the Koreas and northeast China. It's spread primarily by rodents.

"Well, it's a possibility," mumbled Becker. "A witness, a woman who reported Yao's death, said he had a fever, nausea, and initially, a dry cough."

"You've just described the symptoms of virtually all of these diseases," said Harper with a sigh. "Is there anything in the report about a rash. Maybe red spots, for example?"

"Nope. That might rule out HFRS."

"That's what we do. If we can't determine what it is, we determine what it isn't."

For the next few hours, the two discussed their plan of attack, and Harper provided instructions to the two epidemiologists who'd accompanied her. They arrived at the North Las Vegas Airport, where they were greeted by a limousine from the Gold Palace and a police escort. They were pulling into the hotel fifteen minutes after landing, twenty-four hours after Yao had died.

CHAPTER THIRTY-THREE

Gold Palace Hotel
Fremont Street Experience
Downtown Las Vegas, Nevada

The hotel's limousine pulled Harper and her team into a private, VIP entrance of the hotel that was secured away from paparazzi and casual onlookers. It provided their high rollers and celebrities a modicum of privacy, at least for their arrival. Once in the hotel, most of the celebs couldn't help but mingle with their fans although some requested private gaming tables be set up in their spacious hotel suites on the top floors.

As soon as they exited the car, they retrieved their trunks full of PPE gear, sample-gathering equipment, and field-testing devices. They immediately suited up and waited to take an elevator through the hidden service corridors of the hotel to the twenty-third floor. Bellhops were replaced by hotel security. Concierge personnel were replaced by the highest levels of hotel management.

In addition, the presence of beefed-up security did not escape Harper's attention. Since the Mandalay Bay shooting in October 2017, casino hotels in Las Vegas had spent tens of millions of dollars on sweeping new security measures, including armed private SWAT teams trained by former FBI, CIA, and military experts. Most of the teams had K-9 units, undercover detection squads—a staple of hotel security for decades, and hidden metal detectors designed to identify the presence of weapons as they might enter the hotel.

"Welcome to the Gold Palace," a heavyset man greeted them. His gold-plated name tag read Mr. Wallace, General Manager. Harper glanced around the private entrance. It was not unlike the rest of the hotel. Everything, right down to Wallace's name tag, exuded opulence in the form of shiny gold, or at least the polished metal equivalent.

He stretched out his arm to shake hands. Harper didn't reciprocate, but she did smile to the man as she spoke.

"Thank you, Mr. Wallace. I wish we were here under different circumstances. My name is Dr. Harper Randolph. I'll be your point of contact while we're conducting our investigation. My second is Dr. Elizabeth Becker." Harper pointed over her shoulder, and Becker waved at the portly GM.

"Well, I certainly hope you can make heads or tails of what's happened here so we can go about the cleanup process. The local authorities, bless them all, are certainly befuddled by all of this. It looks like a suicide to me. We are the suicide capital of America, you know."

Harper inwardly rolled her eyes, but outwardly maintained her poker face. She wanted to ask the GM why, in his concerted opinion, did more people take their lives in Las Vegas than anywhere else in the nation. *Any guesses, Mr. Wallace? Could it be the loss of their life savings? Maybe dropping the equivalent of their mortgage payment at the blackjack table? Maybe it was the dad who gambled away his paycheck before he bought his baby's formula?*

"Okay, we'd like to get started. Have the bodies remained in place as we requested?"

"Yes, ma'am," a man dressed in a forest green uniform replied from behind Wallace. "I'm Alejandro Figueroa, chief of security. Mr.

Wallace has asked me to escort you through the building to the twenty-third floor."

"Great. If you gentlemen could have someone give us a hand with our gear, we'd like to—"

Wallace loudly cleared his throat, interrupting Harper. "Dr. Randolph, I need to advise you that your movements will be restricted while on the hotel property. Figueroa will escort your people to twenty-three so you can do whatever it is you do. Then we need to get those rooms vacated of the corpses so we can get a cleaning crew in there. We already have a significant room shortage problem because of—"

Harper bristled. "Mr. Wallace, we're wasting time. Let us do our jobs and then we'll determine if our investigation needs to extend to other parts of your hotel." She looked to Figueroa and raised her eyebrows as if to ask, *are you gonna take us, or do we find our own way?*

"I know you have a process, but you also need to understand we have a business to run."

Wallace continued to speak as Harper shoved her way past, with Becker hot on her heels. Figueroa gestured toward the large freight elevator, and the team—along with three uniformed, armed security guards—rode in silence to the twenty-third floor.

The doors opened into a concrete corridor full of room service carts and maintenance equipment. Several locked doors appeared on both sides of them that housed HVAC handlers, water heaters, and supply closets. Figueroa spoke as he escorted Harper down the hallway.

"Let me mention a couple of things before we get to the room. The woman who was with the first dead guy is now being held in one of the rooms near the elevator by the LVMPD. While we were waiting for your arrival, our surveillance video showed multiple contacts between the four men and her. She'd been in the presence of three other Asian-looking women earlier at multiple bars. Possibly South Korean. Anyway, the detectives are trying to determine if she's a professional or not. She's not a guest of the hotel."

"Professional?" asked Harper.

"Sorry. It's a polite way of saying hooker."

Harper jutted her chin out and nodded. "Okay, what else?"

"The four guys checked in together and were here to play in the poker tournament. They played separate tables during the tourney, and all left near the end of the session. During a break toward the end of the evening, one of them went out to the lobby bar to speak with the woman in custody. She ordered them a round of drinks, which he then delivered to his friends."

Harper paused and glanced at Becker. "Was there any indication that she added something to the drinks?"

"Inconclusive," he replied. "There was a point where surveillance was blocked from viewing the four cocktails after they were set in front of her. Doc, this is a city that's known for sleight of hand and trickery. Also, if she was a pro, or even a scammer, you couldn't rule out the possibility she spiked their drinks with something in order to rob them after they passed out or something."

Harper paused as they prepared to enter the hallway leading to the guest rooms. "But wasn't she the one with the first victim when he died? Why would she poison the men and wait until they succumbed to some kind of poison? And then call the cops?"

"Beats me. She isn't speaking, except for bitchin' to high heaven about wanting to leave."

They entered the hallway, and a rush of cool air hit them in the face. The maintenance areas of the hotel were not afforded the luxury of cooler temperatures. Several uniformed officers from the Las Vegas Police Department were stationed in front of the bank of elevators, at the emergency stairwells, and in front of the doors where the bodies were found. They all intently studied Harper and her team as they made their way to Yao's room.

The door to his suite was propped open and Harper glanced inside. Two men in brown suits were milling about the room, opening drawers, rummaging through Yao's belongings, and looking in his pockets.

"Who are you?" Harper demanded.

The taller of the two men responded, "I am Detective Comey and this is my partner, Detective Brennan. We're homicide."

"You're contaminating the scene."

"We beg to differ, ma'am," shot back Brennan. "Our CSI team has finished up, and the ME's office has already gathered what they needed."

"You wanna know something, Detectives? While you two are rustlin' through this man's belongings, you may very well be gathering something for yourselves."

Comey, who stood all of six feet six, was an imposing figure and quite smug. "We don't deal in riddles, lady. Only facts."

"Okay, Detective, here's a fact for you. The deadliest killers on the planet are the ones you can't see. It's quite likely you're covered with them."

"Come on," protested Brennan, but he was ignored.

Harper turned to the chief of security. "Unless you want your entire hotel infiltrated by a deadly pathogen, you need to temporarily place these two men in quarantine in one of the spare rooms. If they won't do it voluntarily, I'll call Atlanta, who'll in turn call Washington, who'll call the United States Marshals to ensure my suggestion is adhered to."

Figueroa chuckled. He didn't like the arrogant duo either. "You heard the Doc, Detectives. You guys need to get comfortable in one of our luxury accommodations."

The men complained as they exited, giving Harper death stares as they pushed their way out of the room. Figueroa gave his security team instructions on where to keep the two, and then he turned back to Harper.

"Well played, Doc. Those two think they've got this thing all figured out anyway. You know how they can be. They come up with a working theory and it's case closed."

"I suppose. Sir, thank you for your assistance, but we need to clear this room and not be disturbed. Will you let your people know that we'll be making our way to the other rooms before we release the bodies to the coroner's office. Also, I'd like to be notified if they send a representative, okay?"

"Sure," he replied. "Anything else?"

Harper was all business. "After we process the bodies, we'll need to interview the girl. Please make sure she doesn't go anywhere."

"You got it," he said, and then he leaned in to take one more look into Yao's room. "Whadya think, Doc? Dead men tell no tales, right?"

Harper studied the corpse for a moment and then casually replied, "This one will."

CHAPTER THIRTY-FOUR

Gold Palace Hotel
Fremont Street Experience
Downtown Las Vegas, Nevada

"Okay, we've got a lot to unpack here," she began after dismissing everyone from the hotel room except Becker and her two epidemiologists. "Let me remind everyone, we don't know what we're dealing with here, so be careful. The white coat you're wearing doesn't make you immune."

Epidemiologists use a systematic approach to disease outbreak investigations. Unlike many scientific studies, or even the tasks undertaken by law enforcement to catch a perpetrator of a crime, the members of the EIS working a new outbreak knew that a speedy solution was essential to minimize the spread of the disease and resulting deaths.

However, they couldn't sacrifice accuracy for speed. The CDC was often under intense pressure from external forces like the media and politicians to quickly identify the disease, its characteristics, and the solutions. It was natural for the public to expect answers. Many would be understandably frightened in the face of a possible pandemic. Getting the wrong answer at any step in the investigatory process would mean the outbreak would continue and the spread could expand.

Harper retrieved a UTM kit from her case. The red-topped viral transfer container, known as a Universal Transport Medium, was part of her standard procedures utilized during the investigation of a patient stricken with a potential infectious disease. Nasopharyngeal swabs were commonly used for the detection of respiratory viruses such as influenza, SARS and coronavirus.

Using a penlight, she carefully examined Yao's nostrils for evidence of excess mucous. Nasal excrements can interfere with the collection of the cells on the swab. Administering the test was much easier on a deceased patient. It was terribly uncomfortable for the living.

She placed the index finger of her left hand on Yao's nose and depressed it slightly. Then she inserted the swab into his nose with a slow, steady motion until it had been inserted approximately two inches into the membrane-lined cavity where the nose and mouth intersect with the esophagus. She rotated it several times to gather a sample and then withdrew the swab. After snapping off the end of the swab containing the sample and securing it in the UTM kit, she turned to Becker.

"How about the poison theory?" asked Becker as everyone unpacked their gear just outside the victim's hotel door.

"The coroner's toxicology report will shed some light on that. I'm not sure its viable."

"Why?" asked one of the epidemiologists.

"The timing, mainly. This woman would have to be a sophisticated killer to know which poison to use and when to administer it so the men would die simultaneously, or close thereto. Then, for what purpose? To steal their chips? Empty their bank accounts?"

"It's possible," added Becker as she opened up her case containing empty vials, scalpels, and syringes, among other things.

"A poison of that nature would be used by expert assassins or our friends at the CIA. They wouldn't do it in a hotel full of surveillance cams, and they sure as heck wouldn't crawl in bed naked with one of the victims. Much less call security when the man died. No, she'd be long gone by now."

"Accidental poison?" suggested the other epidemiologist, who slowly uncovered the corpse but quickly covered the man's genitals with a large gauze pad.

"That's also a possibility, especially if these gentlemen ingested something that was toxic, at least to their systems. Poisons surround us daily. Clearly, too much of a bad thing, like arsenic, can kill us, but too much of nearly anything can as well. Excessive doses of vitamin A can cause liver damage. Too much vitamin D can damage the kidneys. Consuming water in excess can result in hyponatremia." Hyponatremia was the process of diluting the blood's salt content, which could disrupt heart, brain, and muscle function.

Becker discovered the bottle of Brain Buster stimulants. She held it up for everyone to see. "Look at this. It's got a ton of B12 in it."

"Another good example," said Harper as she joined the others by gathering blood samples. She carefully labeled each vial to identify the deceased and the testing she required. "B12 is found in many foods, yet people don't get enough of it. It's important to red blood cell formation, energy production, and nerve maintenance. Yet excessive doses can lead to anemia and even death. Once again, not all at once, like what has happened here."

As they worked, Harper led the discussion leading to the establishment of their own case definition, not the presumed one concocted by the two sloppy detectives. This process of evidence gathering, toxicology, and autopsy of the bodies was just the beginning of a ten-step process that began with identifying the cause of death to be related to an infectious disease. Even if that conclusion was reached, they would have to move with care in identifying this as a potential outbreak. Thus far, there was no indication of any other victims with similar symptoms.

For the next two hours, Harper, Becker, and the rest of the team diligently gathered their samples, recorded their findings, and methodically double-checked one another as they proceeded from room to room. Just as they were wrapping up their investigation of the last body, representatives of the coroner's office showed up through the door leading to the maintenance corridor.

"Who's Dr. Randolph?" a female voice asked politely as she led one of four gurneys into the hallway.

"I am."

"Hi. Um, we're here to load up the bodies to have them autopsied. Doctor, I am sorry if you're not finished, and the ME also sends his apologies, but we're getting a lot of heat from the mayor and, um, probably the hotel management to speed things along."

Harper rolled her eyes. She didn't want to take out her anger on this young lady. She was simply passing on a message.

"I understand. We've just finished processing the last victim."

"Thank you, Dr. Randolph. Two things. The ME wanted me to ask if there was one body you'd like him to examine first, you know, over the others."

Harper pointed down the hallway. "Yes. Start with Yao in room 2311."

"Yes, ma'am. The other thing was he wanted to extend an invitation to you, or one of your people, to be present during any or all of the autopsies."

Harper smiled under her N-95 respirator mask. Harper thought of a statement her former mentor, a Professor at Georgetown, said to her after class one afternoon. *When dealing with pathogens, autopsies may give us the facts, but not necessarily the truth. That is up to you to find.*

CHAPTER THIRTY-FIVE

Clark County Coroner's Office
Las Vegas, Nevada

An hour later, the hotel limousine delivered Harper to the Clark County Coroner's Office, which was only a short drive from Fremont Street on the west side of I-15. Harper changed out of her PPE clothing and pulled a pair of jeans and a tee shirt out of her luggage. She was all about comfort and short on pretense when in the middle of an investigation. When she packed, she'd included the closest thing she owned to a casino-themed tee. It was gray with a pair of red dice on the front. The inscription read *roll them bones*, a reference to an oft-used phrase at the craps table. She had no idea how appropriate it would be.

Harper was met at the entrance by one of the administrative personnel for the county medical examiner. She was escorted through the building, where she was shown into the cluttered office of Dr. Wolfgang Boychuck, the longtime medical examiner. He presided over an impressive operation. The coroner's office was the only one in the U.S. that was accredited by both the International Association of Coroners & Medical Examiners and the National

Association of Medical Examiners. It was a testament to their tireless investigative work and accurate findings.

Their reputation preceded Harper's visit to the ME's office for the first time, and fortunately, she knew of their accolades. Dr. Boychuck had been consulted on a number of high-profile criminal investigations and was considered one of the preeminent forensic scientists in the country. Otherwise, she might have bolted out of there in search of an alternative.

The ponytailed, bespectacled ME presided over the coroner's office in the midst of what might be described as a crazy aunt's attic. Throughout the office, among the stacks of medical journals and hard-covered treatises, was a variety of what Harper could best discern to be trophies.

Glass jars of well-preserved animals in various states of dissection were scattered about on one perch or another. Photos of crime scenes coupled with anatomically correct organs were propped on bookcases. Antique microscopes sat on tabletops next to case files and piles of phone messages. A single computer screen that looked like one of the original IBM monochrome VGA monitors sat on the corner of his desk. It probably hadn't been powered on in a decade, if it worked at all.

"Come in. Come in." Dr. Boychuck frantically waved Harper inside while he finished up a phone call. He held his hand up with an index finger in the air, indicating he wouldn't be long. He wasn't. "Yes. Yes. Yes. Of course. Yes. Goodbye."

"My apologies, um, Doctor? I'm Dr. Harper Randolph with the CDC."

"Randolph. Yes. Yes. Yes. Of course. Thank you for joining us. Are you ready?"

Harper smirked and shrugged. "I'm ready if you are." She was slightly sarcastic in her response, but her tone seemed to soar right past the eccentric ME.

"Good," he said as he pushed files out of the way in search of a white notepad and a pen. He shoved both into a well-worn lab coat that either hadn't been washed in a month of Sundays, or the stains from decades of wear couldn't be removed with the strongest dose of Clorox bleach.

Harper studied the man with amusement. She immediately liked him although she was somewhat relieved that he only applied his expertise to the already deceased.

He gathered up a black medical bag in his arms and nodded toward the other side of his office. "Would you mind assisting me with Squishy? He has wheels, so he shouldn't be too much of a burden."

"Squishy?" asked Harper, somewhat confused. She turned in a circle, and an anatomical model complete with skeletal structure and removable organs grabbed her attention. She turned to Dr. Boychuck and pointed at it. "This is Squishy?"

"Yes. Yes. Yes." He seemed to enjoy confirming his agreement with any statement, times three.

Harper studied the anatomical model, a blank expression on its face, except for the portion that was missing. The rubber and plastic human could've been the inspiration for a walker on *The Walking Dead* except for its accurate coloring to represent the parts of the human body.

She couldn't resist giving the model's forearm a gentle squeeze. The rubber arm gave somewhat, and then the spongy material underneath returned to its original shape.

Harper mumbled, "Squishy."

"Yes. Yes. Yes. Come along, Dr. Randolph."

Harper dutifully followed the ME down the hallway, carefully wheeling the anatomical model by her side. Squishy rolled easily down the pristine, shiny floors of the coroner's office, which stood in stark contrast to the disaster of a space occupied by Dr. Boychuck. However, the man seemed to know where everything was, and that was all that mattered unless someone ever took over his duties. She chuckled as they approached the elevators leading to the morgue in the basement. Perhaps that was the key to job security. Make your workspace so cluttered, disorganized, and utterly disastrous that nobody would want to take it over.

Two coroner investigators exited the elevator as the doors opened.

"Good evening, Dr. Boychuck," said one.

"Hi, Squishy," the other one casually added.

Instantly, Harper wished she were a ventriloquist. She wondered how the young man would've reacted to getting a response to the greeting.

After the elevator doors closed, Dr. Boychuck took a deep breath and exhaled. "Squishy talks, you know. Just like the dead."

Harper wasn't sure what to say, so she agreed by nodding her head.

He asked, "But then I suspect you know that, don't you?"

Harper glanced over at the ME. "That the dead speak? Absolutely."

Dr. Boychuck continued, possibly with the intent to test Harper. "Their language may be different, but they still tell us a lot. Just know, their voice can be harsh at times."

She understood the intent of his statement. "Dr. Boychuck, this isn't my first rodeo. The smell is part of the process."

He tested her again. "Dr. Randolph, I'd be glad to get you some Vicks VapoRub if you'd like." He feigned looking through his notes, but she caught him studying her through the voids in Squishy.

Harper laughed. The use of Vicks was an urban legend found in poorly researched television shows. "No, thanks. All that would do is open up my sinuses more. I'll stick to the smeller God gave me."

He jutted his chin out and nodded.

Harper was curious about the anatomical model, and she suspected Dr. Boychuck was a bit of a storyteller, so she asked, "How did you come up with his name?"

"Go ahead, give him a squeeze."

Harper didn't want to admit she'd already done so. She grabbed Squishy's exposed shoulder and squeezed his trapezius muscle. It gave and then bounced back.

"I see."

"No, I mean grab a fun part," teased Dr. Boychuck with a laugh. "Have you ever held a beating heart?"

"Um, I can't say that I have."

The ME nodded toward the model and encouraged Harper to reach under the exposed rib cage.

She grabbed the heart and quickly recoiled from it. "It's beating!"

Dr. Boychuck began laughing uproariously. "Yes. Yes. Yes. It certainly is. The husband of one of my coroner investigators works for Madame Tussauds wax attraction at The Venetian. He created an exact duplicate that has a mechanical vibration device inside it. It's activated when it's squeezed, as you just learned."

Harper turned red in embarrassment as Dr. Boychuck pulled off the prank for probably the thousandth time.

Ding-ding!

She was saved by the bell.

The elevator slowly opened, and the bright fluorescent lights illuminated the dark recesses of the coroner's office. Dr. Boychuck hustled ahead, and Harper rushed to keep up, lifting Squishy slightly so he could move along with her.

Footsteps and Squishy's wheels rattled along the floor devoid of furniture or other personnel. The sound reverberated off the walls as Dr. Boychuck led Harper to the end. Oddly, and with a bit of macabre drama, the lights began to flicker as they approached the last door.

"Here we are," he announced as he leaned into the swinging door with his shoulder to shove it open. He held it in place with his elbow so Harper and Squishy could join him.

Seconds later, they were standing outside a glass-enclosed autopsy room holding the remains of Yao Qi, their index patient, the first identified case in their group of patients succumbing to this unknown communicable disease.

CHAPTER THIRTY-SIX

Clark County Coroner's Office
Las Vegas, Nevada

"Dr. Boychuck, I have to be honest. I'm impressed that you're handling this yourself. I wouldn't have expected you to take away from your busy duties, especially at this late hour." Harper continued to dress in the PPE provided in the lockers for visiting physicians and law enforcement. Just as she did when she entered a BSL-4 laboratory, she ensured there was no potential for microbes to enter her breathing apparatus or attach to her skin.

"Dr. Randolph, we live in a world where terrorists know no bounds of morality, and pathogens are weaponized. I rang the warning bell more than a decade ago, and the Clark County Commission listened. The result was a federal grant that allowed us to build and maintain this incredible facility that is designed after the biosafety laboratories in which you work."

"Infectious diseases don't die with the patient," Harper noted as she nodded to Dr. Boychuck that she was ready.

"Yes. Yes. Yes. We have to be just as careful with autopsies performed on patients with infectious diseases. A safe autopsy requires a facility that can be effectively decontaminated and that has adequate ventilation and air-handling systems, controlled access, and other design features. Most community hospitals may not have the types of patients necessitating such facilities. However, in a city the size of Las Vegas, and especially since it's frequently mentioned as a target for terrorists, it was not unreasonable to expect this type of facility investment at medical examiners' offices, academic medical centers, and large urban public hospitals, especially with the billions of dollars spent on defense against bioterrorism."

The two, with Squishy in tow, entered the air lock and waited until the green light indicated they could enter the autopsy room. On top of the white sheet covering the stainless-steel table was the first set of remains, those of Yao Qi.

For all of Dr. Boychuck's eccentricities and practical joking, he was all business inside the autopsy room. He sighed as he stared down at the body. "Dr. Randolph, I've studied the dead for most of my life. There is no such thing as a routine autopsy. What I do is provide family members, the deceased's loved ones, answers in some form or fashion. Maybe it's a homicide investigation. Perhaps, like this one, a sudden death of a young man in the prime of his life who is a perfect specimen of health. Regardless, it's my job to destroy this once beautiful body in order to provide answers."

Harper paused for a moment as she took in his words and respected his solemn demeanor. It wasn't often that she participated in the autopsy of an infectious disease victim. To be sure, she anxiously awaited the results, but rarely was she in the room when they were ascertained. She relayed to the ME the types of indicators she was looking for in an autopsy report.

"Most victims of viruses, especially those affecting the respiratory system, die from complications, including pneumonia and swelling in the lungs. These viruses also cause swelling in the respiratory system, which makes it hard for the lungs to pass oxygen into the bloodstream."

"Yes. Yes. Yes. The lack of oxygen leads to sometimes rapid organ failure. If the pneumonia is severe enough, it causes the patient to drown in the fluid flooding their lungs."

She nodded as Dr. Boychuck gathered his tools and retrieved a pocket recorder from his PPE. Harper made a mental note to confirm he decontaminated the device, and Squishy, before it left the specially designed autopsy room. She brought up another common cause of death associated with deadly pathogens.

"There's also sepsis. The human body can have an extreme immune response to an infection, triggering a chain reaction in the body that leads to widespread inflammation. The inflammation leads to blood clotting and leaky blood vessels, which in turn causes poor blood flow. Once again, organ failure can be the result or even a life-threatening drop in blood pressure."

Dr. Boychuck nodded and took in a deep breath. "Let's get started, shall we?"

Expertly using a scalpel, he made a large, deep Y-shaped incision starting at the top of each shoulder and running down the front of the chest, meeting at the lower point of Yao's sternum just below his abdomen. This procedure opened up the breastplate, providing Dr. Boychuck access to the body's major organs.

Methodically, and with Harper's assistance, he removed Yao's organs, including the heart, lungs, liver, stomach, and spleen and arranged them neatly on a stainless-steel cart. Dr. Boychuck stood back from the cart and gestured to Harper with a sweeping motion of his arms.

"I'll let you gather your samples now."

She'd already laid out several UTM kits to be used for the CDC to conduct its own pathologic study. The CDC's Infectious Diseases Pathology Branch would take the results of Dr. Boychuck's investigation and couple it with the samples taken by Harper to issue their findings.

It was rare for Harper to bring a pathologist into the field with her during an investigation. Similar to a criminal investigation in which state and federal agencies were frequently at odds with one another in the early stages of their detective work, local medical examiners didn't appreciate the CDC sending their own pathologists onto their turf.

Dr. Boychuck was actually one of those rare examples who welcomed cooperation among professionals. It was not unusual for medical examiners around the country to call on Dr. Boychuck to participate in a high-profile autopsy. His set of experienced eyes had helped law enforcement around the country solve crimes, as well as identify potential cases of infectious disease.

Harper took a lung swab from the tissue of each lung, the trachea, and the bronchi. She secured them in separate UTM kits and marked them for identification. She did the same for the liver, the kidneys, and the heart. Finally, because so many infectious diseases were respiratory, she took swabs from the rest of Yao's respiratory system.

She set the UTM kits aside and addressed Dr. Boychuck. "Thank you for understanding. We don't want to doubt any ME's ability to gather these specimens for us, but we may be on the cusp of an outbreak, and our pathology branch will want to quickly review the tissue histopathology and conduct molecular testing."

Dr. Boychuck stepped forward. He made a statement that both comforted and impressed Harper. "Understandable. Let's give them plenty to work with. Under the circumstances, we're going to forego the use of the oscillating bone saw since we might be dealing with an unknown pathogen. We have a vacuum shroud attachment to contain aerosols escaping, but as you know, it only takes one of these microscopic creatures to infect the human body."

Harper raised her eyebrows and mumbled, "Creatures, interesting use of words."

"Yes. Yes. Yes. They are creatures, are they not? Oftentimes these viruses enter a human target through the nose and mouth. They are alive, hell-bent on seeking a host cell in the respiratory system. Once they find one they like and latch onto, the cells burst and infect other cells nearby. An army of deadly little creatures on a mission to infect and destroy. Do they have the ability to think and reason? Of course not. But do they have purpose? Absolutely. Nefarious. But a purpose nonetheless."

Dr. Boychuck retrieved a pair of hand shears as an alternative cutting tool to the oscillating bone saw. He started with the rib cage, which clattered like Jenga blocks as he separated the left from the right. Harper was anxious to focus on the lungs, the usual start for a presumed respiratory virus. However, she was patient and considerate of the ME's routine.

An hour later, Dr. Boychuck had completed his autopsy, recorded his notes, and taught Harper a helluva a lot about dead bodies. He then x-rayed the organs, taking extra angles of the lungs. After the X-rays, he obtained samples of the lung tissue to be examined by his team. Biopsies would be performed locally as well as at the CDC, and then the results would be compared.

He gathered another slice of Yao's lung and took it to a sophisticated microscope set up in the corner of the autopsy room. Unlike the antiques that were on display in his office, this device was state of the art.

"No expense was spared here," Dr. Boychuck began as he settled into a chair. "With the use of expansion microscopy, we can expand the lung tissue sample to one hundred times its original volume before imaging it. This enables us to provide an on-the-spot preliminary diagnosis. Time is critical in matters such as these, right, Doctor?"

"Yes, sir," replied Harper, who could feel the clock ticking as she thought of hundreds or thousands of casino visitors pouring in and out of the polished brass-appointed revolving doors of the Gold Palace. Her mind raced as she considered how many people these four men had come in contact with since their arrival in Las Vegas. Who had they spent considerable time with at the hotel? These Asian women? How about their fellow poker players? The servers or bartenders at the restaurant? Beads of sweat began to form on Harper's forehead.

Dr. Boychuck pushed away from the table holding the microscope. The slick floor coupled with the well-oiled wheels on the chair propelled him a little farther than he probably intended. His legs flailed for a moment as he tried to stop.

"Well, I can say this for a certainty. We have a respiratory disease. Take a look."

Harper walked up to the microscope and studied the tissue sample from the lung.

Dr. Boychuck explained, "My belief is that this young man was experiencing acute respiratory distress syndrome. Note the fluid buildup in the alveoli. All of those tiny elastic air sacs are designed to bring oxygen into the blood and expel carbon dioxide. The fluid buildup blocked that from happening, which could've led to cardiac arrest."

"Like SARS," Harper added.

"Yes. Yes. Yes. MERS, too. Even COVID-19. Excuse me." He slipped his chair back into place and retrieved another slide containing a biopsy specimen.

"The liver?" asked Harper. It was the next logical step in studying a potential SARS or MERS outbreak.

"Yesss," replied Dr. Boychuck, uncharacteristically abandoning his customary triple-yes response. Harper was intrigued by his serious demeanor.

"What is it?"

Once again, he pushed back but in a more controlled movement this time. He gestured toward the microscope for Harper to see for herself.

She spoke her thoughts aloud. "That's severe microvascular steatosis. Drug-induced liver injury. Hepatitis C. Reye's syndrome."

Dr. Boychuck interrupted her list of causes with a few of his own. "SARS, MERS, coronavirus."

Harper pulled away from the microscope, looked toward the ceiling, and rolled her head around her neck to relieve some tension. She sighed as she turned to Dr. Boychuck.

"I've got more questions than answers."

"Yes. Yes. Yes. I hate it when that happens."

CHAPTER THIRTY-SEVEN

Las Vegas, Nevada

Harper stared out the limousine window as she sat in traffic. It was Saturday night and residents from Summerlin, a sprawling community in the far western part of Las Vegas at the entrance to Red Rock Canyon, were streaming toward the Strip and Fremont Street for dinner, dancing, entertainment, and gambling.

The two-mile ride was also slowed by traffic exiting the World Market Center, the location of hundreds of exhibitors featuring home furnishings. Harper chuckled to herself as she considered the fact she could've briskly walked the two miles back to the hotel faster than the car traveled. In actuality, she appreciated the opportunity to gather her thoughts.

She'd left Dr. Boychuk to complete the final three autopsies. She trusted him implicitly and left him several UTM test kits for the other victims. He promised to call her if he learned anything new. She, and the agency where she worked, was in an untenable position, as usual.

As the CDC had learned in the past, they were often condemned unfairly for their decision-making as it relates to an outbreak, especially if took place on American soil. There were always two very competing interests involved. The CDC—whose motto could be summed up as coordination, autonomy, and transparency—was most concerned with saving lives. It had always served them well to err on the side of caution in order to protect the public from deadly contagions.

This necessarily required containment orders, including public admonitions to practice social distancing when visiting essential businesses. Under some circumstances, it required quarantine measures involving more than just infected patients. If the disease spread was determined to be high, entire buildings or communities could be placed on lockdown.

This had dire consequences on the impacted economy and the financial well-being of the residents. When the CDC was deemed to have been alarmist, all with the benefit of Monday morning quarterbacking, of course, then the director and his immediate subordinates were blamed for catastrophic economic loss.

If the CDC failed to issue adequate warnings in a timely manner, again based upon the opinions of pundits with twenty-twenty hindsight, they were accused of having blood on their hands.

The same applied to the nation's political leaders. Harper shook her head as she thought about Joe. He chose the life of being second-guessed, criticized and unfairly bashed by political opponents. She frankly didn't know how he did it. And now, based upon his new relationships with rich and powerful people, he was ascending the political ladder to positions of greater power and scrutiny.

All of these factors weighed heavily on Harper's shoulders, as she knew in her gut that these four men were not poisoned or the victims of foul play. There was still more investigative work to do before she could make a recommendation to Dr. Reitherman and, ultimately, to the director of the CDC. She closed her eyes as she came to the realization that it would take days of analysis to make a scientific determination of what they were dealing with. However, a few more full body bags might tip the scales toward an outbreak declaration.

The limo driver made the final turn toward the VIP entrance of the hotel when he abruptly slammed on the brakes. Three emergency vehicles with their lights flashing blocked the entrance. The driver looked in the rearview mirror as he spoke to Harper.

"That's Las Vegas Fire and Rescue. I see an SUV from Clark County's Office of Emergency Management. They're still exiting their vehicles, ma'am."

Harper didn't respond. She flung open the rear door and kicked it with her foot as it tried to spring back closed. She raced around the emergency vehicles and pushed her way past two uniformed LVMPD officers who were trying to restrain onlookers.

"Hey, lady! You can't go in there!"

Harper ignored the order and arrived at the elevator doors just as they were opening. Two firemen pushed a gurney out, followed by Becker.

"Dr. Randolph! Mask! Mask!" shouted Becker.

Harper rummaged through the side pockets of her case and pulled out a paper surgical mask, a quick fix but not her preferred option. "What happened?"

The firemen pushed the gurney in her direction, forcing her to flatten her body against a wall to avoid being struck.

"It's the witness," replied Becker. "She began convulsing during our interview. She'd been cooped up downstairs and then in that hotel room since the discovery of the first body. When I first met with her, she'd complained of body aches, sweats, and a fever."

Harper had heard enough. She spun around and reached out to grab the arm of one of the firemen pushing the patient toward the ambulance.

Becker shouted after her, "Doctor! There are two more coming!"

"Stop them! Nobody leaves!"

"What?"

"Stop all movement!"

The fireman brushed her hand away, but Harper was more

forceful the second time. "Sir, please stop. This woman can't leave like this!"

"She needs to get to the ER!" he shouted back. Neither he nor his partner was wearing a mask, although they did have on nitrile gloves.

"She has a contagious disease that's already killed four men. We have to make quarantine arrangements."

Both of the firemen stopped dead in their tracks and stepped away from the young woman, whose labored breathing was not benefitting from the forced oxygen provided to her.

"Are you kidding me?" said the other fireman, clearly a New York transplant by his thick accent. "Nobody said anything about a disease, lady."

"It's evolving and under investigation. Where are you taking her?"

"UMC Medical is closest."

"Do they have an isolation unit for infectious disease patients?"

Crickets.

"Come on, guys! Do they?"

"I don't know," replied one, finally.

A cop shouted from behind Harper, "Dignity Health on West Sahara does. My wife works there. They have emergency drills for that stuff every summer."

Harper turned back to the firemen. "Go there! Now! Tell them Dr. Randolph with the CDC has identified this patient as possibly being diagnosed with SARS. Do you understand?" SARS wasn't necessarily the disease, but it would get the ER's attention.

The men started pushing the gurney toward the back of the ambulance. "Yeah. Randolph. CDC. SARS. Got it!"

Then the patient was stricken with an uncontrollable seizure. She began bouncing around the gurney wildly, unconsciously pulling against her restraints as she struggled to breathe. Her coughing became out of control, which ultimately forced the oxygen mask off her face.

Then came the foam, the bubbly mix of body fluids, emanating from her stomach, lungs, and esophagus. With one final heave of her chest, she went into cardiac arrest and died.

Harper stood in shock. *It's too fast. Too early. What the hell is going on here?*

The firemen tried to revive her with chest compressions and forced air from a resuscitator, but Harper stopped them.

"You can't help her. She couldn't be saved."

"Maybe if we'd hurried," said one of the men, but Harper reassured him.

"There was nothing to be done for her. Now we have to focus on you guys. Please stay here and wait for—"

Becker was frantically waving to get Harper's attention. "Here are the other two! Old woman and her husband."

She turned to the firemen and yelled, "Stay! Don't move and don't touch anything."

They both raised their hands and looked at one another before focusing on their fellow firemen headed their way.

Harper changed her focus toward the new patients. She stood in front of them and raised her arms high in the air. Her five-foot-ten-inch frame with hands held high created an imposing stop sign.

"Hold up!"

"Move it, lady, these folks need help."

"What are their symptoms?"

"Are you a doc?"

"Yes, CDC. What are their symptoms?"

"Chills. Body aches and pains. Coughing. At their age, the flu can kill, you know?"

"Yeah, I know. Take them to Dignity Health on West Sahara."

"Why? There's a hospital right down—"

Harper cut him off. "I know. UMC. Does it have an infectious disease quarantine unit?"

"Yeah, probably."

"You don't know for sure?"

He shrugged. "Yeah, I mean, no. Listen, we haven't heard anything about a terrorist plot."

"Becker!" shouted Harper, frantically looking around.

Her young assistant had been right behind her. "Yes, ma'am."

Harper addressed Becker and the two firemen. "Listen to my instructions very carefully. Becker, get these guys N-95s." Becker immediately rummaged through her bag and retrieved new masks for the guys.

Harper turned to the security guard for the hotel. "Hey! You! Come here, but no closer than six feet."

The man lumbered close to her, but not too close.

Harper continued. "You have to hurry. Go to the twenty-third floor of the Rush Tower. Find the two doctors from the CDC. Tell them to bring me a roll of Visqueen and two rolls of duct tape. No questions. Go! Hurry!"

He was off and running. Harper turned around and found the third ambulance. Its driver was standing at the front of the truck, observing the action. She waved toward him. He looked around and then pointed his thumb at his chest. *Who me?* He mouthed the words, most likely hoping she meant someone else.

"Come here!" she ordered.

He slowly walked toward her.

"Come on, man. Get the lead out!"

He moved a little quicker. "I'm not medically trained," he began, immediately trying to get out of any involvement with these patients.

"You don't have to be. Listen, I want you to prepare your ambulance to haul both of these patients together."

"I'm not sure there will be room."

"Strip it down to the bare bones. They have all they'll need right here, and one of these gentlemen can watch over them on the way. How far is it to Dignity Health?"

"UMC is—" he replied before Harper yelled to cut him off.

"Aw, shit, man. Dignity Health!"

"That's west, corner of Decatur and Sahara. Five miles, eight minutes with the bubblers and siren blaring."

"Okay, strip down the back of your ambulance. Make sure there is room for both. Then call the Dignity ER. Tell them you are bringing them two infectious disease patients. Possibly SARS. I'm Dr. Randolph with the CDC. Understand?"

"Do you want me to call now?"

"Now. While you get ready, my people are going to seal off the driver's compartment so you're not affected. Turn off the air-conditioning. Go!"

Minutes later, the two epidemiologists arrived from the twenty-third floor. They knew exactly what Harper needed to be done and worked efficiently to prepare the ambulance. One of the firemen escorted the two elderly patients to the Dignity Health Emergency Room, and the other three firemen followed behind in another ambulance. They were destined for quarantine.

Harper caught her breath and looked around at all of the bystanders and hotel personnel who'd come in contact with these three patients. She shook her head as a realization swept over her.

The big question had been answered. They were at the epicenter of an outbreak. They still didn't know what they were dealing with and where it came from. Her focus now turned to possible containment measures. No easy task.

CHAPTER THIRTY-EIGHT

Urumqi, Xinjiang, China

Dr. Zeng paced the floor of his modest apartment although it was somewhat larger than others within his mid-rise building overlooking the hospital campus. The cost of living in China was low. A bottle of purified water was $0.29. A pound of chicken was under three dollars. His two-bedroom apartment ran $550 a month. By comparison to wages earned by most in China, Dr. Zeng's annual salary of seventy thousand dollars afforded him every luxury. He chose not to use it that way. His extended family was large, and there were children who would need college, possibly abroad if they were smart enough for graduate school. He saved his money rather than spending it on the higher rent apartments closer to Urumqi's cultural attractions.

"Husband, can you please find a place to sit down? You are making me nervous."

He turned a deaf ear to his wife's entreaties. He loved her dearly, but he was concerned about the risk both his nephew and he had taken.

As he walked back and forth, he frequently glanced out his living room window toward the courtyard-style entrance to his building. Row after row of bicycles filled the steel-grate racks lining the entry. There was no room for an automobile. Very few city dwellers in Urumqi found a need for one.

Dr. Zeng was looking for the telltale sign of police action. When a dissident was being flushed out of their home, several Volkswagen Santanas or Passats would scream toward the exits to the building. They were all painted white with the customary dark blue swoosh painted on the side. Sometimes, if the raid was intended to abduct whole families for interrogation, a Mercedes-Benz Sprinter patrol van would join the law enforcement personnel.

Thus far, except for the screech of a lone siren roaring past their building on an unrelated matter, there had been no evidence that he had been associated with the post on WeChat that his nephew was making on his behalf.

Fangyu had elected to post a pdf without encryption. Initially, the two of them agreed the inquiry to other members of the chat group was harmless. He was simply sharing symptoms and possible illnesses, asking for feedback from others in return.

He'd already texted his nephew twice to ask whether the post had been made. Both times, Fangyu had admonished him to be patient. After the second message, Dr. Zeng received a thumbs-up emoji, indicating he was clear to follow the post with his own account.

Within minutes, the WeChat app on his phone sprang to life. Notification dings began to grab his attention, forcing him to sit on the sofa, much to the relief of his wife, who was using needle and thread to mend some of their clothing.

Most of the messages came from small community doctors near the border of Tibet and Xinjiang. He began to read the responses as they streamed in, speaking some of them aloud as if it helped him focus. One message in particular caught his attention. It was from Lhasa, Tibet, not that far from the land farmed by the deceased Sherpa.

"I had two patients who died of a mystery illness. Both were men, age sixty-one and sixty-nine. I was instructed by my administrator to declare the cause of death to be pneumonia. That is standard practice of my prefecture. The hospital pathologist informed me about unusual lung lesions. He did say pneumonia is what killed both men, but their bodies were pushed to this point by a severe viral infection attacking the respiratory system."

Dr. Zeng kept reading as other doctors from Tibet and Southern Xinjiang weighed in. He refrained from joining the conversation, following the instructions of his nephew. The police, said Fangyu, will not arrest you for watching. Only for participating.

A microbiologist joined the WeChat session. He lived in Korla, a city of approximately three-quarters of a million people a hundred twenty miles southwest of Urumqi. Dr. Zeng read his post aloud. As he did, his wife looked up from her sewing project from time to time to study her husband.

"I have been studying this virus without the knowledge of my administrator. I remember what happened to others like me who shared their findings on COVID-19. They never returned to their jobs."

Dr. Zeng paused and closed his eyes. *What have I done? I have placed my nephew at great risk.* He shook his head vigorously to erase the visuals of the young man being thrown into a cell at Qincheng Prison, the maximum-security prison belonging to China's Ministry of Public Security. When a new inmate was assigned to Qincheng and there wasn't a bunk available, they would simply kill the longest residing prisoner to make room for the new one.

After a deep breath, he continued. "This virus has the same functional host-cell receptor as SARS—ACE2." ACE2 was a universally accepted acronym for angiotensin-converting enzyme 2, an enzyme attached to the outer cell membranes of the lungs, arteries, kidneys, and intestines. This protein coding gene was prevalent in patients whose immunities were compromised by another ailment.

"SARS?" Dr. Zeng mumbled aloud before he read the rest of the microbiologist's post. After he was finished, he reached his own conclusions. "This would contribute to the ease with which this pathogen could transmit from human to human. It would also explain the deaths of people with weakened immune systems."

He stood again and began to pace. However, his patient was an apparently healthy man in his mid-thirties. *Did he have an underlying predisposition to the disease, or perhaps another condition not discovered by pathology?*

His phone continued to ding well into the night as more physicians around Western China reported similar cases. As his wife finally encouraged him to get some sleep, Dr. Zeng realized he needed to perform more testing on the deceased Sherpa. There would have to be a more detailed autopsy that examined the respiratory system. It required him to get somebody else involved. There was a pathologist at the hospital who was an independent thinker. Would he risk his career and his family's well-being, something Dr. Zeng was already committed to doing?

CHAPTER THIRTY-NINE

First Affiliated Hospital
Urumqi, Xinjiang, China

By the time Dr. Zeng woke up and made his way into the hospital that morning, dozens of other community health care workers throughout Xinjiang and Tibet were expressing their opinions and sharing their own cases within the WeChat group. Similar messages showing concern about the unknown illness were created as top posts by other physicians in Western China. By the time he convinced the hospital pathologist to conduct a thorough autopsy, focusing on the respiratory tract, Dr. Zeng counted at least eight more cases in Tibet and five more in Xinjiang.

"Dr. Zeng, this is novel," said the pathologists as he studied the kidney tissue samples through his microscope. "It is not unlike the human immunodeficiency virus in many respects. See for yourself. Observe the HIV attachment to the white blood cells."

Dr. Zeng took over the microscope from the pathologist. "This is extraordinary. The body's immune system has gone into overdrive, attacking the patient's organs." Dr. Zeng leaned back and wiped the perspiration off his brow. His nerves were shot.

"A cytokine storm," said the pathologist nonchalantly. "The virus signaled the cytokine molecules to mobilize in the body's fight against the strange virus. However, the body became flooded and triggered widespread inflammation. Instead of the white blood cells attacking the infection, they began multiplying and attacked the patient's vital organs instead."

Dr. Zeng shook his head in dismay. "They went berserk."

"A good description, Doctor. It is very much like the out-of-control cytokine response associated with H5N1."

Dr. Zeng glanced through the microscope again and then strolled around the deceased Sherpa's remains. "This is a very dangerous virus that behaves like SARS in many respects, triggering white blood cell activity like HIV/AIDS, and is undiscerning with its victims based upon age, gender, and—"

Suddenly, the doors to the autopsy room flew open and a young man in a pressed suit followed by two hospital security guards strode toward Dr. Zeng and the pathologist.

"What is the meaning of this?" the administrator screamed.

"You must not enter this room without the appropriate protective clothing and masks!" the pathologist shouted back.

Dr. Zeng stepped backwards toward the microscope table. He wished he could blend into the wall to avoid the wrath of the administrator. It didn't work.

"Zeng! You were instructed to return this body to the family in Tibet. You are not authorized to waste hospital time and resources on unnecessary autopsies."

Dr. Zeng didn't dare respond. Nothing he could say or do would protect him against the young man with fire breathing out of his nostrils.

"Sir, it is not safe for you to be around this patient—" The pathologist tried to warn the men who were exposed to the disease. He never got a chance to finish his sentence.

"Enough!" he shouted at the pathologist. He grasped the rolling table containing the remains of the Sherpa and shook it. Clearly frustrated, he stammered as he issued his orders. "Prepare this body for transport. Put it, put it—put it back together somehow."

"Yes, sir," the pathologist replied sheepishly.

The administrator swung his right arm in a wide arc and pointed at Dr. Zeng. "Bring him to my office!"

"But, sir," Dr. Zeng began to protest, "I must change out of these clothes and dispose of them—"

"No! You will come now and explain your actions. Then I will determine if you have a job by the end of this day!"

Dr. Zeng stared at the pathologist. The man was frozen and shaking out of fear. He returned Dr. Zeng's stare with one of anger for involving him in this situation. Dr. Zeng would make sure to explain that the pathologist had no involvement other than to help a colleague out. As he was led out of the autopsy room by the burly security guards firmly grasping him by the arms, he plead once again with the administrator.

"Sir, you do not understand. We may be dealing with a new infection. A virus that acts like three different—"

The administrator, who had the power of the Beijing government—and the military, if necessary—behind him, seemed to enjoy cutting off other people's sentences. "Do you want a raise in pay for your good work? How about a larger apartment? The one you have is not so grand to suit your tastes. Do you want our government to pay for your private practice? Is that what this is about? You are trying to make a name for yourself by defying my authority? We will see about this!"

The man berated Dr. Zeng all the way to the administration office suite near the front of the hospital. Dr. Zeng's colleagues and interns had front-row seats to the demeaning exhibition. That was, of course, by design. Dr. Zeng's punishment would include some type of reduction in his monthly pay and most likely a delay in his plans to enter private practice. But more importantly, in a communist state, the opportunity to make an example of someone was never passed up.

As he was escorted through the corridors to the main floor, his phone continued to buzz with notifications of WeChat messages. He wondered if he would have a chance to read them. He wondered if his wife would be punished, too. He wondered how many people in the hospital were being infected by the submicroscopic infectious agents that had attached themselves to his PPE. He wondered if this novel virus would explode into something much bigger.

CHAPTER FORTY

Chinese Center for Disease Control and Prevention
Changping District
Beijing, China

Dr. Eloise Blasingame was a lonely figure that day within the Chinese Center for Disease Control and Prevention located in Beijing. She was one of three epidemiologists from the U.S. CDC stationed at the main campus of the Chinese CDC located in Changping District.

Dr. Blasingame, like the other two Americans in her cadre, had been embedded in the Chinese CDC as part of a settlement, of sorts, between Beijing, Washington, and the World Health Organization leadership. Following the COVID-19 pandemic of a decade prior, questions were raised about China's coverup of the early cases and the subsequent numbers of deaths. To avoid criticism, and reparations, China agreed to allow up to three American epidemiologists to work at the CDC offices in Beijing in a consulting and training role.

She was not given complete access to their CDC facilities. Her movements were confined and closely monitored. It was assumed by all that Dr. Blasingame would formally be a trainer for the Chinese field epidemiologists who would be deployed to the epicenter of any outbreaks. She would not assist in the tracking, investigating, and containment of the diseases, but she would be kept abreast of her protégé's activities.

As a result, she was in an ideal position to be the eyes and ears on the ground for the U.S. in the event of a new outbreak. No other foreign disease experts were involved in the program, and as a result, she was able to gain the confidence of those she worked with.

Without warning that morning, the dynamic at the CDC in Beijing changed. She was awakened early that morning by her handler, the person identified as a liaison but truly acted as a gatekeeper and monitor to ensure Blasingame's cadre didn't overstep their boundaries. The handler explained that she and the other two American epidemiologists were being recalled by the CDC in Atlanta. She was advised to immediately pack her belongings, and to expedite her departure, two military personnel holding empty plastic bins stood on both sides of Dr. Blasingame's door.

She tried to get answers from her handler and even threatened to resist packing without a better explanation. Then she demanded to make telephone contact with the Atlanta CDC. After she insisted on speaking with the American embassy, she was escorted to an empty office and locked inside with her coworkers from the States who'd made similar demands.

Within hours, they were driven one at a time on a short, seven-mile drive from the CDC to the American embassy complex, where they were dropped off at the gate without explanation. After the CDC personnel were expelled from the Chinese CDC, complaints were registered with the Beijing government, and red flags were raised in the Geneva, Switzerland, headquarters of the WHO. Any efforts to get answers from the Communist government were either ignored or responded to with falsehoods. The Beijing government had a new infectious disease on their hands, and they planned on dealing with it as they always had—internally.

———————

The director of China's Ministry of Agriculture and Rural Affairs had been called into the CDC. He was questioned about the death of the Sherpa as well as other patients in Tibet. He answered truthfully, but it wasn't what the Chinese CDC hierarchy wanted to hear.

"We have conducted interviews with farmers, livestock herders, and the other Sherpas. All have reported instances of flu-like symptoms. Not all of the Tibetan people are in contact with swine or chickens or goats. Yet many are becoming sick."

One of the administrators spoke in a deep, gravelly voice. The very tone of his voice came across as threatening and hostile. "Why are the patients reporting this illness as zoonotic?"

The agricultural ministry official shrugged. "It is all they know and understand. They have seen how swine flu, avian flu, and hantavirus affects others in their villages. They make assumptions."

"Yet, Director, you believe otherwise."

"Yes, because my administrators have interviewed them in an effort to pin down the animal source of the disease. There is no common thread."

BAM!

One of the administrators interrogating the director slammed his fist on the table and raised his voice. "There can be no misunderstanding as to the root cause of this disease. It must be determined to be confined to Tibet and their penchant for eating yak meat. Our country cannot be accused of harboring a virus that may have been generated by meat and poultry, two of our top exports."

The director paused and chose his words carefully. He would be retiring within the year and didn't want to lose his modest pension or expose his family to ridicule.

He spoke in almost a whisper. "With the appropriate assurances, I will do my duty and prepare a report identifying the disease as coming from yak meat."

"You will have your assurances," the deep-voiced man quickly replied. "You are dismissed to write your report."

The director of the agricultural ministry hastily exited the room, leaving the trio of Chinese CDC personnel alone. They turned to one another and began discussing the bigger issue—stifling online conversation.

"These hospital workers and village doctors are jumping to conclusions. The information sharing is going to concern the people of China, possibly causing a panic. We must order all medical personnel to stop discussing this new virus."

A female administrator nodded her agreement. "Orders should be given with guarantees of punishment for noncompliance. Anyone spreading information about the novel virus will face severe punitive measures. Spreading rumors results in fearmongering. This harms stability throughout China and results in panic."

"Yes," began the gravelly-voiced leader of the group. "All medical staff personnel are hereby forbidden to pass messages or images, either directly or via the social media platforms. Further, when dealing with seasonal flu patients or those with colds, to avoid undue panic, they are not to wear protective clothing except for a surgical mask and nitrile gloves. There will be no outward indication of a new disease."

This last declaration seemed to have no effect on the other two people in the room. If this was a highly contagious disease, they were possibly sentencing their health care personnel to severe illness or even death.

The female administrator brought the conversation around to the next task. "The Party has been prepared for this eventuality for many years. They look to us to control the medical personnel. They also look to us to find the explanation for an outbreak. The next step is to bring in for questioning those who are sharing this information on WeChat."

The gravelly-voiced man agreed. "We have identified four physicians involved in the posts who seem to have the most knowledge of the disease. Arrest them and bring them into the Xinjiang Public Security Bureau. I wish to speak to them myself."

CHAPTER FORTY-ONE

Gold Palace Hotel
Fremont Street Experience
Downtown Las Vegas, Nevada

The frenzied activity began to dissipate as Harper saw the last of the ambulances exit the hotel's property. She was left with stunned employees of the hotel, the security team in a dazed and confused state, and one portly, sweaty general manager named Wallace. Harper stripped off her nitrile gloves and tossed them into a trash receptacle near the elevators. She reached into her jeans pocket and pulled out a four-ounce bottle of Purell.

After thoroughly covering her hands with the disinfecting substance, she approached Mr. Wallace. Before she could address him, he peppered her with questions, nervously raising his voice as he spoke.

"Doctor, what is happening in my hotel? Are these people being poisoned? Do they have some type of China flu? I don't know about the elderly couple, but the other five are Chinese, right?"

"Mr. Wallace, I understand you're looking for an explanation and some type of connection between these victims, but we don't have definitive answers for you yet."

"When? When can I know what we're dealing with here so I can calm our guests down? I've got the twenty-third floor empty now. The old people were staying on seventeen in the same tower. They're from Kentucky or some damn place."

"I'll be investigating that next," interjected Harper. "It may be that the seventeenth floor will need to be evacuated as well."

"What? No!" he bellowed. The general manager was incredulous, and it drew the attention of everyone in the VIP entrance.

Becker walked up behind Harper and handed her a fresh pair of nitrile gloves and an N-95 mask, which she quickly used to replace the temporary paper mask. Becker gingerly placed the mask in the waste receptacle.

"And is that really necessary?" he asked, pointing at Harper's mask. "You're frightening our guests. How would you feel if you walked into our hotel and saw people running around wearing surgical masks and rubber gloves?"

"It's not a surgical mask, sir. And in my line of work, it's a tool of the trade."

"Well, can't you at least confine the use of these so-called tools to the rooms involving these dead people."

Harper glared at the man. *The only tool around here is you, Mr. Wallace.* She had several other choice names to pull out of her repertoire, but she resisted the urge to unleash her frustration on him.

"Excuse me, sir. We have work to do. C'mon, Becker."

The two walked toward the elevator, and Harper motioned for Figueroa to join them. The chief of security seemed to be enjoying the exchange, and it was clear he didn't have a lot of respect for Wallace.

"Where to, ma'am?" he asked.

"We need to see the elderly couple's room on the seventeenth floor. Also, can you free up some of your security personnel to review the surveillance footage? I need a precise time and method of contact, if any, between the four Asian men and either the husband or wife. Also, I need to pin down the interaction between the four men and the woman who just died on that gurney. Let's see who she had contact with and when. Please try to determine the whereabouts of the other women."

"You've got it," said Figueroa. "We've already copied the footage of Yao and his companions onto a separate file. We'll review those clips first to see where the interaction might have been with the old folks and also the young girls they had drinks with."

"Can we get LVMPD involved in tracking down the identity of the women? If not, I can call in the bureau." She was referring to the FBI.

"The two detectives are still locked up in one of the rooms on twenty-three, and they're over it, to say the least."

Harper smiled. They had no idea what was in store for them.

"Oh yeah. I'm afraid they're going straight to quarantine." Harper turned to Becker. "Get with Clark County Emergency Management and see what they have set up to quarantine possible victims of a bioterror attack. It's not necessary to send those two to a hospital, but they need to be isolated and observed."

"On it," Becker replied as they exited the elevator and entered the maintenance hallway of the seventeenth floor. It wasn't all that different from the twenty-third except it was crawling with housekeeping personnel and a bellhop.

"Mr. Figueroa, I'm afraid you're gonna have to clear this floor soon. I know that's a heckuva burden, but I don't believe the elderly couple's symptoms are just coincidentally the same as the victims'. It's entirely possible the disease hasn't advanced in their bodies as much as the young woman who succumbed a little while ago. It depends on the timing of contact."

"I'll have my people on that surveillance footage right away."

"Here's the thing, the human body is similar in most respects, but different in many ways. Some people are more susceptible to contracting diseases, and their immune system may be lower than others' for some reason. That's why it's impossible to specifically define a timeline from contact to being symptomatic to contagious to death."

Harper, Becker and the two epidemiologists arrived at the hotel room door and allowed the security chief to open it for them. After they entered, he tried to follow them inside, and Harper quickly stopped him.

"Not a good idea, sir. Please, we've got this. Thank you for helping us review that footage. So you know, Atlanta is gonna ask for duplicates of everything you have."

"Yeah, I expected you would," he said, pointing at Becker. "She told us that already."

She turned to Becker, who peered at them both over her mask. Harper often wondered if there were seven Beckers operating in an alternate universe somehow. Almost like an omnipresent, all-knowing being that was able to appear and reappear in the blink of an eye.

"Good. Well, thank you." Harper gestured toward the door and Figueroa picked up on the hint. He left and the group was left in the room alone.

"I don't think that we're gonna find much in the way of clues in here," said Becker. "Any evidence left with those two as they rode out on the stretchers."

"That's probably true, but let's process it nonetheless. Look for any commonalities. Room service. Drinks. Brain Booster stimulants. Keep a sharp eye out for the unexpected. You know, something out of sorts. If there's nothing here, then we know there must've been some direct contact between these patients and our dead Chinese gentlemen."

"About that," added Becker. "All we got out of the woman before she became deathly ill was that she was an American of South Korean descent. She spoke Chinese, but had never met Mr. Yao or his companions before the other day."

Harper shook her head as she wandered around the room, studying the couple's personal effects. "This just doesn't make sense. Assuming Yao was at the highest point of being contagious, and she contracted the disease during their gathering in the bar, that meant she died within seventy-two hours of contact. That's unheard of."

"Unless there was something else about the young woman's susceptibility we don't know as of yet," offered Becker. "By the way, how did the autopsy go?"

"Very well. Dr. Boychuck is very, um. Well, I think you'd like him," Harper lied. Most likely, he'd drive Becker batshit crazy.

"Cool. Do you think he can provide some insight on the young woman's underlying health?"

Harper nodded and then checked her watch. "The man is very astute." The three-hour time difference wouldn't matter to Dr. Reitherman. She needed to relay what she knew so far so they could decide on a possible containment plan for the hotel, its staff, and guests.

CHAPTER FORTY-TWO

Gold Palace Hotel
Fremont Street Experience
Las Vegas, Nevada

Harper plead her case to Dr. Reitherman.

"These deaths are not coincidental and certainly involve some type of pathogen or site-specific source. Trust me, I've thought about the Atlanta hotel case from years ago in which the housekeepers were rinsing the bathroom drinking glasses out in the sink using toilet bowl cleaner."

Dr. Reitherman had been digesting the information Harper had relayed to him and was also puzzled by the sudden illnesses of the other hotel guests. Bacteria-based illnesses like the Atlanta case couldn't be ruled out.

"Fecal-oral spread of serious diseases is not uncommon, especially in a hotel setting. However, the preliminary autopsy results indicate transfer via respiratory secretions. Your conclusion with Dr. Boychuck from the biopsy would confirm that, am I correct?"

"Yes, sir. My educated guess at this point is SARS simply because the first reported illnesses and deaths came from the four gentlemen who'd just traveled from China to the States. It's just that the next patients to contract the virus throw off the timetable considerably."

"Once again, patients differ. Testing is the answer, together with studying the investigative results from your team and Dr. Boychuck. That's what disease detectives do, Harper. Gather evidence, compare the results to other cases like it, and then construct a case definition. It's a fluid, time-consuming process, as you know."

"Yes, sir. I have Becker creating a line listing, and it changes by the hour."

Whether conducting routine surveillance, investigating an outbreak, or conducting a study, an epidemiologist compiles the information on a spreadsheet to create a line list. It's a logical method of compiling a number of variables, including the patient's characteristics and disease-specific indicators.

"Harper, in order for you to perform the necessary descriptive epidemiology to develop a working hypothesis, you need to come back to Atlanta."

She was afraid of that. The action was here, in Las Vegas. Not sitting behind a computer or hovering over a microscope in Atlanta. There would be more bodies, she was sure of it. She began to make her case.

"Sir, I don't think I'm finished here yet."

"Your team can handle it, and I'll send more foot soldiers from here to pick up the slack."

"But there are interviews to conduct. We need to track down three missing women who came in direct contact with the first four victims. The surveillance videos from casino security—"

Dr. Reitherman interrupted her. "All of that can be done by others. I need you to help me get a handle on this thing. We've got a decision to make, and Washington is aware of what has happened."

"As in the White House?" asked Harper.

"Well, Homeland Security and NIH first, then the president's chief of staff was notified as part of the Presidential Daily Brief. You may not know this, but the president has a tendency to skip those, opting instead to delegate appropriate actions to his cabinet or chief of staff."

Harper was aware. It was one of Joe's primary complaints about the man who occupied the Oval Office. She nodded at Becker, who grabbed her attention and gave her a thumbs-up. They were finishing up their work and packing up their samples. She returned her attention to Dr. Reitherman.

"We don't have much time, sir. If this is SARS, or something like it, we need to notify the locals and quite possibly quarantine this hotel."

"We can't declare an outbreak with six or seven victims," he responded. "Not without a definitive answer as to what we're dealing with first. Gather your evidence. Have your team prepare their reports and email them to you. You and Dr. Becker come back here so we can figure this thing out."

Somehow, she sensed her days were about to get longer. Harper sighed, but she agreed. She was exhausted and looked forward to sleeping on the plane and getting into some fresh clothes. Above all, she missed talking with her husband.

CHAPTER FORTY-THREE

First Affiliated Hospital
Urumqi, Xinjiang, China

Dr. Zeng had been rebuked and reprimanded over the next hour. There would be a payroll deduction to pay the hospital for the unauthorized autopsy. He was forced to write an apology letter and acceptance of responsibility for the delay in transporting the body back to the family in Tibet. The political situation in Tibet was complicated for the Communist Party in China. Tibet was closely monitored by Western media for abuses, and something like this could create an unwanted international incident. Finally, Dr. Zeng was suspended for two weeks from all teaching duties or any hospital activities.

Financially, this was only a slight setback for the man, who was diligent about saving money. The letter was justified, and he was sincere in his apologies to the family. The two-week suspension was welcome. He wanted to learn more about this virus and needed the time to interact with other physicians on WeChat. Much like a grade-school kid who'd been suspended for misbehavior, he looked upon the two-week absence as a pretty sweet deal.

Over his wife's muted objections, Dr. Zeng spent a considerable amount of time on WeChat. He disregarded his nephew's recommendations to avoid using his phone and actual WeChat account to interact. Instead, he went into great detail as he shared the case study he'd undertaken on the deceased Sherpa.

He began to establish a timetable, which indicated his patient might have been the first to contract the disease. As he conducted WeChat conversations with many doctors over the several days following the ill-fated autopsy, he learned a little more about the disease and how it was possibly spread. He was beginning to get a full understanding of the novel virus, and through his extraordinary efforts and the aide of his nephew, he spread the word across China and eventually to Taiwan, where the Western influence was far greater.

He and his fellow rogue physicians knew the risks they were taking. They lived in a Communist country where the central government controlled the content of messages and their dissemination. Dr. Zeng continued compiling information from others and discussing it in many WeChat groups, not just the original one his nephew used.

Then, late one evening, a message came across the original WeChat forum. It was the one group that he did not personally interact with. As his nephew suggested, he'd shown restraint, simply observing the ongoing conversation. The message he read was chilling, and it seemed to be directed at him.

We sincerely warn you. You will stop your impertinence and illegal activity. If you persist, you and all of your associates will be brought to justice. Is that understood?

Dr. Zeng, like a hundred other WeChat users in that group, immediately dropped out until nobody remained.

PART IV

INDEFINITE DOUBT

Being a detective isn't all about murder and monsters. Sometimes it gets unpleasant, especially when the fate of many lives may depend on you.
~ Jack Randolph, Harper Randolph's father

CHAPTER FORTY-FOUR

Australian Federal Police
National Missing Persons Coordination Centre
Canberra, ACT, Australia

Amelia Wharton, deputy spokesperson of the National Missing Persons Coordination Centre of the Australian Federal Police, approached the podium. Her demeanor was always solemn. Her job was to disseminate to the media information on any missing persons reported to the NMPCE.

"Good afternoon. We have an update on a previously reported case, but a related case remains open. The two missing persons registered with us are named Adam Mooy and Trent Maclaren.

"This morning, we were notified by the men's employer that they went on a climbing expedition to Mount Everest and never returned. Investigators at the AFP have reached out to the governments of Nepal and Tibet for assistance.

"They have received information based upon eyewitness accounts that an accident occurred near the peak of Mount Everest, which resulted in injuries and the tragic death of some climbers.

Witnesses identified Trent Maclaren as one of the climbers who slid off an icy cliff to his death.

"His body can be seen from the route to the peak of Mount Everest, but its recovery is deemed too dangerous by Tibetan officials. Because Mr. Maclaren signed a waiver form excusing any duty of local search and rescue parties to retrieve his body, it will remain on the side of the cliff. The family has advised us that a recovery effort can be undertaken for forty thousand dollars AU.

"With respect to Adam Mooy, his coworker and reportedly his best mate, the facts are unclear. The locals who investigated the matter said witnesses were conflicted as to what happened to Mooy. Some thought he perished. Others thought he was rescued. At this time, the focus of the AFP's inquiry had been with the Tibetan government, but they have now been referred to China's Ministry of State Security.

"Also, we've been advised our primary jurisdiction over these missing person cases has been transferred to the Minister for Foreign Affairs. We will update as more information comes into this office. Thank you."

CHAPTER FORTY-FIVE

CDC Headquarters
Atlanta

Harper was a new woman after taking a long shower and getting nine hours of solid, uninterrupted sleep. She took Dr. Dog for a brisk walk and then turned him over to Sally for his breakfast. She then hit it hard, running like the wind for two miles to release pent-up frustration and energy. She wanted to be back in Las Vegas, on the ground, with the fresh set of troops preparing to be sent by the CDC to investigate the mysterious outbreak. The real action was in the field, on the scene of the outbreak. Interviewing patients, contact tracing, and studying the dead. She wanted to stow away with them.

She arrived at the CDC that morning wearing her jeans and a white tee shirt bearing the Georgetown Medical logo on it. Had she known what was in store for her, she might have dressed up. But then again, Harper really didn't care about anyone's opinion of her appearance unless it related to her husband. With her, *what you see is what you get.*

After entering the building, she grabbed an intern who worked on her floor and sent him to Starbucks for her morning caramel latte. Becker would've eagerly volunteered to run the errand for her, but Harper suspected the young doctor had been in her office since the crack of dawn, running numbers.

Becker was one of those people who loved numbers—*a numbers cruncher*. Make no mistake, the role of the epidemiologist was to detect, contain, and eradicate infectious diseases. But part and parcel with that process was creating prediction models to be used by the director of the CDC and related agencies within the government to plan for a spread of the outbreak.

Her young assistant was a walking, talking human calculator. Harper could throw numbers at Becker and she could generate off-the-cuff disease models without powering up her computer. Given time, she could create complex computer simulations that rivaled any mathematician's work. Harper feared there would come a time that word of Becker's talents would slip out of her department and capture the attention of the chief epidemic modeler at the National Institutes of Health. They had a fat budget and could throw lots of numbers with dollar signs attached to lure her right arm away.

"Hello again." Harper greeted her office with a sigh. Like her husband's congressional office, Harper's was equipped with a sofa-sleeper, a small refrigerator, and a sink mounted in a closet kitchenette. There had been occasions when she slept on the sofa to take a catnap in the middle of an epidemic.

She tossed her vintage, oak-brown Mulberry Alexa bag onto a chair stacked with months of the *New England Journal of Medicine*. Her grandmother had given her the satchel-style bag as a present when she graduated from Notre Dame before she left for med school. Harper didn't ordinarily carry a bag with her, but she had mounds of paperwork and notes from Las Vegas to review and later discuss with Dr. Reitherman.

She glanced up at the wall and simultaneously touched her mother's crucifix necklace that had also been given to her by Ma. The Catholic cross was all she had left of her mother, who, for all intents and purposes, was dead.

A sign from her childhood home hung on the wall. It read, *Jesus and germs are everywhere, so wash your hands and say your prayers.*

"Truth," she mumbled with a smile.

Harper had barely gotten settled in her chair and was perusing the dozens of emails in her inbox when her phone rang. It was Dr. Reitherman's secretary, summoning her to his small conference room immediately.

Harper perked up. There was some action. Possibly more cases in Vegas. Maybe internationally? Everything in her gut pointed to China as the source.

She raced out of her office, notes in hand. She almost crashed into the intern who was delivering her coffee. He handed her the latte, and she left him standing in the hall, mouth agape.

"Dr. Randolph, I have your Starbucks card!"

"Put it on my desk!" she shouted back as she rounded the corner and headed for the stairs. There was no time to wait for the always crowded and notoriously slow elevator.

Less than a minute later, she forced herself to slow her pace so she could catch her breath. She adjusted her formfitting jeans and took a quick sip of the caffeine-infused latte before gently knocking on the conference room door.

Dr. Reitherman opened it quickly, as he was waiting for her arrival.

"Good morning, Dr. Reitherman," she said cheerily. But then her attitude quickly changed. "Um, hello."

Two men in dark suits stood on the other side of the room. It never ceased to amaze Harper that men representing a federal law enforcement agency—any of the three-letter ones, your choice—seemed to follow the same dress code. Black suits. Shiny black shoes with rubber soles allowing them to run after bad guys. White pressed shirts and a solid tie—blue, red, or undertaker black.

The *Men in Black* provided Harper emotionless stares in response to her greeting. Dr. Reitherman quickly closed the door and motioned for Harper to sit down.

She was immediately put on alert. Her mind raced, concerned

for Joe. Elected officials had been the target of killers throughout American history, but there had been a war on congressmen. In 2017 a gunman opened fire on the House Republican softball team practicing for a charity event. The ten-minute shoot-out was the first of several other assassination attempts of political officials over the next ten years.

Dr. Reitherman immediately picked up on Harper's apprehension and moved to assuage her fears. "Dr. Randolph, these men are with the Central Intelligence Agency. We need to discuss your findings in Las Vegas."

Harper's anxiety over her husband was alleviated, but her heart rate remained high. Her brain raced as she tried to prepare herself for the conversation with the two agents. *CIA? Poison may have been the cause after all. Bioterror? Nah, that's FBI stuff.*

One of the agents introduced themselves. "I'm Agent Belleville and this is Agent O'Fallon."

Harper suppressed a smirk. She'd traveled to East St. Louis years ago to investigate a possible return of encephalitis. Belleville and O'Fallon were small communities in Illinois near Scott Air Force Base. Harper knew the men were lying about their real names, but maybe that was part of their schtick as spooks.

"How may I help you, gentlemen?"

"We need you to tell us everything you can about the four Chinese victims in Las Vegas."

Harper glanced at Dr. Reitherman. She was not ready to release any official findings as of yet. They were just getting started in their investigation of the Chinese men, as well as the other victims. He winked at her and nodded, providing tacit approval to speak freely.

She took a deep breath and began. "There's a lot to tell, but truthfully, there's even more that I don't know. The four men checked into the hotel together. They have Chinese passports and were apparently there to play in a poker tournament. Based upon my team's interviews of hotel personnel and guests, it was apparent the men were exhibiting signs of a flu-like illness. The dealers at the poker tournament relayed that the men were sweating and coughing from time to time. Hours after their first day's session ended, they were all dead."

"Together? Or, at least, simultaneously?" asked one of the agents.

"Not together, but most likely within a few hours of each other. I believe we identified the first death to be a young man named Yao."

The other agent shifted gears. "Did you go through their personal effects?"

"My team did."

"Did you find anything unusual?"

"Well, first, let me say the CSI personnel on the ground got there first. In fact, they'd released the scenes to the detectives before we were able to begin our work. To answer your question, we did not. You should check with CSI on that."

"What about the men? How would you describe them?"

"Young. Healthy. Muscular and toned. Surprising, actually."

"How so?"

"Generally speaking, infectious diseases, especially respiratory ones, have an easier target in those with pre-existing conditions like heart ailments, diabetes, and lung issues. I assisted in the autopsy of Yao, and I have the autopsy reports of the other three men from Dr. Boychuck, the local ME. There's nothing to indicate they were susceptible to a respiratory disease. That said, we haven't had a chance to run all of our tests yet on the samples. There are a lot of infectious diseases on our planet, both known and unknown."

The other agent entered the conversation. "With respect to the bodies, were there any identifying marks, scars, or tattoos?"

Harper thought for a moment. "Um, yes. On Yao and one other, that I recall. They had tattoos on their right biceps."

Harper paused and closed her eyes, a method she used to visualize something she'd seen but couldn't recall.

"Dr. Randolph?" asked one of the agents.

She held her right index finger in the air and then responded, "A tiger. Siberian, I think."

The two men glanced at each other. One of them leaned forward and asked, "Are you sure? And are you positive it was on both men?"

"And how do you know it was Siberian and not another species?"

Harper realized she'd struck a nerve with her questioners. "Yes, I'm sure it was a Siberian, and it was definitely on two of the men, if not all of them. I'd have to review the autopsies. The tattoos were very detailed. Excellent work and coloring. The artist took great pains to be accurate."

"How so?"

"Siberian tigers generally have a rusty-red coat with black stripes, while the Bengal sub-species have light yellow fur and brown stripes."

"Okay, Dr. Randolph, thank you," said the taller of the two agents. He looked to Dr. Reitherman. "Thank you for your time. We'll need a copy of the autopsy reports and the EIS reports related to these four men in particular."

Harper was impressed the agent was familiar with the abbreviation of the Epidemic Intelligence Service. However, she was not ready to be dismissed because she had a job to do as well.

"Quid pro quo, gentlemen," she announced bluntly. She'd always wanted to use the famous line from the classic movie *Silence of the Lambs*, and this was the perfect opportunity.

"Excuse me?" asked the lead agent.

Harper stood to make eye contact with the agents. "Clearly, there is something more to these four poker players from China that warranted you two to fly all the way here from East St. Louis. Am I right?"

The taller agent scowled, but the other man leaned back and grinned. He seemed to appreciate Harper's ability to bust them on their contrived last names.

"That's need-to-know, Dr. Randolph. Thank you for your time."

"I have things I need to know, too," she countered. "Whatever happened to interagency cooperation?"

"Classified, ma'am."

Harper shook her head and stood her ground. She leaned on the table to make closer eye contact. "Here's the thing. I have a novel virus that could at this very moment be running through people's bodies in Las Vegas and halfway around the world if these four guys from China came in contact with others while contagious. We have hours, not days, to identify the disease and determine if containment measures are necessary, or it could blow into an epidemic or worse."

"Noted," he said as he tried to round the desk and head for the door. Harper moved to block his path.

"Tell me something about these men. I need to have our people conduct contact tracing to determine who they've been in contact with both before and after they arrived in Las Vegas. I wanna know the details of their flights. Points of origin. Where did they work? Family life. Everything."

"We're not at liberty to release that information at this time," he replied calmly.

Harper was fuming. She gathered up her files and coffee without saying another word. She winked at Dr. Reitherman in a way the CIA agents couldn't see. As she reached for the door, the other agent spoke up.

"Where are you going?"

"I've got a disease to identify, and I don't have time for this."

"What about the information request?"

"Put it in writing and we'll get to it in due time. However, if you can provide me something in return, I will most certainly speed up our response to your request."

The men looked at Dr. Reitherman, who shrugged. Harper would later thank him for backing her up.

The standoff came to an end.

"Fine. Fine. Let us explain."

CHAPTER FORTY-SIX

CDC Headquarters
Atlanta

"Chinese military? Bioterror plot? They can't be serious."

Harper paced the floor of Dr. Reitherman's office as she recounted the details provided by the CIA agents.

Dr. Reitherman remained calm in an effort to ease Harper's frustration. "They didn't tell you everything. You know that, right?"

"Aw, shit, sir. I know that. Listen, I've been around these Secret-Service-CIA types throughout Joe's career in Washington. The FBI folks are a little easier to read. The others are like robots with no soul. They're experts at saying nothing. It's aggravating."

Dr. Reitherman. "I'll give you credit. You effectively called their bluff. You know I would've been forced to make you comply."

"I know that," she said with a laugh. "Those two didn't."

"All right, based on what they told us, has your hypothesis changed?" he asked.

Harper exhaled and sat in a chair across from his desk. She crossed her legs and fiddled with her crucifix necklace as she spoke. "I can't rule out a bioterror weapon. You never can. If there's a deadly contagion, some immoral, unscrupulous scientist will find a delivery agent and kill unsuspecting people."

Dr. Reitherman nodded in agreement. "Think about it. These four guys may all be military. It's possible they were intentionally infected by the Chinese government because they were headed to Las Vegas, a city that hosts millions of visitors a year from all over the world."

Harper scowled and shook her head. "Including China. It doesn't make sense to come to a gambling mecca frequented by Mainland Chinese citizens, expose them to a novel virus, and then watch them all fly home with the disease coursing through their bodies."

"You've got a point. There's also the possibility they were exposed to the disease by accident. There was always the theory that the coronavirus pandemic was caused by a laboratory accident in Wuhan. It was never proven, nor was it disproved."

Harper remembered 2020. It was the year she and Joe got married, virtually. Their big wedding she'd planned for a year was scrapped. Their guests couldn't attend. They lost the deposit on the venue they'd chosen because the company never reopened. It was a debacle that she'd always blame on Beijing.

"That's because the Chinese government hid it away under lock and key. They never let information out of the country, even if it's necessary to save lives."

Dr. Reitherman understood. He'd been in the trenches during the pandemic and almost lost his life had it not been for the well-trained doctors at Emory Healthcare. Harper was frantically typing on her smartphone and then ran her fingers across the screen to navigate to a web page.

"Harper, what is it?"

"Sir, the Chinese military has a special forces unit called the Siberian Tigers. They're the baddest of the bad. You know, throw them into the frozen tundra with nothing but a loincloth and a hunting knife and they can survive. Those types of guys."

"Are you thinking zoonotic? That's the likely culprit for any disease arising in China."

Harper didn't respond. She'd zoned him out and was taking in all the information found on the website she was perusing.

He tried to get her attention. "Harper?"

"Oh, yes, sir. Sorry. Um, I need to get to work on something. Anything else?"

Dr. Reitherman looked at his watch. "Yes. I've assembled a team to travel to Vegas. Brief them. Give them their marching orders. Let me know when they're ready. I'll need to charter a plane for a group that large."

"Great! So we're going back later today?"

"Not you, Harper. I need you here to quarterback this thing."

"Please, Dr. Reitherman. I'm going stir-crazy."

"You've been here less than two hours, for Pete's sake. You haven't even finished your coffee."

Harper stared through the tiny hole on the lid of the Starbucks cup and quickly gulped down the last of her now-cold latte. She tipped up the cup so he could see that it was empty. "There, all done. Now can I go back to Vegas?"

He laughed. She was the only one under his supervision who could smart-off like that.

"No. Not yet, anyway. Help me get a handle on this thing; then we'll decide."

Harper pouted and then exhaled. "Okay. I do need to do some research on something, and this new information on our index patients might help."

Dr. Reitherman stood and crossed his arms in front of him. "Listen, I know you. You're like a darn thoroughbred ready to bust out of the gate, but I've gotta pull back on the reins sometimes. Help me get this investigation on the right track, and then we'll see what's next. Deal?"

"Deal."

CHAPTER FORTY-SEVEN

Urumqi, Xinjiang, China

Dr. Zeng sat down with his wife of forty years to come clean on all the secrecy. The two had been alone together for the past two decades after their only child, a son, died in a military training accident. The couple had only had one child in accordance with the Communist government's birth-planning program designed to control their overpopulation issues. It had first been introduced in 1979 after ten years of a two-child policy and was later modified to allow two children if the firstborn was a daughter.

The one-child policy in China did not make exceptions for the death of the first. Besides, under the policy, women were forced to either be sterilized by tubal ligation or have an IUD, intrauterine device, surgically installed to prevent additional pregnancies.

After their son died, they'd lived alone and were each other's primary means of emotional support. Their life together was mundane and uneventful. Dr. Zeng rarely discussed his work at the hospital, and his wife, who didn't work, spent her days doting over their nondescript apartment.

Despite their relative isolation socially, the two managed to love one another and enjoyed each other's company. There were no secrets between them because their outside lives never presented the opportunity to hide anything from the other. Until now.

Dr. Zeng, out of fear for his wife's reaction, had not disclosed his involvement in the examination and study of the deceased Sherpa. She first became aware of the matter the night he was pacing the floor and staring out the window. Still, she didn't quiz him about it. She'd trusted his judgment in all matters pertaining to their lives together and knew he'd confide in her when the time was right. That time was now.

"Wife," he began out of character. They rarely spoke to one another using any form of name or designation. This immediately grabbed her attention. "I have become involved in something that has placed us at great risk."

"Can you tell me what it is?" his subservient wife replied. She patted the seat on the sofa next to her, encouraging him to relax as he spoke. Dr. Zeng glanced out the windows for what felt like the hundredth time that day and sighed as he sat down.

"I am sorry, my wife. I am very sorry."

"What is troubling you?"

"I should have minded my own business. I have a good job and a good life. I did not have to concern myself with the affairs of others."

She delicately probed further, encouraging him to speak freely. "Let me help you, if only to hear your troubles."

He stood and glanced over the back of the sofa to catch a glimpse of the roads leading to their apartment building. Nervously, he sat back down and began to rub his hands together. Perspiration broke out on his forehead.

She patted his forehead using a cloth handkerchief she'd embroidered and then took his hands in hers. She gave him a reassuring smile. Sensing he was in serious trouble, she thought to herself, *Now is not the time for hand-wringing but, rather, a time for hand-holding.*

The words poured out of her beloved husband. "I have been

conducting an investigation into a patient who died of a mysterious illness. Many years ago, I vowed to help our medical community avoid the kind of devastation felt in Wuhan. I did it for you, our family, and the innocent people who were intentionally kept unaware of that deadly disease."

"I know you were distraught over how that was handled. I did not know you still fostered such strong feelings about it."

"I had pushed it out of my mind until recently when a seemingly healthy, viral young man from Tibet was sent to the hospital for analysis. He was a goat herder and a Sherpa from an isolated family near Mount Everest. He died of a mysterious illness. The more I learned of his case, the more I wanted to examine the evidence."

"What have you learned?"

"He died of complications from a virus I am not familiar with. In fact, it resembles several respiratory diseases, including SARS and coronavirus, but it attacks the body like HIV/AIDS."

His wife had no medical training nor much schooling, but over time she'd listened and learned from her husband on those occasions he did relay his daily activities. She was unsure of the science behind his revelation but presumed an unknown disease with the attributes of three deadly killers was not good.

"It appears you have made a wonderful discovery that should be shared."

Dr. Zeng exhaled and flopped back against the sofa. "Yes, but I did not share it with my administrator or the proper authorities. I chose to share it with my colleagues on WeChat."

"Why?"

"Because I feared a cover-up like what happened in Wuhan."

His wife grimaced and jutted out her chin. She squeezed her husband's hand and then smiled. "I understand. You are a principled man and I stand by your choices. Are you in trouble?"

Dr. Zeng rarely showed any emotion. However, he couldn't stop the tears from flowing out of his eyes. "Yes. I have been questioned by my supervisor. My time at home with you has not been a vacation. It was a suspension. My pay has been reduced to pay for my unauthorized examination of the body."

He began to sob and she comforted him. She stayed strong and held her husband while he let out days of fear and sadness. When he calmed himself, she looked him in the eye.

"We will get through this together. Do not fear, my husband."

Dr. Zeng addressed his wife by her first name for the first time in years. "Ying, it is not over. With the government, it never is. It is a matter of time before they come for me. And ..." His voice trailed off.

"For me as well," she concluded in a solemn tone of voice.

"Yes. Maybe."

He began to sob again and buried his hands in his face. Ying wasn't going to allow him to wallow in self-pity.

"Husband, it is time for you to listen to me. I love you. I trust you. I will protect you just as you have protected me these many years. I am not a porcelain doll that breaks easily. Do you believe that?"

He chuckled and hugged his wife. "Yes. I am sorry. It appears I am made of porcelain."

She wiped away his tears and studied his face. "No, you are the strongest man I know. If what you say is true, we need to make—"

She abruptly stopped her sentence as she heard sirens in the distance. It was not unusual for emergency vehicles to speed past their apartment building, as they were located near a busy highway. But, now, with her husband's revelations, she was also hyperaware.

Dr. Zeng pushed off the sofa and sprang to his feet. His greatest fears were realized.

"They are coming. You must go!"

He raced to the kitchen table and opened his laptop. He navigated through the folders of documents on his computer. He transferred one after another onto an external hard drive.

"Come, husband, we must leave now."

"I am staying. If we both leave, they will hunt for you as well." He handed the hard drive to his wife. "Find our nephew. He will be at the university today."

"I know his schedule. I take him lunch sometimes."

He placed his hands over hers as she gripped the portable hard drive. "Tell him to find a place to keep you safe. Then he is to publish my findings to WeChat."

"This?" she asked, holding up the hard drive.

"Yes. Tell him to share all of it. Encrypted. Do you know what that means?"

She nodded. As more sirens could be heard, he turned to kiss her. "I will always love you, my wife. Please hurry and be careful."

"I love you, but how will you find me?"

"Fangyu. He is a very smart young man and knows what to do. I will find you through him."

Ying gathered her composure, kissed her husband goodbye, and slipped out the door. Dr. Zeng left the door slightly ajar. He watched her move quickly down the hallway toward the emergency exit. Just as the stairwell door closed, the elevator arrived and the doors began to open. Leaving their hallway door ajar, he raced back to the kitchen and hastily fixed a bowl of Asian gazpacho soup. The cold, sweet delicacy was typically consumed as a dessert.

The fist pounding on the slightly opened door jolted Dr. Zeng even though he expected it. He took in two quick spoonfuls of the scrumptious soup. Not because he wanted to lend authenticity to his attempt to appear calm and therefore not guilty in the eyes of the police. But rather, because he thought it might be his last meal.

CHAPTER FORTY-EIGHT

Urumqi, Xinjiang, China

Urumqi was located far away from Beijing, the center of the Communist Party's centralized government. However, the city on China's Central Asia frontier may be one of the most closely surveilled places on earth. Security checkpoints with identification scanners guard train stations and roads leading into the city. Facial scanners track comings and goings at shopping malls, banks, and hotels.

Police use handheld electronic devices to search citizens' smartphones for encrypted chat apps, dissident videos, and other social media content labeled as subversive by the Beijing government.

The simple act of topping off their vehicle's gas tanks required the driver to swipe their identification cards and submit to a facial-recognition scan.

Decades ago, a separatist movement by a mostly Muslim ethnic group had turned the city into a test laboratory for high-tech social controls being developed by the Chinese military and law enforcement.

Longtime residents remember the strife created by some of the more violent separatists and the Xinjiang police. The WeChat service was used as a method of communication between the separatists. Soon, the police put its foot down and demanded the proprietors of WeChat grant the government unfettered access in order to monitor the activity of its users.

Labeling content they deemed contrary to the government's best interest as *malpractice,* a taskforce was enlisted to tamp down so-called *rumors and information leading to violence, terrorism, and pornography.*

The surveillance state expanded across China, but Urumqi was the testing ground. It was also the place where enterprising Chinese students learned ways around the government intrusion. At first, like Western hackers, it was a game to see how they could circumvent the surveillance. Later, it became a movement as more and more young people sought the types of freedoms enjoyed in the West.

It also became lucrative. Enterprising hackers like Fangyu were paid by businessmen to hide financial transactions from prying government eyes. They helped abused women find safety from their husbands who enlisted the assistance of police to track them down. They even opened up internet portals to Taiwan, considered by Beijing to be a part of China, but whose people believed themselves to be an independent, free country falling under the protection of the United States.

Ying was worried about her husband. She hid herself outside the apartment building, where she could observe the activity of the police. After fifteen minutes, her husband was led out of the building in handcuffs, and one of the uniformed officers had his laptop sealed in a large plastic bag. Several residents stopped to gawk at Dr. Zeng as he was forcefully taken across the small courtyard and thrown into the back of an unmarked sedan. Seconds later, he was gone.

She began to cry for the first time. She wanted to appear to be strong for him in his time of need, but she was fearful they'd never see one another again. She put a death grip on the portable hard drive in her coat pocket. She wanted to squeeze the life out of it as if the information contained on the hard drive was responsible for her losing her beloved husband.

She finally gathered her thoughts and suppressed her emotions. She put on a scarf and a pair of dark sunglasses to trick the many surveillance cameras that were located between their apartment and the university. It was a long walk for her, one that would take an hour, but she did not want to risk retrieving her bicycle. Besides, she knew several routes through retail store buildings that allowed her to avoid cameras. It was a method many residents used to mislead the massive computers that stored the whereabouts of nearly every resident.

An hour later, after taking a roundabout route to the university, she was sitting on a park bench outside Fangyu's dormitory. She sat stoic, staring ahead and not making direct eye contact with anyone. At her age, she was somewhat out of place at the university campus, but because she didn't draw attention to herself, nobody approached her.

It took another hour for her nephew to emerge from his dorm. She casually walked ahead until her path intersected his. Fangyu, like so many students his age, walked down the sidewalk with his attention and face buried in the display of his smartphone. He was startled when his aunt suddenly appeared in front of him.

"*Gaisi de!*" Damn it.

"I am sorry, nephew," she whispered as she reached out to touch his forearm.

He stared at her. He'd never seen her in dark sunglasses and a scarf before. "Aunt, is that you?"

"Of course, nephew. Your uncle has sent me to you. He is in trouble. So am I."

"What happened?" He nervously looked around the grounds.

"He was interrogated by his administrator first. Now he has been arrested. He told me to seek you out for help."

"Yes. I can help. Come with—"

She gripped his arm again. Ying glanced around and saw the cameras affixed to the light posts. She wrapped her arm through his and led him down the sidewalk. Casually, like an expert in the art of espionage, Ying slipped her hand into her coat pocket, retrieved the hard drive, and transferred it into Fangyu's olive drab green military-style jacket.

She whispered to him, "If you see police coming, leave me on the sidewalk. He wants you to publish everything on this hard drive. Encrypted, he said."

"When?" asked Fangyu as he pretended to laugh as if they were having a casual conversation.

"Immediately. All of it."

"I will do this without a problem. First, I need to get you to safety."

They walked a few more paces until he leaned his body to guide her through a grove of trees out of view of the surveillance cameras. The two of them continued their casual, unremarkable stroll together until they joined hundreds of residents walking down the road toward a residential district featuring low-income, high-rise housing.

Without speaking, they entered the building and rode up to the third floor. Fangyu led his aunt down a darkened hallway to the emergency stairwell. From there, they walked down five flights of concrete stairs until they reached the bottom of the structure. The basement contained furnaces, boilers, and plumbing servicing the building.

They continued their silent trek through the bowels of the building until Fangyu came to a steel door at the end of a barely lit corridor. As he opened it, a rush of cool, stale air struck them in the face. A small darkened utility room contained a handful of wooden crates, and steel shelves were strewn about.

Ying was genuinely concerned and her tone of voice reflected it. "Nephew?"

"Shhh," he admonished her to keep quiet. "Trust me." His tone toward his aunt would be considered disrespectful under any other circumstances.

He shoved two of the crates out of the way and opened a steel hatch door embedded in the concrete floor. More stale air greeted them, but Fangyu moved quicker now. He descended the steel rungs of the twenty-foot ladder and assisted his aunt until they'd reached the dusty rock floor. When she was comfortable, he scampered back up the ladder to slide the crates around the opening, and then he pulled the trapdoor closed.

"What is this, nephew?"

"Aunt Ying, welcome to the Underground Great Wall."

CHAPTER FORTY-NINE

CDC Headquarters
Atlanta

Harper was still perturbed that she was sidelined when she returned to her office. She put it out of her mind for the moment and immediately began doing some internet research on the four victims' military unit. She learned that the Siberian Tiger special forces unit was based in Shenyang located in the northeast part of the country in Liaoning Province. Located on the Yellow Sea near North Korea, historically, the region had been known as Manchuria.

This was consistent with Yao's passport. However, as Harper thumbed through the notes provided by the other epidemiologists in Vegas with her and Becker, she noticed their plane tickets revealed an itinerary returning them to Urumqi in Xinjiang.

"That's a long way from your home base, gentlemen," Harper muttered aloud as she continued to read about the Siberian special forces. They were highly regarded by the world's military leaders. They'd performed admirably on behalf of the Chinese military in the Middle East in the past. Harper cursed under her breath at the secrecy maintained by China. If it were almost any other nation, she could pick up the phone and have details on these men within hours.

"There you are!" Becker announced herself rather than politely tapping on the door. Her hands were full with two glasses of some kind of drink adorned with a straw and an orange slice. "After Vegas, I thought it would be a good idea for us to build our inner armor."

"Huh?" asked a puzzled Harper. She had no intention of drinking whatever the puke-green-looking concoction was in Becker's hands.

"Inner armor. You know, immune system. Immuno-booster drinks are full of super-healthy, disease-fighting goodies that actually taste pretty good, too. Here." She extended her arm to hand Harper one of the glasses and waited.

"Um, no, thanks. I got boosted with my latte. Go ahead, you can have them both. Double the armor, right?"

Becker scowled at her boss and then came closer. Her voice lowered to an almost demented, insane tone. "I don't insist upon much, do I?" she snarled.

Harper's eyes grew wide. She had to think for a moment. That was probably true, but she didn't want to admit it, especially when the consequences meant she had to drink the glass of puke-green unknown something or other.

"Maybe." She leaned forward and looked at the drink from above. Her nostrils flared in an attempt to sniff it. She'd never smelled baby diarrhea, but the immune-booster drink certainly gave her the visual.

"Seriously, it's good. It has honey in it."

"Is that supposed to sell me on it?" Harper was being a smart aleck, but deep inside, she knew Becker liked the playful back-and-forth.

"Partly. Come on, it's good for you. You'll see."

"What's in it?"

"Well, honey for sweetener. Watermelon, carrot, beet, ginger, kale, turmeric, tomato, celery—"

Harper raised her hand. "Aw, shit, Becker. What did you do? Rummage through the garbage in the cafeteria?"

Becker liked a challenge, but she was growing exasperated with her boss. "If you try it, I'll give you an update on a new related case that just came in to us."

Harper didn't hesitate. She took a small sip through the straw. She raised her eyebrows and shrugged. "It didn't kill me. Yet."

Becker smiled and put her left hand on her hip in her customary I-told-you-so stance. "Admit it. It's good, right?"

"Okay, not too bad. It could use a little more turmeric, though." Harper started laughing, as did Becker. She took another sip of the drink and motioned for her assistant to sit down. Becker had to set her drink on Harper's desk and move a stack of folders out of the chair opposite the one holding the medical journals.

After getting settled in, she anxiously shared the news with Harper. "We have two more locals who've been admitted to Southern Hills Medical Center in the suburbs of Las Vegas. Our people learned of them through a conversation with Figueroa. He's been very helpful."

"What's their status?" asked Harper.

"Our people confirmed they'd been at the Gold Palace the afternoon our four Chinese poker players were circulating through the casino. Figueroa has his surveillance people trying to establish a contact between the couple, from Summerlin, by the way, and the Chinese men."

"I gather they're alive."

"Oh, yes. Sorry. They both complained of a persistent cough and a low-grade fever, as well as difficulty breathing. They are in their mid-forties. The man is a cigar smoker and his wife is actually very healthy. She's a mom and a yoga instructor."

"They're both hospitalized?"

"Yes. She's afebrile and all of her symptoms have resolved with the exception of the cough. Even that is decreasing in severity."

"Is he a heavy smoker? What about cigarettes?"

"She claims he's never touched one. He smokes occasionally when playing golf or at the casinos. That's it."

"She provided the information?"

"He's on a ventilator and in isolation. His condition is labeled critical, and his doctors say he's day-to-day."

Harper shook her head in disappointment. The disease was likely transmittable between humans, which meant hundreds of people could be infected and outside any possible containment zone.

"Becker, see if the woman will release their medical records to us. If she won't, I'll take it to Dr. Reitherman. Find out how the physicians treated her. We might be able to learn something from that."

"I'm on it."

"What else?"

Becker leaned forward in her chair and looked at Harper's drink. "Did you finish?"

"C'mon, Becker. Okay." Harper slurped the last of the greenish smoothie down and stuck out her tongue. Unbeknownst to her, it was now colored baby-diarrhea green, or puke green, if there was a difference.

"I've assembled a team in the large conference room. They're geared up and ready to fly when Dr. Reitherman gives us the thumbs-up. They're waiting for you now."

"That's it? I finished that mess so I could send them off to have fun?"

Becker stood and smiled. She grabbed Harper's glass. "In Vegas, I learned the art of deception. It's a powerful tool, wouldn't you agree?"

"Whatever," Harper grumbled. "Let's go." She grabbed her notes and sneered at Becker as they left her office.

CHAPTER FIFTY

CDC Headquarters
Atlanta

"Good morning." Harper greeted the group of a dozen recruits who would join the other epidemiologists already deployed to Las Vegas. She knew them all by name but realized only a few had worked abroad. Nine out of twelve had never been deployed to a hot zone, ground zero of an infectious disease outbreak.

While Becker was handing out packets of materials that included up-to-the-minute updates from those already in Las Vegas as well as the new autopsy reports from Dr. Boychuck, Harper decided to change her approach to the meeting. These people had been handpicked by Dr. Reitherman with Becker's input. It wasn't necessary for Harper to state the obvious regarding what their duties were once they arrived at the hotel. *They need something more. A reminder. Or a warning.*

"I know all of you are excited to get to Las Vegas and hit the ground running. I wish I could be on that charter flight with you."

"We thought you'd be with us," one of the newer CDC epidemiologists groaned. If any of the newbies could pick one of their superiors to work beside during an outbreak, it would be Harper. Her experiences working in Africa were invaluable. Passing on the benefit of her work at ground zero of an outbreak was better than all the books written on the subject.

"Trust me, I'd like to be there in the trenches with you, and most likely, I'll see you soon enough. As you know, Becker and I just spent twenty-eight grueling hours there. It was fast paced, and frankly, we didn't stop for a moment, much less sleep.

"In the hot zone, whether it's Africa or Las Vegas, you finish your day and you barely feel human. There will be deep marks on your face from the elastic bands of your N95s. Your hair will be damp with sweat. Your eyes will barely be open. Seriously, when we boarded that jet to return to Atlanta, I was no longer a woman or a doctor. I was a foot soldier in the war against an unknown enemy, a virus, that I'd never seen before.

"Make no mistake, when you start your day, you'll feel an adrenaline rush like no other. You'll gear up in your PPE, surrounded by your colleagues. You'll try cracking jokes, but your eyes will tell the truth. They'll reflect the worry as to whether you've protected yourself adequately. You'll reconfirm to one another as you carry out the steps we've all practiced here in Atlanta. Gloves, gown, second pair of gloves, glasses, cap, mask, visor, shoes, shoe covers and then tape over tape over tape to keep everything sealed.

"Why? Because you know what it means to make a mistake. These viruses don't mess around. There are no do-overs. Your partner is more than someone who works by your side in a hot zone. They are the ones who write your name on the back of your PPE in a big red Sharpie. When you're geared up, nobody recognizes anyone else.

"You feel like a paratrooper with the 101st Airborne about to jump out of an airplane. You hope that chute will open. In the hot zone, you hope that tape is secured. You hope the mask is properly covering your face. You hope your gloves won't rip. And you pray that nothing comes in contact with your body.

"Before you know it, a ten-hour, or twelve-hour, or fourteen-hour day is over. Time flies in the hot zone because there is so much to do. Your mind races as it processes the data while reminding you to follow proper safety protocols. Remember, there are no do-overs in our jobs. Mistakes mean death, not just for you, but for everyone you come in contact with. Your coworkers. Your friends. Your family.

"You're disease detectives. The evidence is gathered methodically and efficiently. But the sheer volume of information will seem overwhelming. That's why there is a team behind you, here at the CDC, to compile your findings and construct a case definition.

"And when your day is done, you step aside for the next team to do their part. You're not finished, nor will they be. The thing I want to emphasize to you is this. When you're dealing with an emerging infectious disease outbreak, especially a novel virus like this one, you're always behind where you think you are. Each patient can infect three or more. Each of whom can infect three or more, and so on. It doesn't take long before a handful of contagious individuals have multiplied to thousands or tens of thousands. *Or millions.*

"This is why we do what we do at a somewhat frenzied pace. Infectious diseases don't give a damn about lack of personnel or budget cuts or long hours. Viruses are always winning the race until you stop them from reaching the finish line. He who wins the race survives. It's truly us versus them.

"And when it's over, you realize the fight has just begun because there is always one more disease out there waiting to see how fast you can run. To see if you are capable of catching them. There is no margin for error. You don't get a head start, they do. It's a race to the finish that we cannot lose."

Harper exhaled and exited the room without another word, leaving Becker and the dozen epidemiologists destined for Las Vegas in stunned silence.

CHAPTER FIFTY-ONE

Xinjiang Public Security Bureau
Urumqi, Xinjiang, China

If Dr. Zeng was fearful when meeting with his administrator at the hospital, he was downright terrified he'd lose his life when confronted by the officers of the Xinjiang Public Security Bureau.

"We have eight unfounded rumors attributed to you, Dr. Zeng!" one of the officials circling the room screamed.

Dr. Zeng was strapped to a chair with his ankles and arms bound to the point his extremities were going numb. He tried not to show his discomfort and did his level best to remain emotionless. However, the interrogation had been ongoing for three hours, and the police showed no evidence of growing weary of their role. He just wondered when the physical abuse would begin.

Another official took a turn, spitting in Dr. Zeng's face as he yelled the questions. "There is no unexplained virus, is there? All you want to do is make a name for yourself, correct? Who is assisting you? You will answer us!" The official hissed the last sentence, causing the hair on Dr. Zeng's neck to stand up.

The first official was back. "You signed a letter of apology to the family of the patient. You admitted to your administrator that you were in the wrong. You forced the pathologist to assist you with threats. You have poisoned the minds of physicians all across the People's Republic!"

Dr. Zeng stared ahead, refusing to provide them any satisfaction. If he was going to die, he'd die keeping his secrets and protecting those who helped him, especially his wife and nephew.

Suddenly, the cell door was flung open and crashed against the concrete wall behind him. The force of the air physically shook his body, and the impact of the door almost caused him to urinate in his pants. He cringed as he prepared his body to be struck by the brute who entered the room.

Nothing was said. The two men who had been interrogating him calmly walked around the chair. Dr. Zeng resisted the urge to follow them with his eyes. Thus far, he had effectively remained zombielike, staring beyond the men at the mirrored glass he was certain contained observers.

The men stepped outside and pulled the door until it was only slightly ajar. Dr. Zeng strained to listen to their conversation. It was not heated, but was certainly serious. A minute later, the interrogators returned with the third man, who wore a CDC identification badge.

"Dr. Zeng, my name is Chen Shengwei, the chief technology officer for the CDC. The time for games is over. We are not barbarians here, and now we need your cooperation."

Dr. Zeng studied the man and suppressed a grin. Good cop, bad cop. He'd never seen an American television drama, especially one involving police procedurals. But the practice of an interrogator beating down a captive who was then offered an olive branch if he'd just come clean was a universal concept.

The man leaned across the desk and locked eyes with Dr. Zeng. For an awkward minute, nothing was said and neither of them blinked. Then he slowly reached into his suit jacket pocket.

Dr. Zeng took in a deep breath. He expected to die in that moment. He silently apologized to his wife and all of his extended family. He congratulated himself for keeping calm in the face of death. He prepared his mind for the crushing blow that certainly was about to be delivered.

But, instead, the CDC technology officer retrieved a Huawei smartphone and held it in front of Dr. Zeng's face. As he studied the display, a slight, imperceptible grin came over his face. If he was to die, he'd die a hero.

发口哨の人

反神经　今天

2030年04月30，芬曾份肺病病检测，她用红色出「冠病」字，当学同学7，她份拍传给了同生同学。当晚，份传遍了生，转发份括8被警方训生。

给芬了烦，传播源，她被谈，了「有、斥责」，她专。此些，芬被「有割被训生浮出面」，她「吹哨」，芬正了割说法，她说自吹哨

"What does this mean, Dr. Zeng?" the man ostensibly from the

CDC asked. "There is no doubt in my mind you are the author of this post."

Dr. Zeng fought back the urge to laugh. He stared at the combination of Chinese characters and emojis. Some were bizarrely associated with others. It was most likely that many had no meaning whatsoever other than to throw off anyone attempting to decipher the code. It was also likely some of the emojis were triggers, objects embedded in the post to instruct the recipient to look elsewhere or to await further posts.

Dr. Zeng's nephew was a genius, and his captors, including the chief technological officer, were confounded by the apparent gibberish.

"I will make him talk," said the largest of the three men as he balled up his fists.

"No, not yet," countered Chen. "Dr. Zeng is a reasonable man, are you not? You want to take credit for this great find, don't you? Please, tell me of your work. Give me the details so that I may give you credit with your peers at the CDC. Then we will let you go."

Dr. Zeng stared at the post. As the display was held in front of his face, he watched the number of WeChat users who liked and interacted on it. Comments were in a similar language. Some were simply sad faces shedding tears. Others were written in Chinese characters, encouraging the poster of the message to continue. Most of the comments insisted on more information and vowed secrecy.

Then, unbeknownst to the CDC man, the post disappeared from the screen, apparently deleted by the Chinese government. Dr. Zeng looked up to the man's eyes and blinked. There was no meaning behind it. He never intended to antagonize the man. However, immediately after he looked away from the phone, the technological officer turned the display around and cursed loudly. Then he gave the other two men the directive they'd been waiting for.

"Beat it out of him!"

CHAPTER FIFTY-TWO

CDC Headquarters
Stephen B. Thacker CDC Library
Atlanta

Albert Einstein once said *the only thing you absolutely have to know is the location of the library.* As a kid, Harper grew up in the library. In the small town where she was raised, most entertainment options for children were outdoors. There were no shopping malls or movie theaters to hang out in. Most of her friends spent their time outside their homes. They'd make the hour drive to the Savannah River and hang out in the many inlets. Some would play sports while others enjoyed hunting. To be sure, Harper did all of those things. But while most kids her age spent half their days on some form of computer device, either playing online games or interacting on social media, she went to the local historic library.

Spending a considerable amount of time in the library, holding actual books and turning the pages, shaped her studies for the rest of her life. Harper always knew where the library was, just as Einstein had suggested. While others conducted their research online at a much faster pace, Harper preferred to find a quiet spot, snuggled out of the way in the stacks. While others occupied tables and chairs in the center of the building, Harper would find an empty cubicle, where she could focus on the task at hand without distraction or social interaction.

During her studies at Georgetown, she'd learned there were medical treatises and journals that were not available online in portable document format, or pdf. Diseases were older than mankind, and it wasn't beyond the realm of possibility that some could be resurrected from days when computers and eReaders didn't exist.

She'd let Becker know she'd be at the Stephen B. Thacker Library main branch located at CDC headquarters. Since its inception in 1946, it had been relied upon by CDC researchers, scientists and public health officials as a valuable resource in the fight against infectious diseases. Over time, fewer of these professionals utilized the library in person, opting instead to access its database online.

Harper traveled light, carrying only her cell phone, which she muted, a notepad, and her leather-bound copy of *Gray's Anatomy*. The illustrated classic written over a hundred years ago was given to Harper by her great-grandmother Mimi when she left for undergraduate school at Notre Dame. Both her grandmother and great-grandmother were profound influences on her life, gently nudging her away from following the career path of her father. The exquisitely designed antiquity was well-worn and cherished by Harper because of how it had influenced her life, in addition to the medical information it contained.

Something was disturbing Harper. The evidence related to this disease came from so many directions, and she was, for the first time, stumped by what she knew so far. Naturally, as was the case with any outbreak of a potentially novel virus, the passage of time would reveal more information to tighten up her working hypothesis. Unfortunately, more people would have to be infected and quite likely die before she could truly identify what they were dealing with.

Suddenly, her concentration was broken. She looked up from an old issue of the *Journal of the American Medical Association*, or *JAMA*, a medical journal published since 1883. The library was mostly empty, not unusual in an age of computer technology in which virtually everything could be accessed via a few strokes on a keyboard. Harper had retrieved two chairs from a nearby table, one for her tush, the other for her Nikes.

A bright flash of light caught her attention, followed by a thunderous boom. Her eyes searched for a window. Craning her neck, she saw water dripping down the outside of the glass. A pop-up thunderstorm had crossed over Atlanta while she was conducting her research.

The thunder served to break her out of her trance. She set the *JAMA* journal from 1919 aside. It was published the year the planet was in the throes of the first H1N1 influenza outbreak turned pandemic. She stretched her arm to pick up a massive, nine-and-a-half-pound virology treatise and thumbed through the index. Her body was sore from her two-mile sprint earlier that day. She'd forgotten about easing herself back into a routine. In reality, the run was less about exercise and more about relieving stress.

Harper scribbled a few notes on her pad, which was rapidly filling up with research combined with question marks and reminders to follow up on other possibilities. She set aside the virology textbook and pulled up a pamphlet-style journal published through the NCBI, the National Center for Biotechnology Information.

She muttered the title out loud, "'Detection of Biological Warfare Agents in Virology.' That's some heavy shit." Then again, every aspect of Harper's job was.

Her phone buzzed, indicating a text message had arrived. It was from Joe, causing her heart to immediately leap. Suddenly, biological warfare agents weren't all that important.

JOE: I miss you and I love you!

That was all it took to give Harper a boost to continue. Simple words, yet full of devotion and heartfelt.

HARPER: Save me! I'm buried in the stacks.

JOE: You love the library, admit it.

HARPER: I love you more.

JOE: More than Dr. Dog?

Harper decided to tease him. She didn't respond for a minute. Predictably, her husband fell into the trap.

JOE: Hello?

HARPER: Hold on, It's a tough choice.

HARPER: Ha ha! I love you both equally, although Dr. Dog's snoring is just a little worse.

JOE: I wish I could be home with you. Do you know when you have to go back to Vegas?

HARPER: TBD. How are the budget negotiations? Will the government shut down again?

JOE: We're close to an agreement, but TBH, it doesn't look good for the extra funding to the CDC. Status quo seems to be the fallback position for both sides.

HARPER: So typical. All of this drama to do what everybody could have done to begin with.

JOE: It's how we dance in DC, fighting like a bunch of ferrets in a sack over who gets to spend taxpayer dollars.

Harper glanced up at the window and noticed the rain had dissipated. A voicemail notification came in, and she swiped the text message stream off her screen to see if it was Becker calling for her. It wasn't.

HARPER: Hey, can you call tonight? I just got a phone message from an old friend.

JOE: A boyfriend?

HARPER: Yeah, the same clean-shaven brute who ravaged me last weekend.

JOE: Ha ha! I wish. I do miss you a lot. One of these days, we might at least work in the same city.

HARPER: When we move into the White House?

JOE: Yeah, sure. You wouldn't stop what you're doing even if we did. Love you!

HARPER: Love you back!

She studied the transcription of the voicemail she'd received. "Hmm, from one man in my life in Washington to another."

She put away the books and journals before making her way outside, where she could have some privacy. Under the low, gray skies hovering over Atlanta, she studied her phone, and then she pushed the call-back icon to call another man whom she missed.

CHAPTER FIFTY-THREE

CDC Headquarters
Atlanta

Harper nervously waited for him to pick up the call. They hadn't spoken in almost a year, and their last conversation had been somewhat heated. Like so many relationships around the country, whether family, friends, coworkers, or strangers, the politics of the time had driven a wedge between her and her mentor.

"Greetings, young lady!" he answered. Harper immediately beamed. Her old medical school professor had not disowned her, nor had he deleted her phone number from his cell phone. More importantly, he was willing to let bygones be bygones.

"Dr. Maxwell!" she said loudly, grabbing the attention of two passersby. The drizzle began again, but she didn't care. She wandered the sidewalk, speaking to the aging professor and department head at Georgetown Medical.

"It is I! The reincarnation of Louis Pasteur!"

Harper let out a hearty laugh. Hearing his cheerful voice lifted her spirits. He was just what the proverbial doctor ordered.

"How are you, *Monsieur Pasteur?*" she asked, using her best Southern-girl French accent.

He laughed before speaking. "Tenacious as ever. A thorn in every side of my colleagues. But I continue to instill in the young minds of Georgetown University they should be prepared to recognize good fortune when it slaps them in the face."

"Professor, you taught me I didn't have to distance myself from God just because I became closer to science. The more I've studied the wonders of the natural world, the more I've become amazed at the spiritual one." Dr. Maxwell, like Harper, was a devout Catholic.

"This is why we were a perfect team. Our minds were one when we conducted our research on *C. albicans*. The antifungal drug protocols you helped create are now used to help people around the world."

Candida albicans, a yeast pathogen, was the most prevalent cause of fungal infections in humans. Although *C. albicans* was a part of the human body's natural microflora, its overgrowth leads to infections of the gastrointestinal tract, the mouth, and the urinary tract. Antibiotics were often prescribed until Dr. Maxwell and Harper conducted their clinical studies. By focusing on the gene functions, they were able to identify antifungal drug protocols to give millions of people relief.

Harper's face beamed again. She was proud of her work, and it was always nice to get a pat on the back from her professor. She couldn't help but get in a snarky dig at her private sector counterparts.

"Thanks, Dr. Maxwell. Are you still receiving your checks from big pharma for those antifungal drugs? I think they lost my address."

He let out a hearty laugh. "Same here. I need to look into that."

The two laughed for another moment and then Dr. Maxwell continued. "I hear you've got something brewing out in Sin City."

She sighed before responding, "It's made the media. Dr. Maxwell, there's so much to tell about these cases, yet I have absolutely nothing. It's the damnedest thing."

"The police issued a statement that poisoning is a likely cause.

When they were quizzed about other cases in the valley, they demurred, claiming coincidence and happenstance."

Harper shook her head and looked skyward. Local law enforcement was sticking to the poison theory regardless of facts and unanswered questions to the contrary. "I disagree with their analysis of the deceased gamblers."

"Apparently, the local medical examiner does, too. I saw an interview with him as he was leaving the coroner's office. In response to the questions regarding poison, he simply said, wrong, wrong, wrong. Then, when another reporter shouted a question about a contagion, he said—"

Harper cut him off. "Let me guess. His response was yes, yes, yes."

"Oh, you saw the interview?"

"No, but I know the man. In fact, I assisted him with the first autopsy."

"And?"

"Inconclusive. We've got samples and findings here in Atlanta with a dozen people assigned to study them. We've got another dozen en route to Las Vegas to investigate the new cases."

Dr. Maxwell paused. "I think I hear rain on your end. I take it you're not in Vegas." It only rained in Las Vegas about twenty-six days a year, and even then, the total accumulation was around four inches.

"No, I'm here *quarterbacking*." Her tone of voice reflected her frustration.

"Reitherman has you chained to his side, doesn't he?"

"He says it's short term until he can get his war room set up here. Then I'm going back in."

He hesitated again. The second time, it caught Harper's attention. "Why did they pull you from Africa?"

Harper stopped wandering the sidewalk and immediately scowled. "You know about that?"

"I hear things. I live in Washington, remember?"

Harper explained, "The president pulled the plug on the

operation. He said it was too dangerous and didn't what our people hurt."

"It is dangerous, Harper."

"So? I can handle myself. I'd go back if Reitherman would let me."

Dr. Maxwell began to have a coughing fit. He struggled to compose himself. After a moment, she could hear him gulping down a glass of water.

He returned to the call. "Um, sorry about that. Sometimes, I talk too much and it aggravates my throat. How do you intend to proceed in Las Vegas? If this is a contagion, more cases are sure to follow."

"They already are, and the fact we can't identify it has me concerned about the potential spread. My assistant is working on the R-naught now. It's still too early to identify a case fatality rate much less create an exponential curve."

"Do you have any cases outside the outbreak location?"

"Only in downtown Las Vegas and the suburb to the west toward Red Rock Canyon. It's too early to consider containment measures, but that time may come soon."

"A nightmare, to be sure," quipped Dr. Maxwell. "The city has hundreds of people coming and going every hour. You and I both know a novel infection will spread. You can't board up a germ. It will get out. It always does."

Before Harper could agree, a text message came in from Becker.

BECKER: 911! Vegas is exploding. More cases. More poker players. The two detectives. First responders. Where are you?

"Aw, shit, Dr. Maxwell. I'm sorry, but I've gotta go."

She disconnected the call without saying goodbye.

CHAPTER FIFTY-FOUR

Urumqi, Xinjiang, China

Police brutality exists in every corner of the world, but the *Chengguan* were a particularly Chinese phenomenon. Formerly known as the Urban Administrative and Law Enforcement Bureau, the Chengguan were established to clamp down on illegal street vendors who came from rural areas to sell their livestock, produce, and handmade goods. In addition to ridding the streets of unpermitted vendors, they were authorized to use any means necessary to put unlicensed taxi cabs out of business as well as disrupt potential protests.

The Chengguan were experts at inflicting harm using brutal force upon the subject of their wrath. When hired, they were trained using a manual entitled *Practices of City Administrative Enforcement*. This manual contained intricate descriptions and photographs in dealing with their targets, advising them how to inflict their methods of punishment without leaving visible blood, wounds or, at least initially, bruises on the body.

Those considered the best at their craft were often hired by public officials and agencies to encourage Chinese citizens to perform desired functions or behave in a certain way. The men locked in the room with Dr. Zeng were two of the best and performed exactly the type of function the CDC needed at the moment: administer a bruising beatdown of the stubborn doctor until he was ready to speak.

However, he refused.

After sporadic beating and beratement sessions, the CDC official gave up on extracting information from Dr. Zeng and ordered him to be released. He was thrown into the back alley of the Public Service Bureau, gasping for air, but alive.

Two hours later, doubled over in pain, Dr. Zeng made his way back to his apartment building. Despite the intense beating he'd received, he remained aware of his surroundings. A light, misty rain had settled in over the city, and most everyone donned some sort of simple raincoat or parka. However, two men leaning up against a tree across from the entrance to the building were not. They had most likely been stationed there before the rain began. Dr. Zeng considered that he might just be paranoid, but he had to assume they intended to watch him in case he met up with anyone else involved.

When he entered his apartment, he didn't call out his wife's name. For all he knew, surveillance devices had been installed in the space. Instead, he immediately went to take a long, hot Epsom salt bath to soak his battered body.

As he lay there, he devised a plan of escape. He had to assume that yet another agency of the Communist government would be around to have their turn at him. He needed to find his nephew and reunite with his wife. He thought of every possible diversion to get away.

After getting cleaned up, he applied an analgesic balm his wife used for her arthritic elbow, and then he took a double dose of generic Excedrin. He'd never had to treat a bruised body at home, but headaches from long hours at the hospital were common.

In his bedroom, he approached the windows of his apartment overlooking the courtyard. The two men continued to stand under the tree as the mist turned to rain. They were both smoking but stayed on duty as the cold front passed through the central part of Xinjiang.

Dr. Zeng considered sleeping, then thought of something. The men watching his building had undoubtedly been briefed on his condition. They might have expected him to be returned to the apartment by taxi or some type of medical vehicle. Either way, he had to assume they'd seen him return, especially walking in a hunched-over fashion.

They expect me to sleep, he thought to himself. *The last thing they would presume is an attempted escape.*

So that was exactly what he prepared to do. With a newfound sense of purpose, he took some vitamins, fixed a pot of herbal tea, and changed into clothes suitable for traveling in inclement weather. He studied the two men through the curtains of his apartment, trying not to be obvious in his surveillance of the surveillers.

He would pass by the windows from time to time, making himself seen in case they were using binoculars to watch his movements. He turned lights on and off to indicate activity until he moved into the bedroom. He left those lights on for half an hour, and then his spirits lifted when the rain came down in torrents. It was time to go.

Dr. Zeng turned out the bedroom light, indicating to all who might've been watching that he was turning in for the night. Instead, he was going to slip out of the complex through the utility yard, a task that involved dropping from a fire escape twenty feet into an open dumpster.

It would hurt and he might stink from the garbage. But it gave him a chance to escape his watchers.

CHAPTER FIFTY-FIVE

Urumqi, Xinjiang, China

As uncomfortable as the driving rain was, and despite the painful beating he'd endured, Dr. Zeng arrived at his nephew's dorm in fairly good spirits. As he fought through the wind-blown rain that stung his face, an odd sense of relief came over him. He wasn't exactly free, as no citizen of China was. In a way, he'd cast off the burdens that plagued him.

He knew his career as a physician in China had come to an end. He would be blackballed and ostracized by his colleagues, not out of contempt, but out of fear for their own careers should they attempt to befriend him.

His wife had shown a strength and moxie that he never gave her credit for. She never questioned his request to help. She never judged or condemned him for the troubles he'd brought upon their marriage. And, when he saw the WeChat post most likely authored by his nephew, he knew she was safe somewhere, awaiting him.

He kept his face completely covered as he traveled, using a turtleneck sweater and a vintage baseball cap from the old Chinese baseball league. The cap bore the logo of the Jiangsu Pegasus, literally translated as huge horses. The mythical winged horse that sprang from the blood of the slain Medusa was symbolic of a reach-for-the-stars imagination.

It was always Dr. Zeng's dream to be his own man and not another tool of the Communist state. He wanted his own practice. His own patients to care for that didn't require him to get an administrator's approval. He would find that somewhere. Maybe in Turkey. Maybe in the United States. Pegasus would take him high into the sky to another place. But first, he would have to go underground.

He waited until a group of students were hustling toward the dormitory entrance, and then he cut in behind them. One of them scanned their student identification card to gain access to the building, and the others simply piled in behind the first in line, as did Dr. Zeng.

Once inside, he kept the bill of the cap pulled over his eyes and the turtleneck covering his chin. His eyes darted around, searching for any university security personnel or dorm administrators. There were none.

He moved deeper into the building until he found a common area where some students were studying and others were congregated as they accessed their social media. On a hunch they might be familiar with his nephew, he approached the social group first.

"Excuse me. Will you help me locate my nephew, Fangyu?"

The three young men and their two female companions looked at him with skepticism. He was nervous, apparently giving away his apprehension because his eyes were constantly darting around the room.

"If you are not a student, you are not allowed inside," said one of the students. "You must call for admittance using the phone outside. Come with me. I will show you."

Dr. Zeng sighed. "Please don't make me go back outside. I am old and have the chills. I need to speak to my nephew because I have locked myself out of my apartment and he has a spare key. Please, it was a three-mile walk."

"No. You need to—" the young man began to insist as he rose out of his chair. He was cut off by one of the girls at the table.

"That is silly, Nan," she said before turning to Dr. Zeng. "I will text him for you. What is your name?"

"I am his uncle."

She giggled. "Uncle. That is all?" She sent the message to Fangyu.

Less than a minute later, Fangyu bounded down the stairs, not bothering to wait for the elevator. He was already dressed in a black parka with matching black accessories. He appeared nervous as he approached.

"Hello, nephew," Dr. Zeng greeted him matter-of-factly. "Um, I locked myself out of the apartment."

Fangyu managed a pensive smile. "Aunt just called me. She was worried about you."

"Oh?"

"Yes, Uncle. Come with me. I will walk you back."

He thanked the group for sending him the text, and he quickly escorted Dr. Zeng outside. Once they were clear of the building, Fangyu pulled his uncle by the arm into the thicket of trees to the side of the building.

Dr. Zeng groaned from being brusquely handled.

"What is wrong?"

"I was beaten, but nothing is broken. Where is Ying? Is she safe?"

"Yes, Uncle. We will go there now. I have to tell you. The interest within the WeChat groups has mushroomed. I made a post that—"

"I saw it just before I was beaten. I did not know there were so many emojis."

Fangyu stopped under a tree. "Uncle, there are more dead from the mysterious disease. You are considered a hero. A whistleblower."

"I am not a whistleblower, Fangyu. I merely provided you the whistle."

"Not just me, Uncle. There are many more involved now. It is the most exciting disclosure in a decade."

They began the long walk towards the same entrance to the

Underground Great Wall that Ying had entered. Fangyu monitored his various WeChat posts as they moved through the shadows of Urumqi.

Just as they approached their destination, Dr. Zeng asked, "Where are the dead located? Tibet?"

"Yes, mostly. There are others, including the military installation at the Lhasa Gonggar Airport."

"An airman?"

Just before they entered the building, Fangyu stopped. He turned to his uncle. "It may not be connected. It is an odd post, one that is encrypted in part and otherwise it is not."

"Nephew, is the post reliable or not? What do you know?"

"It is not from a physician, but from the family of a helicopter pilot who died suddenly at the base. They do not fully understand our encryption techniques, but they were able to decipher it with the help of someone."

"What did they write?"

Fangyu looked around and then leaned in to his uncle to whisper, "The pilot flew a rescue mission to Mount Everest. Days later, he was dead."

"When, exactly?"

"The day before you came to see me with your first message."

CHAPTER FIFTY-SIX

CDC Learjet
Final Approach to Las Vegas, Nevada

"I'm exhausted," said Harper as she pressed her nose to the glass to gather in the views of the Grand Canyon and Hoover Dam. The water levels upriver from the dam built during the first Great Depression had continued to drop. "But I'm not as tired as the Colorado River is. Look at the banks."

"I see them," said Becker. She wiped the crumbs off her lips after she polished off the last of a slice of banana nut bread she'd packed in her briefcase. "They're more of a grayish-brown compared to the canyon walls. The red clay stops a hundred feet or more before the water level."

"California and Arizona are drinking it dry," opined Harper. "I read the other day that they're just a few feet away from having to make a shortage declaration."

"What happens then?" asked Becker. She guzzled down the last of an immuno-boost drink. Harper, reluctantly, drank one as well.

"Water wars, I guess," said Harper half-jokingly. "Joe said it's a big political issue out here. I guess the governor has been in a scrap with the governors of Cali and Arizona. He wants to cut off the flow downstream."

"But wouldn't that screw the rest of Nevada? Like Boulder City?"

Harper shrugged. She was about to give her opinion when the copilot made an announcement over the communications system.

"Ladies, we've just received an advisory from the North Las Vegas Airport. They've rerouted our flight to McCarran International. Please stow your belongings and fasten your seat belts. We should be on the ground in under ten minutes."

As soon as he completed his instructions, the pilot took a hard left turn over Lake Las Vegas, the luxury golf community located on the east end of the valley. The setting sun glistened off the many lakes dotting the landscape.

"I wonder what's up?" asked Becker.

"Who knows? I'm surprised they'd let us land and mingle with the big boys." McCarran was capable of handling the largest commercial jets in the world. For five years, they'd been accommodating the Airbus A380, a superjumbo passenger jet that carried almost six hundred passengers and crew members.

The pilot slowly descended to McCarran, flying directly into the blinding sun setting over Mount Charleston to the west. Harper and Becker couldn't see due to the brightness, so they focused on gathering their belongings. Becker readied her cell phone to arrange for transportation as soon as the pilot gave her the all clear.

After an uneventful landing, they were escorted off the plane near hangars designed for cargo aircraft. Normally, all inbound executive aircraft landed at North Las Vegas or thirteen miles south of the city at the Henderson Executive Airport.

They casually walked down the portable stairs pushed up against the aircraft. A member of the airport's ramp crew motioned them toward a steel door where a security guard stood waiting. The two women were almost there when a black SUV sped toward them. Harper saw it first and immediately stopped, grabbing Becker's arm. She wasn't sure if the driver saw them crossing the tarmac.

Seconds later, the truck parked between them and the door.

"What's this all about?" mumbled Becker.

Two men exited the vehicle and quickly approached.

"More men in black," responded Harper.

"Huh? Whadya mean by more?"

Harper didn't respond as the men quickly closed the gap. Harper instinctively looked around for witnesses.

"Dr. Randolph, we need you to come with us, please."

Becker stood between the approaching men and her boss. She stood as tall as her five-foot-three frame would allow. "She isn't going anywhere with you two. Take off your sunglasses and identify yourselves!"

"This doesn't concern you, ma'am," said the burlier of the two. "Please, Dr. Randolph, this way."

Becker didn't back down. "Please ain't gonna cut it, pal. Let's see some ID."

The men retrieved their bifold leather identification wallets out of their suit jackets and held them up for the women to see. Harper immediately recognized their IDs as being with the Secret Service. She'd accompanied Joe to a number of events over the years in Washington. Anytime they were in the presence of the president or vice president, the Secret Service was everywhere. She glanced around the tarmac, looking for Air Force One or AF2.

"It'll be fine, Becker. I recognize their IDs."

"But, Dr. Randolph ..." Becker began to protest as her voice trailed off.

Harper gently touched her on the shoulder. "It's okay. Seriously."

"Well, I'm going too," she countered.

"No, you're not," said the two Secret Service agents in unison.

This infuriated Becker, and she was about to hurl f-bombs and all manner of expletives before Harper calmed her down.

"No worries, Becker. I've got this. You go ahead and let the team know we need to find a stopping point for the day. Bring everyone into the hotel and ask Figueroa to set us up with a conference room of some kind."

Becker snarled at the agents, and Harper swore one of them snarled back. "Okay. Um, do I need to call Dr. Reitherman or Joe?"

Harper stepped past Becker and stared into the men's sunglasses. "I don't know. You tell me, gentlemen. Does my security detail need to call my husband the congressman?"

"I don't think so, ma'am. If so, the president will be glad to help you make that call."

Becker lost it. "What a load of horsepucky!"

Harper was also skeptical, but then she started to think about the change of airports and the men in black cutting them off before they could get off the tarmac.

She touched Becker on the shoulder. "It's fine." Then she approached the SUV. "Okay, let's go. I've got work to do."

CHAPTER FIFTY-SEVEN

McCarran International Airport
Las Vegas

Harper sat in silence as the Secret Service agents drove her to Air Force One on an isolated part of the runway. Several black SUVs surrounded the aircraft, and half a dozen military Humvees with machine guns mounted on their turrets were at the ready in case a terrorist tried something stupid. She was astonished at the mammoth aircraft. As they got closer, she immediately recognized the light blue and white paint scheme of the modified Boeing 747-200B aircraft.

The Air Force designation for one of the most recognizable symbols of the presidency was VC-25A. Emblazoned across the fuselage were the words United States of America, the American flag, and finally, the presidential seal. It was an undeniable presence of America wherever it was flown.

Harper had never seen Air Force One in person, but she'd heard Joe talk about it. Not in the sense of what it was like inside, but rather, how it was used by the office holder. It was often used as his office when the president flew for security purposes. But, as

Joe put it, a visit to Air Force One could be far more intimidating than a trip to the White House. Once on board, you were effectively the president's captive until he was done with you. Suddenly, she wished she'd instructed Becker to make that call to her husband.

Her escorts pulled the vehicle to a stop and they motioned for her to exit. She stared up the steep gangway at the bulging hull of the aircraft. She momentarily felt the urge to run.

"Come with us, Dr. Randolph. The president is waiting for you."

Why? What does he want with me? Why not Reitherman or, better yet, the director of the CDC? I'm just a foot soldier.

Harper had read once that the flying Oval Office contained over four thousand square feet of interior space, including four bedroom suites, private sleeping berths for its twenty-six-member crew, and galleys capable of serving fifty.

As she climbed the stairs, the last vestiges of daylight disappeared over the Spring Mountains. She moved quickly up the stairs, but the Secret Service personnel were directly behind her. She felt pressured by their close proximity and, for a moment, wondered if they were checking out her ass in her Levi's.

At the top of the portable gangway, she stopped and took a deep breath. She forced herself to relax, making every effort to slow her pulse rate.

Easy, Harper. It's just a plane.

The inner debate raged.

And the President of the United States.

Oh, yeah. Good point.

A female Secret Service agent greeted her immediately. "Dr. Randolph, I'm Agent Free. I'm sorry to ask you to submit to a search, but it's required by our security protocols. Please step into this room with me. We'll wave you with the wand and look through your belongings. Lastly, I'll pat you down. I promise not to be intrusive."

Harper smiled and shrugged. She appreciated the agent's professionalism. They all had a job to do, and it wasn't their fault the president was up to something. The more time she had to think about it, the more guarded she became.

She'd read that the interior was designed to provide the passengers and visitors alike a sense of calm. Air Force One was a workspace, but it was also living quarters for the president, his family, and key staff. Also, a contingent of reporters frequently traveled with the president, so they also were made to feel at home.

Right now, the last thing Harper felt was calm. Her mind raced from the magnitude of the moment. World leaders and multiple presidents had stood in the very spot where she awaited being escorted deeper into the aircraft. Decisions were made in times of crisis that shaped world history. *What the hell am I doing here?* Her heart began to race again.

"Dr. Randolph." A man's voice startled her. She immediately recognized the balding head of the president's chief of staff, Steve Powell. He motioned for her to accompany him. "Let me take you to the president. This way, please."

"Why?"

"What's that?" He turned and glanced over his shoulder.

He's stalling.

"Why does he need to—" Harper began to ask her question again when he cut her off.

"Here we are. Mr. President, this is Dr. Harper Randolph."

President Jon William Taylor had his back to Harper as she entered. He stood at a bar containing an ice bucket with the presidential seal, an eagle clasping arrows and olive branches, engraved on the side. He dropped a couple of cubes into an etched glass and poured himself a drink. Most likely bourbon, if Harper remembered correctly.

She'd never met President Taylor, but she certainly had heard a lot about him from Joe. The leader of the free world was unremarkable looking. He was slight of build, wore glasses, and had thinning gray hair. He was in his early seventies and slouched somewhat as he stood. Harper was every bit as tall as the president.

"Thanks for coming," he said, extending his hand to shake.

Harper customarily avoided shaking hands, but the president, the consummate politician, couldn't help himself. When she hesitated, he chuckled. "Oh yeah, you folks don't shake hands, do you?"

"No, sir, not really. It's safer not to."

"Do you do the elbow thing?" He tried to make light of her refusal to shake hands.

Harper ignored the question and stood in silence.

He shrugged and sipped his drink. He motioned for her to sit in a chair across from his desk. Harper thought it was odd and somewhat rude that he didn't offer her a drink, not that it mattered. She would've politely refused. If she'd walked into an ambush, she wanted to keep her faculties about her.

"In a way, that's why I've called you here, Dr. Randolph. Let's talk about what's happening downtown."

Harper swallowed hard and then spoke. "Sir, I'd be glad to tell you what I know thus far, but, um, shouldn't this be a conversation between you and the director or even my boss, Dr. Reitherman?"

He took another sip and peered at her over his glass. He was sizing her up, like a boxer trying to identify weaknesses in his opponent. "Aren't you the one quarterbacking this thing?"

There was that word again. Harper had come to hate that word. This wasn't football, nor was it a game.

"Yes, sir, I am the lead representative on the ground here in Las Vegas, but generally all communications, you know, of this nature, would involve people higher—"

He cut her off. Despite his smallish stature, when sitting behind the desk as President of the United States, his steel blue eyes pierced her soul. He was dangerous. "Do you not have a grasp of this situation? Do you want me to get you some help? I can make a call." He feigned reaching for a phone.

Harper glanced around, searching for Chief of Staff Powell. He'd slipped out while she was distracted. Being left alone with the president made her feel even more uneasy. Not that she was physically afraid of him. She wished there were witnesses to their conversation.

257

"No, Mr. President. That won't be necessary. What would you like to know?"

Her eyes darted around the president's office aboard Air Force One. It was cozy. Furnishings were not ornate like those she'd seen in photos of the Oval Office. His desk was mounded with folders and newspapers.

"What are we dealing with here? I want your learned opinion, not the bullshit being spouted off by police spokesmen."

"Sir, I assume you're referring to the poison theory."

"Yeah. That's a bunch of garbage. First, is this some intentional attack, or do you think it's random? Well, before that, are we dealing with a bug of some kind, and if so, what? Swine flu? SARS?"

"Okay, first, it is not poison. I believe it is a pathogen that is likely transferred by human-to-human contact. It may even be an airborne virus. We simply don't know yet because we're too early in our investigation."

"When will you have some answers for me?"

Harper took a deep breath and exhaled. She had relaxed somewhat because now she was in her element. She'd been grilled by news reporters before, as well as her superiors. Maybe the president just wanted to hear it from the lead investigator on the ground.

"Mr. President, in the initial stages of an outbreak, we're getting our information a step or two behind the pathogen's spread. It takes time and, sadly, more cases to reach an accurate case definition. I'm here this evening because there are more patients in the area who are showing comparable symptoms to those of our deceased index patient."

He was brusque in his questioning. His words weren't quite hostile, but when they were delivered in combination with his piercing eyes, they delivered a powerful effect. "You must have some kind of timeline. The people of Las Vegas have a right to know."

Harper stood her ground to his full-on attack. "Mr. President, this is just the beginning. We don't make the timeline. The virus makes the timeline."

"What are you doing to contain this unknown virus?" he asked. He sipped his drink again, but his eyes stayed focused on hers. She didn't blink.

"Sir, there are lot of unknowns still. It's true that after identification of the pathogen and its potential spread rate is determined, decisions can be made about containment. However, hitting that sweet spot is difficult. Early is better, but too early can end up having devastating effects on the economy and a potentially negative emotional impact on the residents of the city."

He finished his drink and Harper noticed a smirk seem to come across his face. "Okay, Dr. Randolph, you need more time to study these dying patients in order to make a determination. You think the economic factors need to come into play, as well as the psychological impact on a major city."

Harper couldn't stop the scowl that came over her face. "No, sir. Really, I think we need to finish our investigation. Gather the facts. Perform our contact tracing. Coordinate with medical personnel. And then we can provide you better answers."

"Meanwhile, we do nothing?" he asked.

"No, sir. I didn't say that. But we can't let the mere idea of a possible pandemic create chaos. We need to stay settled down, be vigilant, and use reason as we analyze the evidence. If we show panic on our side, you'll have a repeat of 2020. People will be chasing after toilet paper and face masks. Grocery stores will be cleaned out of Lysol wipes, bleach, and hand sanitizer. But worse, a premature lockdown, without laying a foundation for it, will cause people either to rebel or scatter. That has the potential of sending the disease in all directions in a very short period of time."

"In the meantime, unsuspecting people are getting infected and dying."

"Some, yes. These new hospitalized patients may or may not be related to the outbreak. That's part of the reason why I am here. If they are, it gives us more evidence to work with."

"Are you okay with that?"

"No, sir. I don't want people to die. But it's a process."

The president stood from behind his desk and smiled. "That's all, Dr. Randolph. I look forward to following your progress. Steve!"

He shouted for his chief of staff, who opened the door separating the president's office from a conference room. It happened so quickly that Harper wondered if the man had his ear pressed to the door. The president motioned toward Harper, who felt compelled to add one more thought.

"Mr. President, please. Let me reiterate. It's too early to be making decisions about this potential outbreak. I'll make sure my boss and the director keep you informed."

"You do that," he said as he turned away from her. As Chief of Staff Powell began to escort her to the front of the plane, the president barked, "Close that door, Steve."

Harper wasn't aware of what happened next, although it would come to light very soon. The president immediately picked up the phone. His words were ominous and foreboding.

"She's on her way to the hotel. You know what to do."

PART V

PANIC IN THE STREETS

Panic is highly contagious. When certainty doesn't exist, panic takes hold and is as dangerous as the unseen enemy.
~ Unknown

CHAPTER FIFTY-EIGHT

"Okay, guys, catch your breath and then let's move this along to the next topic." Harper strode along the front of the conference room secured by Becker. The Gold Palace hotel hosted large gatherings and weddings from time to time, but uncharacteristically, there were no special events in the hotel that evening, as it was midweek. Becker, who was always thinking of details, chose the Augusta room located in the center of the building because she thought it would make the CDC team feel closer to home. It was also far away from the hustle and bustle of the casino, which allowed Harper to work with her team without distractions.

She scribbled some notes on the whiteboards located at the front of the room while Becker stood off to the side, ready to jump if Harper made a request. During the pause while the disease detectives compared notes and gathered their thoughts, she approached Becker.

265

"They're exhausted," commented Harper as she stood next to her equally worn-out assistant. "I don't want to keep them too late, but we still have to put our heads together on a number of things."

Becker sighed. "I know."

Harper looked down at her iPad. "What are you researching?"

Becker tried to hide the screen, but her brain was too slow to cover her tracks. "I'm trying to figure out why the president was here. That whole thing stinks."

"I agree. Frankly, I think it was all show. Joe is cleaning his clock during these budget negotiations, and the president figured out a way to show him who the leader of the free world is by picking on me."

"Bullying son of a bitch!"

"That he is. He's also good at it. He didn't scare me, though. Really, I left there wondering what the point of it all was."

"I can't figure out why he was here. I think it might've been for a private fundraiser or something like that. He's due back in Washington for a joint news conference in the Rose Garden at nine tomorrow morning with some foreign ambassador or something."

"Good, go home and let us do our job," said Harper with a chuckle. She glanced over her shoulder at several rolling tables and carts brought in by hotel personnel. "Do we still have plenty of drinks and snacks for everyone?"

Becker studied the refreshments furnished with the help of Figueroa. "Except Red Bull. Your army doesn't like that Monster Energy swill they serve around here."

"They'll survive. Let's get started again."

Harper left Becker's side and returned to the whiteboards. The group piped down and readied themselves. Their respect for Harper and her capabilities was evident. They were completely focused on her as the briefing continued.

CHAPTER FIFTY-NINE

8:41 p.m
Nevada Army Guard
North Las Vegas Readiness Center

Formed in 2009, the 17th Sustainment Brigade of the Nevada Army Guard performed an important mission in Southern Nevada. Las Vegas was always considered a high-profile target for terrorist groups or even nuclear missile attacks. The 17th provided command and control for special troops battalions as well as readiness forces to accompany joint, interagency responses to a terrorist attack.

The brigade commander, Lieutenant Colonel Henry Scarbrough, was the fourth brigade commander to lead the 17th and oversaw fifteen hundred soldiers. In addition, the 17th had multiple military police companies specializing in crowd control and quick response to societal unrest.

Lt. Col. Scarbrough had received the call from the governor's office two hours ago. After confirming this wasn't a drill, he immediately ordered the mobilization of his Guardsmen, who staged their vehicles at the North Las Vegas Readiness Center. The

$25-million, sixty-five-thousand-square-foot facility on Range Road near the Las Vegas Motor Speedway had ample room for a wide variety of military hardware and transportation.

After he gave orders to the battalion and company commanders, he took a moment to check the internet news for a terrorist attack or some other reason for the extraordinary measures. He was aware of the reports concerning illnesses occurring around the valley, but most of the local news stations were downplaying the deaths as a late-season flu bug or even legionnaire's disease. Neither of which, in his mind, justified the orders he'd been given.

But, as a good soldier, he readied his troops for the mission. He'd been in the Nevada Army Guard long enough to recognize this would be the largest activation in Nevada history. The logistical challenges were daunting, but they'd war-planned this activity multiple times.

The colonel tried to remind himself that the underlying reason for the governor's directives didn't matter. He'd always taken the position that deploying the Army Guard on American soil was simply a matter of Nevadans helping Nevadans. His soldiers, the men and women of the Guard, lived in the communities in which they served. They were prepared, ready, and qualified to undertake the responsibilities assigned to them. Like all good soldiers, they would follow orders without question.

One of the battalion commanders, a major, knocked on his open door and requested entry. Lt. Col. Scarbrough turned off his computer monitor and stood to greet his second-in-command.

"Colonel, we're ready to roll out."

"Thank you, Major. The governor's office is setting up a communications link between us, the Nevada National Guard Joint Operations Center, and the state's Emergency Operations Center. I'll remain here to relay information from our end to yours."

"Sir, what about the local law enforcement and the Clark County Emergency Management people? Are they in the loop?"

"I don't think so, Major, at least not that I know of. This has happened on very short notice, as you are aware. At this point, I'm following our procedures and leaving coordination of other agencies to the EOC."

The major stood quietly for a moment and was about to ask another question when he caught himself. "Thank you, sir. I'll provide you a report once we've arrived."

The two men saluted one another. In their minds, they both wondered what their guardsmen were walking into.

CHAPTER SIXTY

9:00 p.m
Nevada Governor's Mansion
606 Mountain Street
Carson City, Nevada

Driving along Mountain Street, the Nevada Governor's Mansion in Carson City stood out among its surroundings. The elegant two-story mansion featured a wraparound porch supported by fluted columns, ornate trim, and a wrought-iron-protected stairwell. The two-story, twenty-three-room home featured a large grand entry area, a formal dining room, a pair of salons, living quarters, and a private den, where Governor George Rickey sat behind his desk, staring at a solitary television camera pointing at him.

A makeup artist applied a final dusting of powder to his face to hide the beads of sweat on his forehead and to take away the shine on the end of his nose. Since he'd received a second phone call from the president almost three hours ago, he'd consumed several drinks despite knowing he'd be appearing on local stations in Las Vegas, pre-empting regular programming.

The mansion had hosted twenty governors and their families

since it was built in 1909, but there had never been an address of this magnitude delivered in those one hundred plus years. After receiving the phone call, the governor met with his political team and his chief of staff. Then he summoned the head of the DEM, Nevada's Division of Emergency Management.

He immediately tamped down their questions and skepticism about the decision he'd made. They had no knowledge of Governor Rickey's conversation with the president. His political advisor, in private, pressed him hard for answers and explanations. The governor resisted and eventually erupted with anger in order to shut down the inquiries.

Afterwards, the governor turned to the bottle of vodka he kept hidden in his desk drawer, a secret to no one. This kept him steady when he needed it, especially when he felt intense pressure. This was not the first time the president had called upon him for a favor. He'd intervened several times to assist the unions in tough negotiations with the casinos. He often wondered, including tonight, when the president planned to return these many favors he'd been granted.

The state's communications director stood alongside a producer and a camera operator. They constantly checked their watches to make sure they were ready for the nine o'clock start. The local networks had been notified just moments ago and were prepared to switch from regular programming to the governor's address.

"Okay, sir. You'll be going on in one minute."

The governor gulped and his forehead immediately broke out in a sweat. The makeup artist scampered around his desk and touched him up again. With less than thirty seconds to go, she pulled herself out of the shot. The governor, however, continued to perspire. Later, many pundits questioned whether he was nervous or ill.

"Five, four," the producer counted down, switching to a finger count as he indicated three, two, and one. He pointed at the governor and the camera rolled.

CHAPTER SIXTY-ONE

9:04 p.m
Gold Palace Hotel Sports Book
Fremont Street Experience
Las Vegas, Nevada

The Gold Palace sportsbook boasted more televisions per square foot than any comparable book in the state. Luxurious booths, a laid-back candlelit vibe, and a well-stocked bar, including crystal glasses, provided comfortable environs for their high-rolling sports bettors.

The multicolored OLED screens showed the sporting events of the day as well as futures bets available to the gamblers. The NBA season was in full swing and approaching the playoffs. Major League Baseball was underway. For football fans, preseason college and NFL bets were also available.

Many of the people in the sportsbook were enjoying a quiet drink and taking in the many different events playing on the monitors. The scantily clad cocktail servers moved through the sportsbook, serving food and drinks, pausing at times to interact with the patrons. Unlike the boisterous gamblers around the craps table or the oftentimes overexuberant slot players, the bettors were more subdued and relaxed.

That was about to change.

As was customary, at least one television on each wall of the sportsbook was tuned to Las Vegas One, a twenty-four-hour news channel that had gone defunct ten years prior when it was owned by Cox Communications. The rights to the channel were later purchased by One America News Network, who simulcast their internet news broadcasts on local cable channels like LV1.

Promptly at 9:00, the top-of-the-hour news was interrupted by the governor's address. At first, many of the bettors were unaware of the change, as they either focused intently on the sporting event they'd wagered money on or they socialized with their friends while consuming cocktails.

In the casino itself, there were no televisions. A casino operation wanted their gamblers feeding those gaming machines, rolling dice, and busting at the blackjack tables. They were unaware of the governor's address at first.

The sports bettors were the first to begin to take notice. One of them read the closed-captioning of the governor and then shouted at the sportsbook personnel to turn up the volume, which they refused to do. The sportsbook was for gambling and ambience, not dissemination of the news.

That did not deter several of them from loudly relaying the gist of the governor's address. The bettors, overwhelmingly men, began to stream out of the sportsbook. Many skipped out on their tabs, resulting in the cocktail servers waving down the security personnel stationed near the entrance to the sportsbook to apprehend the deadbeats.

Others panicked as they picked up large stacks of casino chips off their tables and headed to the single cashier's cage in the book. Soon, the gamblers grew frustrated at the delay and rushed out of the sportsbook into the casino, where they hoped to exchange their chips for money faster.

They would be disappointed.

CHAPTER SIXTY-TWO

9:09 p.m
Gold Palace Hotel Convention Center
Fremont Street Experience
Las Vegas, Nevada

"Let's shift gears for a moment," continued Harper. She'd now kicked off her Nike running shoes and walked around the Augusta Room in her bare feet. Many of the epidemiologists had done the same. They'd continued working nonstop since their short break at 8:30. Harper planned on giving them an opportunity to stretch so they could use the restrooms down the hall at the bottom of the hour. "Now that we've established a case definition, we need to give Becker the numbers she needs to begin her forecasts. This leads us to contact tracing."

Harper knew the group was tired, and they'd spent a long day both in the field and in the hotel, but she wanted to reiterate why the rest of the week's activities were so crucial.

"I'll never forget when I was in between my third and fourth year as a medical student at Georgetown. My professor arranged for a monthlong rotation at the CDC. You guys know what I'm talking about. Unglamorous shit work. I sat in a cubicle, crunching numbers about some fungus or another caused by saltwater in people's toes."

She glanced over at Becker, who'd put away her iPad to charge some time ago. She remained on her feet, however, leaning against the wall near the refreshments. The gal never sat down. Harper took a playful dig at her to see if she was paying attention.

"The kind of stuff Becker truly enjoys."

The group laughed. Becker flipped her boss the middle finger.

Harper continued. "When my direct supervisor asked me to help investigate an outbreak, I did a little jig in my cubicle and happily agreed. My task, he said, was to track down people who'd been in direct contact with a confirmed measles patient. At the time, the spread of measles had become a big thing because of the trend against vaccinating children for measles, mumps, and rubella. The antivaxxers changed their tune, of course, after the coronavirus pandemic. Everyone was lining up for shots after that.

"In any event, he said there was a cluster of measles-related cases in the Midwest. I immediately puffed out my chest and thought, hell yeah, I'm gonna jet around America's heartland, swabbing people in hospital rooms."

The epidemiologists laughed as they enjoyed the lighthearted moment.

"Instead, I never left the campus. I was moved to another cubicle on a different floor. I was handed a dozen case files and told to smile and dial. It was pure drudgery."

Becker chimed in. "Dial? What's dial?"

Harper laughed. "Zip it, Becker. That was before your time."

The playful back-and-forth reinvigorated the team and they focused on Harper as she continued.

"During an outbreak like this one, we have to make a diagnosis as early as possible so we can get health care assistance to those who need it most. Contact tracing is a big part of that. In a situation like the one we face now, it will help shed light on how a novel virus like this one is spread."

Harper turned to the whiteboard, where the passport photo of Yao was enlarged and taped to the board. She took a marker and scribbled the words *index patient* next to his photo.

"As we've all agreed, Yao is our index patient, but it's doubtful he's our patient zero. We'll talk about that in a moment. We've barely begun to learn about this index patient's background and movements. It's making it near impossible to identify all of his close contacts. We've done well with the surveillance video inside the hotel. But prior to his arrival, we have very little to work with because he came from Mainland China. The same is true for the other three traveling companions who died in the same time frame as Yao."

Harper paused and took a deep breath. Something distracted her and she furrowed her brow to focus in an attempt to recreate the sound or movement that caught her attention. After being unsuccessful, she continued.

"We can do some of it by phone, but the hospital contacts are done most efficiently in person. Tomorrow, we'll split you guys up into teams to focus on these contacts. Know this. They'll add up fast depending on how widely these patients traveled throughout Las Vegas before showing symptoms.

"Knock on wood, this outbreak has not yet outpaced our contact-tracing efforts, but I feel time is running out based upon the conditions of the four Chinese men and their date of death. The local health care community has panicked, which can happen, and they're reporting cases to us that are wholly unrelated. This will be the challenge those of you assigned to conduct contact tracing in the hospitals will have. For that reason, you'll need to have your track shoes on in the next few days."

CHAPTER SIXTY-THREE

9:11 p.m
Fremont Street Experience
Las Vegas, Nevada

The major leading the Nevada Army Guard contingent down Interstate 15 was naturally concerned. All of his experience and training in the Middle East theater taught him that preplanning was necessary to cordon off any part of a major city. Prior to the mission, operational risk assessments and procedures would be addressed, and plans would be drawn accordingly. They would evaluate it again as suitable control measures were agreed upon. None of that was done in this case. He was flying blind and he didn't like it, despite the fact it was in his hometown. Or maybe it was because it was where he was raised.

His first task was to set up an initial cordon with the assistance of the Las Vegas police and fire departments, who had been brought on board in the last thirty minutes. They were given precise locations to stage their personnel and understood they'd be given direction by the captains of the companies assigned to each location.

The major was told the use of temporary barriers like caution or traffic tape could not be used. Physical barriers like A-frame barricades resembling a sawhorse and the Army Guard's trucks were the primary methods of blocking the roads. Each place of ingress and egress would include armed military personnel and Humvees. Every member of the 17th was provided masks, goggles, and gloves to wear. They were instructed to tape their sleeves to their gloves to prevent skin exposure.

As the guardsmen arrived and established a perimeter around the Fremont Street Experience, they ran into difficulty unloading their barricades. The visitors to the downtown casinos were in a panic, streaking out of the hotel exits and knocking one another over in an effort to get to the parking areas.

The guardsmen attempted to contain the throngs of people who fought past them, disregarding their uniforms and weapons. The colonel had not issued any rules of engagement in terms of crowd control. They had no tear gas. No rubber bullets. They had no explanation as to why they were there.

The major reported the situation to the colonel. After a brief moment in which the colonel took the information up the chain of command, the major witnessed fights breaking out as people knocked each other down in an attempt to leave the casinos.

Then his revised orders came through. Focus on creating an inner cordon around the Gold Palace Hotel. Block all visitors from leaving. No exceptions.

The major felt he was still able to do both. He had nearly eight hundred guardsmen continuing to get into position around the Fremont Street Experience, which stretched five blocks from one end to the other. Bullhorns were in use throughout the entertainment complex, advising people to move away from the barricades.

As the major led the effort to block all exits from the Gold Palace, shots rang out, causing bullets to ricochet off the ceiling of the Viva Vision, the largest video screen in the world, which acts as a canopy enclosure over the street and the entrance to the hotels.

The major wasn't distracted by the gunfire. He could tell from the report that it was a handgun, and the fact that it wasn't accompanied by the return fire from his guardsmen's automatic weapons indicated nothing had escalated. Yet.

Using the threat of force and the barricades, by 9:15 p.m., the Gold Palace was secured. Mostly.

CHAPTER SIXTY-FOUR

9:13 p.m
Gold Palace Hotel
Office of the Culinary Union 226
Las Vegas, Nevada

At sixty thousand, the Culinary Workers Union, Local 226, had more members than any other in Nevada. Their presence was such a large part of casino operations that all of the major casino hotels complexes provided a union representative from CU226 office space so management had easy access to resolve disputes with their employees before any matter escalated.

Bea Warren, the union rep working in the office at the Gold Palace that evening, had spent the last fifteen minutes gathering up her subordinates, individuals who were assigned as the various types of hospitality workers in the hotel, from housekeeping to food service to maintenance workers.

"Thank you all for getting to my office so quickly," she said. "About ten minutes ago, I received an anonymous phone call from the governor's office. They were giving me a heads-up. We need to leave the hotel immediately."

"Why?" asked a person from the food service department.

"It's too late," said another quickly.

"What do you mean, it's too late?" asked Warren.

"Haven't you heard? The National Guard is trying to shut down Fremont Street." The man was remarkably calm.

"Now?" asked Warren.

"Yeah. I was gonna leave out the back when I got your text. I figured you didn't know."

Warren rolled her eyes. She sighed and a look of determination came over her face. "You said out the back. What do you mean? Which exit?"

The man paused as screams could be heard coming from down the hallway leading to the administration offices. "I self-park at the lot across Bridger. If we take the maintenance tunnels through the back of the hotel to the Carson Tower, it dumps out at First Street and Bridger. Others told me the barricades haven't been set up there. They're all closer in at Main, Carson, and the north side."

Warren patted the man on the shoulder and thanked him. "Okay, all of you. Send out a text message blast to everyone on your contact list. Tell them to leave their post immediately. No exceptions. Drop everything and make their way to the tunnel connecting the main building with Carson Tower. Got it?"

"Yeah," replied one.

"Okay," confirmed another.

"What about those on the floor who don't have their phones?"

"I'll take care of that right now. Go!"

They rushed out of her office and Warren sat at her desk. She'd learned how to access the hotel's intercom system years ago and hoped the method still worked. It was a hidden trick she was saving for a rainy day. Tonight, it appeared to be raining trouble.

She punched in a series of numbers interspersed with the pound sign into the telephone keypad. She took a deep breath and blew into the handset. She heard her blowing sound through the speakers in the hallway just outside her office.

"All members of the Culinary Union and the UAW, please listen up," she shouted. Gaming dealers had joined he United Auto Workers Union a decade ago.

Her voice boomed through the speakers. "In accordance with the terms of our contract and federal law, we have declared this facility to be an unsafe work environment. It's our opinion that you are in danger of serious injury or even death as a result of the present conditions within the hotel and casino. Accordingly, under the Occupational Safety and Health Act, we are declaring a work stoppage and insist that you leave the premises immediately. Please follow the directions sent to you by text and voicemail messages by your union supervisor or contact person."

Her message was heard in the kitchens, the maintenance hallways, the casino, and the administrative offices. Union employees responded without hesitation. They checked their phones and rushed for the maintenance tunnel leading south out of the hotel. Unfortunately, not everyone heard the notification.

CHAPTER SIXTY-FIVE

9:15 p.m
Nevada Governor's Mansion
606 Mountain Street
Carson City, Nevada

The governor had regained his composure as the planned fifteen-minute address came to a close. As instructed, he saved the punch line until the end. The *coup de grace*. The defining blow. He hoped President Taylor would appreciate his efforts.

"During the evening, my staff will be reaching out to the chief medical officers of all Las Vegas hospitals to recommend a thirty-day cessation of all nonessential surgeries and medical treatments. I will further advise them to place stringent restrictions on anyone attempting to enter their facilities. This is absolutely necessary to provide protection for existing patients and any new ones who may have come down with this unidentifiable disease."

The governor, a politician, was in his element now. He adopted that look of concern that played so well to the electorate. He took a deep breath and exhaled, allowing emotion to be felt through the cameras and into the homes of Las Vegans.

"I truly regret that this action is necessary. We simply must take this step for every Nevadan's health and safety. Lives are at stake, and with each passing day, it's possible more people will be infected. My ultimate goal here is to come together as Nevadans to save lives. This requires aggressive strategies aimed at mitigating community spread. It also takes decision-making and action, something that we have not received from the agency of the federal government paid an enormous amount of taxpayer dollars to protect us."

He furrowed his brow and leaned forward toward the camera. His demeanor turned from compassionate to angry.

"We should have been warned and provided guidance on how to help our citizens. Failure to do that is, in my opinion, inexcusable. I hope this is a lesson learned for other governors who may someday be similarly situated. The ball was dropped by the CDC, or at least by the people sent to Las Vegas charged with the responsibility of investigating this unnamed disease. Frankly, the loss of life of any Nevadan exposed to this contagion is on their hands!"

CHAPTER SIXTY-SIX

9:17 p.m
Gold Palace Hotel Convention Center
Fremont Street Experience
Las Vegas, Nevada

"And all of this leads us to the importance of identifying our patient zero," Harper continued. She'd been working with her team of epidemiologists as if they were students in a classroom but helped them to stay organized and on track. Just like any outbreak investigation, there were steps to take and checklist items to mark off. Harper didn't want to leave any stones unturned or rush to a hypothesis without all the facts. To do otherwise would be irresponsible and incite panic.

"We have to identify the point of origin for this disease. The main player in this cat and mouse game is patient zero. Why? Determining the first person whom the disease attacked paves the way for control and prevention of a more serious epidemic.

"It requires meticulous and arduous detective work on our part. We have to go from case to case where the disease made its first appearance. Here, for example. Then we retrace every victim's steps.

"This disease may have originated with our index patient, Mr. Yao," said Harper as she tapped on the whiteboard and pointed at his passport photo before continuing. "Doubtful, however, considering so many diseases originating in Asia are zoonotic. Whom did he have contact with? Was it airborne? How long does it live in the environment, or does it only pass by direct contact within hosts? If so, can it survive outside a host? For how long?

"We have to have that information to guide our efforts in determining the appropriate containment measures of the outbreak so we can keep it from spreading further.

"Once we identify patient zero, then the work continues. We look at their lives. Where did they work? What do they eat? What animals have they come in contact with? We can identify likely candidates for animal hosts, and then we have to venture into the wild to collect those animals and determine whether they have our novel virus."

Harper paused and glanced at her watch. It was time for a break for all of their sakes. She glanced toward the doors where Becker waited. She added one final thought before she released the team to stretch their legs and use the restroom.

"I know many of you feel like we've been chasing our tails, running one lead down after another, and we're still no closer to identifying patient zero. I get it. It's frustrating not to have all the information out of the index patient's home country of China to help us define this disease.

"Some of you have voiced genuine concerns that what has happened here in Las Vegas is the tip of the iceberg. The real question is how big the iceberg is. How much is happening outside Las Vegas that we have not yet seen?"

"Exactly," said one of the epidemiologists. "How do we answer that?"

Harper shoved her hands into her jeans pockets and slipped her shoes back on before walking across the room. "I think I know, but the answers aren't here. Let's all take a ten-minute break, and then we'll finish up for the day."

Harper approached Becker and pulled open the double doors that led to the hallway.

Becker clutched her iPad in front of her and looked up to Harper. "What are you thinking?"

"I have to go to China."

Suddenly, a captain in the Nevada Army Guard appeared with two armed guardsmen behind him. His deep voice bellowed for all to hear.

"You're not going anywhere."

The hunt for a silent killer continues

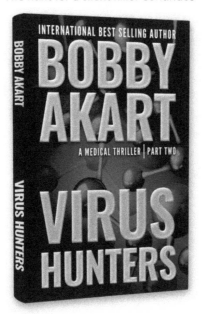

Race, gender, age.
It doesn't matter. Everyone may be a victim.

AVAILABLE ON AMAZON

NOW AVAILABLE ON AMAZON: *VIRUS HUNTERS PART 2*, the second installment in the Virus Hunters trilogy. You can purchase it by following this link to Amazon: *VIRUS HUNTERS PART 2*

A NOTE FROM THE AUTHOR

First, let me take a moment to thank you for reading my first novel featuring Dr. Harper Randolph and the Virus Hunters! These characters and their story have been planned for three years since the success of my Pandemic series published in May 2017. During the course of my research, I became thoroughly convinced that our world was wholly unprepared for a global pandemic. Here's why.

In the mid-twentieth century, a new weapon, the atomic bomb, shocked the world with its ability to destroy the enemy.

For centuries, another weapon has existed…

One that attacks without conscience or remorse…

Its only job is to kill.

They are the most merciless enemy we've ever faced…

And they're one-billionth our size.

Be prepared to become very, very paranoid.

WELCOME TO THE NEXT GLOBAL WAR.

Over the past half century, the number of new diseases per decade has increased fourfold. Since 1980, the outbreaks have more than tripled. With those statistics in mind, one had to consider the consequences of a major pandemic and now we're living the nightmare.

Death has come to millions of humans throughout the millennia from the spread of infectious diseases, but none was worse than the Black Death, a pandemic so devastating that uttering the words the plague will immediately pull it to the front of your mind. From 1347 to 1351, the Black Death reshaped Europe and much of the world.

In a time when the global population was an estimated four hundred fifty million, some estimates of the death toll reached as high as two hundred million, nearly half of the world's human beings.

This plague's name came from the black skin spots on the sailors who travelled the Silk Road, the ancient network of trade routes that traversed the Asian continent, connecting East and West. The Black Death was in fact a form of the bubonic plague, not nearly as contagious and deadly as its sister, the pneumonic plague.

Fast-forward five centuries to 1918, an especially dangerous form of influenza began to appear around the world. First discovered in Kansas in March 1918, by the time the H1N1 pandemic, commonly known as the Spanish flu, burned out in 1919, it took the lives of as many as fifty million people worldwide.

A hundred years later, in 2020, the COVID-19 pandemic swept the planet destroying lives and the global economy. As of this writing, the death toll is still climbing as a treatment protocol hasn't been established; there is no vaccine, and testing is in short supply.

Why does the history of these deadly pandemics matter?

Because it has happened before and it will happen again and again—despite the world's advanced technology, or because of it. People no longer stay in one place; neither do diseases. Unlike the habits of humans during the Black Death and the Spanish flu, an infection in all but the most remote corner of the world can make its way to a major city in a few days. COVID-19 has proven that.

Terrible new outbreaks of infectious disease make headlines, but not at the start. Every pandemic begins small. Early indicators can be subtle and ambiguous. When the next global pandemic begins, it will spread across oceans and continents like the sweep of nightfall, causing illness and fear, killing thousands or maybe millions of people. The next pandemic will be signaled first by quiet, puzzling reports from faraway places—reports to which disease scientists and public health officials, but few of the rest of us, pay close attention.

The purpose of the Virus Hunters series is not to scare the wits out of you, but rather, to scare the wits into you. As one reader said to me after reading the Pandemic series in 2017, "I now realize that humans can become extinct." Not a comforting thought.

This series is also designed to give you hope. You see, the stories depicted in the Virus Hunters novels are fictional. The events, however, are based upon historical fact. Know this, there are those on the front line of this global war. The burden lies on the CDC and their counterparts around the world who work tirelessly to protect us. This series is dedicated to the Virus Hunters—the disease detectives and shoe-leather epidemiologists of the CDC's Epidemic Intelligence Service who work tirelessly to keep these deadly infectious diseases from killing us all.

If you enjoyed this Virus Hunters novel, I'd be grateful if you'd take a moment to write a short review (just a few words are needed) and post it on Amazon. Amazon uses complicated algorithms to determine what books are recommended to readers. Sales are, of course, a factor, but so are the quantities of reviews my books get. By taking a few seconds to leave a review, you help me out and also help new readers learn about my work.

And before you go ...

SIGN UP for my mailing list at BobbyAkart.com to receive a copy of my monthly newsletter, *The Epigraph*. You'll also learn about special offers, bonus content, and you'll be the first to receive news about new releases in the Virus Hunters series.

VISIT my feature page at Amazon.com/BobbyAkart for more information on the Virus Hunters or any of my other bestselling survival thrillers listed below which includes over forty Amazon #1 Bestsellers in forty-plus fiction and nonfiction genres.

Lastly, for many years, I have lived by the following premise:

Because you never know when the day before is the day before, prepare for tomorrow.

My friends, I study and write about the threats we face, not only to both entertain and inform you, but because I am constantly learning how to prepare for the benefit of my family as well. There is nothing more important on this planet than my darling wife Dani and our two princesses, Bullie and Boom. I've always said, one day the apocalypse will be upon us. Well, sometimes I hate it when I'm right.

Thank you for supporting my work and I hope you enjoy the next installment in the Virus Hunters series.

CPSIA information can be obtained
at www.ICGtesting.com
Printed in the USA
BVHW082214301121
622866BV00011B/506/J